EXECUTION

The Divine, Book 6

M.R. FORBES

Published by Quirky Algorithms

Seattle, Washington

This novel is a work of fiction and a product of the author's imagination.

Any resemblance to actual persons or events is purely coincidental.

Copyright © 2016 by M.R. Forbes

All rights reserved.

Execution

1

I could feel Elyse and Rose's hands on my arms, though my body slumped forward, hanging from their grip as every muscle lost rigidity. The demon's voice was soft in my mind, and at the same time the power of it was almost deafening.

"You made a promise, diuscrucis," Abaddon said. "I have no wish to return to this horrible place."

I blinked my eyes, fighting against the threatening unconsciousness.

"Can you hear me?" I asked, pushing my words inward to the place where I could feel him. It was a dark place in my soul, a place I had closed off to heal.

"Yes. I hear you. What has that demon done?" he said. "Diuscrucis, I will not be controlled."

It was the connection that allowed us to speak. The one we had forged inside the Box. It was the promise I had made, to see him destroyed so completely that his soul would no longer be tormented in Hell, or brought back to this world to even greater torment. These things had bound us, linked us together through that black pit. The distance from Hell to where I was had been too far. Now we were together. Closer than I would have guessed.

"A summoning spell," I said. "I tried to stop it. I was too late."

He howled in my mind, the power of it nearly knocking me out.

"I can't help you if you kill me," I screamed at him.

"I hate this place. I hate this body. I hate this power. I hate. I hate."

"Landon?" Rose said. Her voice sounded as if it were a million miles away. "Landon? What's happening?"

I ignored her.

"Abaddon, I will keep my promise. I will find a way. Tell me where you are."

The demon's power eased in my head. He could have destroyed me had he wanted to. The connection was strong enough, and he had the ability. He didn't want me dead. Maybe I was the only thing in the world that he didn't want dead.

"Dark. It's still dark. I don't know. Find the demon. Make him tell you."

"I will. You have to back off. You're going to destroy me. I can't even stand up right now."

The pain lessened immediately, my blurred vision regaining focus. I found my legs, getting them under me and using them to stand. Rose and Elyse sensed my return and released their grip.

"Landon?" Rose said again. "Are you okay?"

I looked over at her, blinking a few times. There was a sudden dark hue to the world that I had never noticed before. It hung in front of me, like a shadow that was in the wrong place.

It was Abaddon. Watching me? Or just leaving me a reminder?

"Keep the promise."

I would never be free of him until I freed him from the universe.

"No," I said to Rose. "I'm not okay. None of us are okay. Abaddon is free. We have to stop him."

2

"Free?" Rose asked. "What does that mean, Abaddon is free?"

"Nothing good," Elyse said. "Abaddon was made in the likeness of the Beast. He has the power to destroy every living thing on Earth. The question is, how did he get out of Hell?"

"Randolph Hearst summoned him," I said.

"Hearst?" Elyse replied. "That lowlife? He doesn't have the power to pull something like this off."

"Not on his own. I'm betting he had help."

"Gervais?"

"No. Gervais wouldn't want to share in a play like that."

I turned my attention to the UPS delivery man. Alyx was still holding him up against the wall, the strength in her tiny hands almost comical. The man didn't move. His face was bleached white, and he had a stain on the front of his pants.

"You son of a bitch," I said. "What's your motive, Gervais?"

"What?" the man said. "Look, mister, I don't know who you think I am, but-"

"Cut the shit," I said, moving in closer to him. "You remember Alyx, don't you?"

She bared her teeth for me. They elongated into fangs as she did.

The man looked terrified, and he tried to run, his legs moving futilely along the ground while she held his neck.

"Judging by what Abaddon said to me, he didn't come across at full strength. I know you know what the hell is going on here. I know there's a reason you came to deliver that message personally, and I know there's a reason you let it happen in the first place. Stop playing games, or Alyx here is going to play one of her own."

The man's eyes shifted from me to Alyx, and back. Then he sighed loudly.

"Oh, fine. Have it your way, Landon."

He morphed in front of us, returning to the thin man with the curly black hair and the accent that I loved to hate.

"How did you know it was me?"

I smiled. "I didn't. I figured if I was wrong, at worst I would have scared the crap out of a deliveryman."

"Bah, I should have guessed. What did you mean, judging by what Abaddon said to me?"

"You aren't the one asking questions here. Tell me what your game is, Gervais. I know you will because you don't want to die, and you aren't powerful enough yet to prevent Alyx from killing you."

"Can you at least put me down?" he asked. "I will explain everything I know, but it would be so much nicer to sit and chat."

Alyx looked at me. I nodded. She released her grip, and Gervais fell to the ground. He reached up and rubbed at his neck.

"That's going to leave a mark," he said.

"Where have you been for the last three weeks?" I asked.

"Oh, here and there. You know how it is for demons."

"Gervais," I said.

He gave me his little French laugh and shrugged. "You defeated the Fists of God and kept your part of our bargain. You didn't need me around anymore."

"You tried to take Zheng's memories. His knowledge of how to make them."

Execution

"Well, of course, I did. That is how this works, isn't it, diuscrucis? I already told you I want to return to my former glory. I can't do that unless I have an ulterior motive. In this case, I was hoping to take our friend's memories and use them to make Fists under my control. It was a bit of a risk, but it was win, win as long as you defeated that stupid Angel."

"And now you hacked your bonded promise so that Hearst could bring Abaddon back into this world. Why?"

"I want to use his power."

"I don't need you to tell me that part. Hearst summoned him. Hearst is in control of him. That's how it works, isn't it?"

"Yes. Mostly. There are ways." He smiled the annoying, mischievous grin that I hated so much. "There are always ways. So, let me tell you why you want to keep me around."

"Good idea," I said. "Though after the last time, I'm considering taking my chances without you."

"As well you should. But it would be a mistake. You see, I know where he summoned the demon. I know where they are keeping him. You're right when you say he isn't at full strength just yet. Except it isn't because his power didn't come across. It's because they are holding it. They don't want Abaddon free in this world. They don't want to destroy every living thing. If they did, what would they feed on? No, they have managed to contain him and his power. Now they will work to extract that power and use it to their own ends."

"You seem to know a lot about it," Rose said.

"Of course I do, my flower."

"How?"

He changed shape again, turning into a fat man with a short beard. "I can be anyone as long as they are human. This one was one of Hearst's. He had access to the Solen Intranet." He changed back to himself. "It is funny, the things that can be found on intranets these days. Such high security from outsiders, but nothing once you are inside. Especially if you're the administrator."

"So you got Hearst's secret hideout for Abaddon from the intranet?" I asked, skeptical.

"No. I got the names of a few demons who had access. That is the thing about lesser demons, Landon. They are very easy to seduce if you have the right body." He morphed into Rose's sister again, sticking out his hip and grabbing his breasts.

"You asshole," Rose said, her face twisting in anger.

"Gervais," I said, putting out a hand to hold Rose back.

"It was a little distasteful, what I had to do for the information, but worth it in the end. A demon with sexual mores is a bit too ironic for me in any case."

"Get to the point," I said.

"Ah, yes. The point. The point is, I know where they are storing Abaddon. You do not. Therefore, you need me to help you."

"I wouldn't have if you had kept our first bargain."

"No."

"And if I make another bargain with you, you're going to renege on that, too."

"Likely."

"So why wouldn't I just find Abaddon on my own? I'm sure Hearst would be happy to tell me where he is."

"Go ahead, Landon. Go to Hearst and ask him about Abaddon. See what you get from him. Why don't you take your harem with you? I will wait here for you to come back and ask me to make a deal." He paused, looking smug. "You will come back to make a deal. I'm certain of it."

I stared at him for a good minute. It sucked to know the demon was up to something and at the same time have the niggling feeling that he had me right where he wanted me. Of any demon I had ever met, Gervais was the most accomplished manipulator of them all.

"Alyx, stay here and keep Gervais company. If he tries to do anything other than watch television, tear his throat out."

"Yes, Master," Alyx said. I looked over at her. "Yes, darling," she said instead.

"Rose, it's your call if you want to come along," I said. "Elyse, I would appreciate your company."

"Sure," Elyse said. "I'm in."

Execution

"I'll go," Rose said. "I need the practice."

"Aren't you afraid I'll steal your girlfriend while you're gone?" Gervais asked, clearly amused.

"Go ahead and try," I said. "Let's go."

3

We took ten minutes to change from workout clothes to street threads before heading out from my apartment, taking to the streets on foot. I would grab a cab to Hearst's place soon enough, but I wanted to get Rose and Elyse up to speed first.

"Apparently, I can hear Abaddon can speak to me," I said. "Through the connection we made while I was in the Box."

"But you destroyed the Box," Elyse said. "How did the connection survive?"

"Part of our souls were both trapped. I made him a promise there, binding his soul to mine. That binding survived after I escaped. Somehow, he can speak to me and push his power through the link."

"He can send his power through the link?" Elyse said. "You mean he could kill you?"

"If he wanted to, yes. All he wants is for me to keep my promise."

"What was your promise?"

"To destroy him. Except he's already told me, he won't go willingly. I need to earn it."

Elyse grabbed me by the arm, turning me toward her. "Are you serious?"

Execution

"Unfortunately, yes. I made the deal because it was the only choice I had. It was the only way I was getting the Beast in the Box. To be honest, I didn't think I would have to make good on it already."

"Shit," Elyse said.

"Yup. So, do you have any idea how to kill an unkillable demon?"

Elyse laughed. "Not yet. One thing at a time."

"So if Abaddon wants you to kill him, why didn't he tell you where he was?" Rose asked.

"I don't think he knows. At least not yet."

"Do you even want to find him before you can destroy him? I mean, it seems to me that he's better off being held somewhere while we figure out what to do. If he's as powerful as you say, it can't be a bad thing that the power is being contained."

"It isn't a bad thing the power is contained," I said. "It is a bad thing that Randolph Hearst is containing it, especially since he has a currently unknown accomplice. I'd be happy to find out where Abaddon is and take control over his imprisonment, if that becomes an option."

"Accomplice?" Rose said. "You said it wouldn't be Gervais, but can you be sure? That demon is the slimiest little worm I've ever encountered."

"You haven't encountered enough demons," Elyse said. "Gervais is too smart to be a worm."

"And if he had a hand in summoning Abaddon, he wouldn't have come back to me. No, he needs my help for something, and in return I'm going to set him up to make a move. We probably won't figure out what that move is until it's too late."

"Then how do you know we won't end up worse off than we already are?"

"I'm linked to one of the most powerful demons that Satan ever created, and he can end me with a thought. How does it get worse than that? At least for me."

"Point taken," Rose said. "Do you know where we're going?"

We had been walking aimlessly while we chatted. It was a couple of miles to Hearst's brownstone, a distance I would normally cover on foot if I were being sneaky. Having Abaddon's power in my soul, a constant buzz of dark energy, was killing my mood for sneakiness.

"Hearst has a brownstone on 93rd and Broadway," I said.

"Do you think he'll be home?" Rose asked.

"Probably not. His cronies will tell us where he is."

"Are you sure?"

"If they enjoy their continued existence, yes." I motioned to Elyse, who plucked a stone from her pocket. The stone could be replaced with a four-foot obsidian roman spatha with both demonic runes and angelic scripture on the blades with little more than a thought. "You brought your knives?"

Rose spread her shorter coat to show me the weapons. I was unarmed myself, figuring to let her get the experience she needed.

I whistled for a cab, waving it down and opening the door for Rose and Elyse. Then I slipped in on the front passenger side. I made eye contact with the driver, checking him for Divinity. It had been easier when I could sense them from a distance, but it had meant they could sense me, too.

"You don't want to sit in the back?" he asked, surprised. He was a younger guy in a sweater and stained jeans.

"I'm good up here," I replied. "Ninety-third and Broadway, please."

I watched his face. His eyebrow twitched just a little. Most people probably wouldn't have noticed.

"Elyse," I said. "Do you know our driver?"

The truth of it was that cabs were very common targets for both the Divine and the Nicht Creidem. They were an easy excuse to criss-cross the city, eavesdrop on conversations, and pass messages from place to place. Things like Lyft and Uber had only made that part of the Divine spy network that much more effective.

"I don't recognize him," Elyse said, leaning forward. As the daughter of the Nicht Creidem's former leader, she would have known most of their crew. "They've been recruiting outsiders lately, though. Kind of like you." She looked over at Rose, smiling.

"Is there a problem?" the driver asked, looking nervous.

"I don't know," I said. "It depends on why you know the home address of Randolph Hearst."

His eyes narrowed. "Who the hell are you?"

"Someone you don't want to screw around. Are you Nicht?"

His hand shifted on his left side. I took hold of my power, using it to pull his hand up hard enough that he cracked himself across the jaw.

"Don't," I said.

"You're him, aren't you?" he asked me, rubbing his jaw. "The one they warned me about."

"Yes. So you are Nicht Creidem?"

"They told me not to talk to you."

"There are three of us in the cab and only one of you. Considering you aren't Divine, and you don't appear to have any tats, I recommend doing what's best for your own safety. And don't even think about reaching for the gun again. You can't kill me with it anyway."

"Yeah, I'm Nicht," he said. "I only joined a few months ago. They put me on this route after I got them some good intel on a demon that was trying to smuggle a runestone. I know Hearst's address because I end up going that way a lot."

"I guess it's my lucky day," I said.

The Nicht Creidem weren't friends of mine, but we weren't total enemies, either. They wanted to destroy all Divine, and at the same time keep all of the power that was stored in the artifacts the angels and demons had created over the ages, like Elyse's sword. I killed Divine to keep humanity from being consumed by them, for better or for worse. There was some overlap there.

"What do you want?" he asked.

"I told you. A cab ride up to Hearst's. I need to talk to him."

"What about?"

"He has something I'm interested in."

His ears perked up. I knew they would. "Oh?"

I smiled. "Stick around, and I might give you something to take back at the end of your shift."

"Okay, sure. Just reporting a diuscrucis sighting will get me a nice bonus. Anything else will be gravy."

"Then let's go," I said. The poor kid didn't know that I would make sure he forgot all about having seen any of us by the time he was three blocks from Hearst's residence.

The cab pulled away from the curb, cutting off a livery in the process. He was a good driver, quick and efficient, and we reached Hearst's brownstone in no time.

4

"What's your name?" I asked the driver when we stopped at the curb a block away from Hearst's place.

"Joey," he said. "Joey Lincoln."

"Nice to meet you, Joey. Come on."

He looked over at me. "You want me to come with you?"

"You wanted the information, didn't you? I'm not going to sit here and tell you something you can hear for yourself."

Joey didn't look happy about the idea, but he unbuckled himself and climbed out of the cab. Rose got out on his side while Elyse joined me on the curb.

"What are you doing?" she asked in a whisper.

"With him?" I motioned toward Joey.

"Yes. We don't need him. I don't get it."

"Abaddon is back on Earth," I said. "I want your old team to know about it. They'll do their due diligence on exactly how and where that happened. Best case, they'll align with us to help me destroy him."

"Worst case, they'll get to him ahead of us and use his harnessed power."

"Yup. Better them than Hearst. If the Solen family gets their mojo back with Abaddon's power behind them, it will be tough to dislodge them again."

"I assume it's also better than Gervais getting his way?"

"Definitely. Besides, we need a ride for the night. I can make him forget everything if we need him to."

"Right. I forgot about that." She smiled. "Hey, do you know if Rose likes flowers?"

"You're asking me this now? Her name is Rose; I assume so."

She punched me in the arm.

The four of us made our way down the street. As we approached Hearst's brownstone, I noticed a group of men sitting on the steps of the block of townhouses across the street. None of us were Divine, so we didn't show up on radar as out of the ordinary. Even so, the way they watched us was too intense to be typical.

"Keep an eye on the Goombas behind us," I said to Rose as we climbed the steps. She looked back at them, earning herself a whistle.

"You can't walk anywhere in this city," she said as I knocked on Hearst's door.

We waited a dozen seconds before we got an answer. A serious looking blood-sucker in a tuxedo blocked the space between door and frame, his eyes flicking over each of us.

"Ah, diuscrucis," he said. "Mr. Hearst has been expecting you."

"He has?" I said casually.

"Of course. Please, come in." He moved aside. I stepped over the threshold, and he repositioned himself to block the entrance. "Just you."

I could have made him let the others in. I still wanted the Nicht Creidem to know what was going down. It wasn't worth making a scene, especially with the guards across the street. I knew Elyse could handle them, but it just wasn't worth it.

"Sorry, I guess you should hang out here. Maybe make some friends."

Elyse rolled her eyes. "We'll be on the steps." She looked at the butler. "If those mongrels come over to bother us, they won't live long enough to have to hide from the sunrise."

"Understood," the vampire said, his eyes casting a tangible warning across to the group. "We don't want any misunderstandings at this delicate juncture." He closed the door, separating us, and then began walking ahead of me. "Follow me."

I trailed the butler through an elegantly appointed lounge so a mahogany staircase and up to the top floor. We bypassed a simple bedroom draped in heavy, sun-blocking drapes, and made our way into a rosewood and green office.

Randolph Hearst was sitting behind the desk.

"Landon," he said with a smile, his head tilting as he tried to remember the last time he had seen me. "How long has it been?"

"Do you remember the night you had to walk home?" I asked.

His smile faded. "I thought that might have been you. Come on in, have a seat." He waved at a chair in front of the desk.

I walked over to it and sat, keeping my posture casual. There was nothing about Hearst that frightened me. He was a two-bit vampire who happened to have a good head for schemes, not unlike Gervais. His physical attributes were less than intimidating.

"I'm sure you've heard by now that I've summoned the demon Abaddon back to this world?"

It had been all of twenty-four minutes. "Why would you assume that?" I asked.

"You don't tend to drop in for tea," he replied.

"I don't like the additives. To be honest, I'm surprised to find you here. I thought you would be wherever your new pet is being held."

"I would, but I needed to be here to deal with you."

"Which meaning of deal with are you going for?" I asked.

He laughed. "You're always so sure of yourself, aren't you?"

"I held the power of a God in my hands and let it go," I said. "It did wonders for my confidence."

"I mean bargaining with you."

"Tell me where Abaddon is, and I won't kill you," I said.

"Cute, Landon. You know I'm not going to do that. And you also have to know I wouldn't have let you this close if there was any chance you could hurt me right now."

I raised an eyebrow at that, taking a quick glance around the room. The edges of demonic runes were visible beneath the rug and behind the bookshelves. They wouldn't affect me.

"How are you planning on stopping me?" I asked.

"That's part of my deal."

"I'm not following, Hearst."

The smile returned to his face. "I have Abaddon, Landon. I can do one of two things with him. One, I can keep him locked up and work on siphoning his power. Yes, my associate and I are going to use it to solidify our position in the Divine hierarchy. But what's the harm in that? Two, I can set him free."

"Why would you set him free?" I asked.

"Because you weren't willing to listen to reason."

I hated dealing with demons, and Hearst and Gervais in the same day gave me a sudden headache. "I'm listening right now."

"The terms are simple. You let my associate and me do what we need to do, and you keep your business out of ours. In return, we keep Abaddon locked up. Or, you insist on making trouble, and I let him out."

"I can't let you upset the balance," I said. "You know that."

"I'm aware of that. Look, I don't want to mess up this world. I like it here. What I want is to take over some of the, shall we say, assets. That's why we summoned the demon. With his power, we can remove certain obstacles, including you."

I was silent for a minute while I considered it. I didn't need to kill Hearst just yet, and there was no real downside to letting Abaddon stay under house arrest while I figured out how to destroy him.

"Well? What do you say?"

"Those are all the terms? I let you kill some competition, and in return you don't let Abaddon roam the Earth?"

"Yes."

"For how long?"

"Indefinitely."

"The balance," I said.

"You can cull when you need to, but you cull from the opposition."

Execution

"You're buying me?" I said.

"That was the idea."

"Who is your associate?"

"They prefer to remain anonymous at this time."

"You know this deal is only good as long as I don't have a way to destroy him," I said. "Once I can, I don't care if you set him free."

"You can't destroy him, Landon. At best you can send him back to Hell, and we can summon him again. You see, the summoning isn't something you can stop, no matter what Gervais says." He laughed, noticing the change in my expression. "Oh, you didn't think I knew he was trying to stick his claws in this game? I know a lot more than you think I do. So, tell me. Yes or no?"

I stood up. The motion caused Hearst to shrink back. He wasn't as confident in the outcome as he was trying to make me believe.

"Yes," I said. "You have a deal. If there's a way to kill him, I'll find it."

"There isn't," Hearst said, satisfied. "The Box is gone. The Blades are gone. You can't kill him. That's why he's so valuable." He stuck out his hand, using a sharp nail to open his skin and draw blood. "Shake on it?"

"You have a knife?" I asked.

He took my hand in his, cutting me with a nail. We clasped hands.

"I won't come after you or try to stop you, so long as you keep Abaddon imprisoned," I said. "At least until I find a way to destroy him."

"And I won't free Abaddon as long as you stay out of my way," Hearst said.

I felt the slight pull of the binding, weakened by the fact that I wasn't really Divine. I could renege if I wanted, but there was no motivation to right now. Besides, I had only promised that I wouldn't butt in. I hadn't said anything about Rose, Elyse, Alyx, or even Gervais.

"Good doing business with you, Landon," Hearst said. "Now get out of my house."

5

"Well?" Elyse asked when I returned to the street. The vamps on the other side had vanished into the night, no longer concerned that we would give them any trouble.

"It could have been better. It could have been worse."

"Did you kill Hearst?"

"Not yet. I made a deal with him. I leave him to his business; he keeps Abaddon locked up."

Elyse made a sour face. "That's why he summoned Abaddon? To get you out of the game?"

"And to make a move on the other demons. Or so he says."

I looked over at Joey. He was listening intently, ready to bring the information back to the Nicht Creidem. The outcome of my conversation with Hearst changed my mind on that front.

"We'll walk from here," I said.

"Aren't you going to tell me what's going on?" he asked. "I understand that Hearst summoned a demon, and he's got him locked up somewhere. What else can you tell me?"

"Nothing. Go home."

I was in a foul mood. Why shouldn't I be? I didn't trust Hearst, despite our agreement. I especially didn't trust his unnamed associate, whoever they were. And I still had to deal with Gervais before the night was over.

"What? You said-"

"I recommend going home," Rose said, showing one of her knives.

"Fine. I'll be happy with what I've got." He made a dirt face at me and headed back to his cab.

"Is he going to remember any of this?" Rose asked.

"He'll remember driving over here and waiting. He won't remember with who, or why. Let's walk."

The three of us made the way back to my apartment on foot. I moved ahead of Rose and Elyse, giving them some space so they could talk a little more privately. Elyse asking me about flowers had proven that there was a mutual interest there though I hadn't realized they had a compatible view of sexuality. Whatever. Who was I to judge? I had bigger problems.

Hearst claimed there was no way to destroy a soul like Abaddon's, and unfortunately, I was inclined to agree. The Beast had only been destroyed after he had been captured in Avriel's Box, and only because I had managed to take his power. Even then, it had taken six blades of both demonic and heavenly power to get the job done. All of that was gone now. As far as I knew, Elyse's spatha was the most powerful artifact still on Earth, and she hadn't corrected me. I trusted her opinion on that. She had been her father's best collector, and she knew Divine trinkets like a Great Were knew how to tear out throats.

Even worse, I knew now that the whole thing with Matthias Zheng and the Fists of God was just the beginning of something bigger. When it rained, it poured, and I was about thirty seconds away from a nor'easter.

"If you two want to grab a bite, or whatever, I can handle Gervais on my own," I said once we had reached the steps of the apartment.

"And miss the fun?" Rose asked. "It's always such a pleasure dealing with that little French shit."

"I'm sensing a bit of sarcasm."

"Who? Me?" She laughed. "What do you say, El?"

Elyse reached into her pocket and tossed me her stone. "In case you need it, Landon. I could go for some Chinese."

"Thanks," I said, catching the artifact. "I'll see you two whenever."

I waved goodbye to them, watching for a few seconds as they headed down the street together. There was good Chinese everywhere in Manhattan and an especially good place two blocks from the apartment.

I climbed the steps to my apartment, opening the door and finding Gervais sitting on my sofa, watching television, as ordered. Alyx was standing in the corner, her eyes piercing into him, her body completely still. She was the best guard I could have hoped for.

"You're back," she said when I entered, her face beaming.

She came over to me, wrapping her arms around my waist and squeezing. I felt my bad mood fading away in an instant.

"Hi, Allie," I said.

The television went off. Gervais got to his feet. "Ah, Landon. You met with Hearst, I assume?"

"You knew he would be there?" I asked.

"Of course. I knew what he wanted."

"Then you also know I don't have any use for you."

"Au contraire mon frère. You need me more than you did before."

"Do you care to explain how, exactly?"

"For one, you can only trust Hearst as far as it suits him, but you already understand that. If he aims to make a power play against bigger demons, and you can't do anything to stop it, it will only end up badly for you in the end. Especially if he manages to harness Abaddon's power. Think about it, Landon. Picture Hearst controlling the demon's shadows."

I had thought about it, every step of the way back to the apartment.

"I know," I said. "But having Abaddon loose is a worse choice. Hearst will at least be a little picky about who he ends."

"For now," Gervais said. "You know what they say about absolute power, and demons are the most easily corrupted."

"Oh, please. You're no different from Hearst, and you're already corrupted."

"True. That is the chance you might have to take. Think about it, diuscrucis. And while you're at it, think on this: I know how you can get Abaddon away from Hearst without releasing his power on the world."

Execution

I stared at the demon. I had enough experience with the Divine to know everything he had said up until the last part was true. Hearst knew I would come after him and Abaddon the moment I felt I had the upper hand. I knew Hearst would break our deal the moment he thought he had the edge. Demons rarely held fast to their deals, as Gervais had proven.

It was all part of the balance.

The question then was whether or not to believe Gervais when he said he had a way to steal Abaddon from the vampire.

"You know how to destroy Abaddon?"

Gervais laughed. "Destroy him? Why would you want to do that?"

"I promised him I would. A bonded deal."

Gervais' amused demeanor vanished. "What?"

"You heard me. This throws a wrench in your plans, doesn't it? You're being a little too transparent right now, Gervais. I'm sure you want Abaddon's power for yourself. Knowing that I'll have to keep coming until it's gone will make things harder for you."

"Harder, but not impossible." His face changed again, returning to its general look of joyful superiority. "My plan may, in fact, meet the requirements of your bargain."

The statement piqued my curiosity, and he jumped on it.

"I see you're interested now, Landon. I knew you would be from the moment I came."

I heaved a nice sigh and rubbed my temples. I knew this was going to give me a headache. "Fine, spill it."

He smiled, a predatory smile because he knew he had me right where he wanted me. I had gotten used to being forgotten by the Divine, and since they couldn't remember seeing me to kill me, they were all trying to use me instead.

That was balance, too, I guess.

"Do you remember back at {name of the demon}'s mansion in California, when you fought the Fists of God?"

"Yeah, I remember. It was only a few weeks ago."

"Do you remember how one of the suits of armor was missing?"

"Yes," I said, playing along. "Did you take it?"

"No. But I know who did. If you recall, the armor is powered by the soul of a demon, held encased in scripture."

I could see where he was going. "How does trapping Abaddon's soul in a Fist of God count as having fulfilled my promise?"

"Well... Okay, technically, it doesn't."

"It doesn't at all."

"Technically, it doesn't," he repeated. "If his soul is trapped by scripture, the link will be broken. You won't need to keep your promise."

I could still sense the dark pallor over the world, offering a different hue through my eyes and caused by my connection to the demon. I wondered if he could hear what Gervais was saying. I didn't imagine he would be too happy with the idea of being trapped in yet another prison.

"And then what?" I said. "I get Abaddon into the FOG, and you steal it?"

"Yes."

I felt my face wrinkle up at the absurdity of it all. He wasn't even trying to be sly.

"Oh, come on now, Landon. Just because you know what I plan to do doesn't mean you know how I would do it or that you would be able to stop me."

"I'm trying to figure out the part where this is better than letting Hearst hold onto him. Whatever the Devil did to you before he sent you here, I still give you credit for being more underhanded and conniving than Hearst could ever be."

"Thank you."

"You're welcome. Seriously, Gervais. Tell me why I would team up with you to stick Abaddon in the FOG."

He was prepared for me to say that.

"Three reasons, diuscrucis. One: as I said, the link will be broken, and you'll be free of the demon. How long do you think he will wait for you to find a way to kill him before he decides to kill you? Two: I would still have to take the FOG from you, which leaves you with more control over your destiny. Three: you can't destroy Abaddon. It is impossible. Which means this is the only way you get out from under him."

Execution

I glanced over at Alyx. She was still glaring at Gervais, remaining silent and watchful. I hated that the demon was making any sense at all. I hated that his points were valid.

"One more question, then," I said. "If you know where to get the FOG, and you know where to find Abaddon, then what do you need me for?"

"That is a good question, with a very simple answer. I don't have the power to get the FOG back from the one who holds it. You do."

"And who is that?"

"Cain. The son of Satan."

6

"The son of Satan?" I asked. "Are you kidding me?"

"Do I look like I'm kidding?"

"You always look like you're kidding. I didn't know Satan's son was on Earth."

Gervais' smile shortened to a sheepish smirk. "He isn't."

"Hell?" I asked.

"Yes."

"You want me to go to Hell?"

"That is where the Fist of God is."

"My powers don't work in Hell."

"Again, I say au contraire mon frère. Your Divine powers did not work on the other planes; that is true. As you like to tell me, you aren't Divine anymore. At least not in the traditional sense. Your power is all stored within you, like a nuclear reactor. You don't need to be on Earth to use it."

I had never considered it that way. It was an interesting twist. Even so, I wasn't exactly keen on the idea of going to Hell on purpose. "I've never been to Hell."

"Which is why you need me. I will bring us to a demon who can open a Rift from here to there, and I will get us back."

Execution

"What I'm saying is, I don't want to go to Hell. I certainly don't trust you enough to let you take me there. Besides, you told me you aren't welcome there anymore."

"It will be fine as long as nobody recognizes me. Believe me, Hell isn't as bad as you might be imagining it."

"So Dante's Inferno was completely off the mark?"

"Not completely, but he did embellish a little bit. Besides, that was hundreds of years ago. Things change there as they do everywhere else."

"We should go," Alyx said, speaking up for the first time. "I can protect you. I don't want Abaddon to kill you."

"See, Landon. Listen to your girlfriend."

I glanced back over at her. I knew she was only concerned for my continued existence, but she wasn't helping. "Have you been there before?"

She shook her head. "No. It can't be worse than living with Espanto."

I was willing to bet it could be worse.

"I need time to think about this," I said.

"Of course," Gervais replied. "Don't take too long. The longer we wait to move on Hearst, the stronger his position becomes."

"Gervais, could you wait downstairs or something?"

"Yes. Fine. Find me outside when you've realized that I'm right."

He bowed to me, blew a kiss to Alyx, and left the apartment. I could hear him whistling while he wandered to the stairwell.

"Landon, I don't want you to die," Alyx repeated.

"I know. I don't want to die either. But Gervais can't be trusted. He's liable to bring me to Hell and leave me there. The entire thing about the Fist of God could be nothing more than a misdirection."

"I understand. Espanto also lied often to get what he truly wanted. If you're worried that Gervais will double-cross you in Hell, then we can go without him."

For whatever reason, the idea of going to Hell without Gervais almost made me more nervous than going with him. At the very least he was an experienced guide. If I could trust him even the smallest amount, I wouldn't have to make this kind of decision.

"Who do you know that can guide us?" I asked.

"Espanto knew a lot of demons. One of them was a fiend named Damien. He traveled between the worlds quite often."

"Why does he go back and forth? Is he some kind of messenger?"

"Something like that. He transports artifacts from Hell to Earth. Runed blades, mainly."

"A Divine arms dealer?"

"That's a good way to put it."

"Can we trust him?"

She smiled mischievously. "You know you can't fully trust any demon. He's weak enough that we can keep him in line, and we can give him enough incentive to stay as honest as any fiend can."

"What kind of incentive?"

"Me."

"What?"

"I'll promise to sleep with him if he helps us. I saw the way he looked at me when Espanto visited him. He'll do it."

I froze in place. It was hard for me to see Alyx as a demon. She was so sweet to me and so innocent about how normal human life worked. It was incredibly endearing and occasionally shocking. Despite what Espanto had put her through, and could continue to put her through if he got close enough that his brand put her back under his control, she had a freeness of both sexuality and violence that made me uncomfortable. Maybe my human morals were off-kilter with the reality of the situation. I didn't care.

"No," I said. "I'm not trading any part of you."

She didn't seem disappointed, but she was confused. "Why not?"

"You aren't a thing to barter. You're a living creature. You have a soul."

"A demonic soul."

"I don't believe souls are good or evil. Or if they are, I believe they can change from one to the other. You get to choose what kind of soul you have. You're protective of me because you don't want me to be hurt. I'm protective of you because I want you to be able to make that choice with a full understanding of what it means."

"But you said you don't love me. Why do you want to keep something

Execution

you don't love to yourself?"

"I don't want to keep you to myself. It's your choice to be here or not. Just because I don't love you doesn't mean I want to see you make decisions that will hurt you. I don't love all of the humans who are out there. I still protect them from the Divine because I believe in their freedom to choose to be good or evil."

She pursed her lips, considering my statement. "I think you do love me," she said at last.

I didn't say anything. Most of our conversations seemed to go this way.

"It is my choice to stay here with you. I will never change my mind. It's also my choice if I want to make a deal with Damien."

She threw me again, turning my words against me.

"I'm asking you not to. We can find some other way to pay him. You're too valuable to spend like currency."

She smiled, her entire posture melting into something entirely different. It was all I could do to keep my heart from pumping right out of my chest, and my arousal was impossible to prevent.

"I love you," she said, noticing my reaction. She was doing it on purpose.

"I know," I said.

In her own way, she did. I didn't feel the way I needed to use those words. I didn't deny that she was incredibly sexy, in part because of how ferociously protective she was over me. I didn't deny that I had come to desire her more and more over the last three weeks. But I was still a virgin because that wasn't a good enough reason for me. There was a huge gap between love and lust that would have to close.

"I'm going to head up to the roof for some air," I said. "I'm not taking Damien out of the equation, but if we need to pay him, we'll find some other way to do it, okay?"

She hesitated for a moment and then nodded. "Okay."

I leaned in and kissed her on the cheek. She nuzzled her face against me.

"Keep an eye on Gervais for me?"

"Of course, Mast... Landon."

I left her in the apartment, moving to the fire escape and climbing it to the roof. Once there, I pulled my cell from my pocket. I needed a little more advice than the people around me could offer.

Execution

7

"I appreciate that you trusted me with this, Signore," Dante said.

"I know we've had our differences over the years. This one is too big for me to manage on my own."

We were standing together on the top of my building, standing near the edge and looking down at the street below. When Dante wasn't writing notes of our conversation down on a small pad he had brought; I could tell he was keeping his eyes on Gervais, who was standing in front of the deli smoking a cigarette and looking smug as usual. I was switching my attention between the demon, the poet, and Alyx, who was sitting with her legs dangling from the fire escape and keeping close tabs on everything.

"Well, of course, you know the last thing I think you should do is trust that demon," he said. "That one fiend should cause so much strife among the Divine is an offense to the balance."

"To be honest, all of his schemes haven't come to that much. I mean, he had potential with Sarah, but Josette messed him up on that angle."

"I would argue that Sarah tripped him up herself. People make their decisions in life. Even though her mother was an Angel, she could have decided to seek evil."

"I'll accept that. So, what do you think about Gervais' plan?"

"I'll have to consult Alichino about the specifics, but on the surface I believe it would be possible. There is no way to say for certain, however. Your situation is unlike any I have encountered before. Going to Hell, on the other hand? Signore, you do not want to do this thing."

"I've already established what I don't want to do. But I might need to do it. Is it really that bad? Part of the reason I called you was for a straight answer."

"It has been many years since I was there last. Heaven and Hell are a reflection of humanity as much as anything else. For me, this representation took the form of circles, as I wrote about in the Inferno. You have seen for yourself in Purgatory how things change based on perception. Both Heaven and Hell are no different."

"So everyone experiences it differently?"

"In a sense. What will make Hell dangerous for you is that every being there is a demon. You can trust no one, and they will all be seeking to take advantage of you. Every last one, in one way or another. You must also steel your will against the torments you will see, and remember that these souls are cast down for a reason."

I knew that would be the hardest part. To see people suffering and recognize that it was deserved.

"What about Cain, and Lucifer himself?"

"You will not see Lucifer. He remains in his palace at all times, though his consciousness is everywhere."

"So he can see me?"

"He knows every soul that arrives in his realm. He might be amused by your presence, and he might entertain himself by watching you. As you are a visitor and not one of the damned, he will not intervene in any way. Cain, on the other hand, is dangerous. Very dangerous. I will be honest with you, Signore. I don't know if you can defeat him if it came to a battle of power. You may not have kept enough of it to battle the son of Lucifer."

"I don't want to fight him. I want to sneak in, grab the FOG, and go."

"That may be difficult considering the size of the armor."

"I should be able to carry it. So, you agree with Alyx that I should cut Gervais out of this?"

Execution

He nodded. He looked energized to be involved again. "Yes. Even if the demon doesn't plan to leave you there, you will be better off with a guide you can control."

"I still need him to lead me to Abaddon's prison."

"I will work on that, Signore. With Alichino's help, we may be able to determine the location of the demon. Any prison that is strong enough to hold him will have made waves somewhere."

I put my eyes on Gervais again. He was watching a woman who had just come out of the deli. She was black, well-dressed, with a large chest and a plump rear. He dropped his cigarette butt, stamped it with his foot, and began walking along the street behind her.

"What do I do with him?" I asked, switching my attention to Dante.

Dante rubbed his chin. "Hmm... I'll speak to Alichino about that as well. Perhaps we can fit two souls into the Fist of God." He smiled as though he had made a joke. He looked too hopeful to be kidding. "Leave him be for now. You may need him in case we can find no other option. Have your people keep an eye on him, and I will try to help you do so as well."

"Okay. If you learn anything useful, and I'm still in Hell, you can trust Rose or Elyse."

I looked back to the street. Both Gervais and the woman were gone. I knew he had to feed to keep his strength up, and I didn't like having to let him.

"I believe I can trust Rose. The Nicht Creidem are only a little better than the Divine."

"Dante," I said, turning back toward him with the intention of starting an argument about Elyse.

Of course, he was already gone.

8

I went back down the fire escape, meeting Alyx there.
"He is feeding," she said. "I can smell the blood and sex from here."
"Don't remind me," I replied. "Come on, we're leaving."
She pushed off with her legs, easily jumping into a stand. "Are we going to Damien?"
"We will, yes. We need to connect with Rose and Elyse first."
"Okay."
I looked her over. She was wearing short shorts that revealed the crease between her behind and her legs, and a tight halter top that did nothing to hide the shape of her breasts below it. I knew she wasn't dressed that way to be overtly sexual. It was the way Espanto had always wanted her to look and she didn't know any better. I'd tried to explain the different kinds of clothes to her, and she sort of understood, but being able to change into a massive werewolf and shred anyone or anything that offended you to pulp made the point moot under most circumstances.
"Go change into something more suited to traveling," I said. "We don't want to attract a lot of attention, and you will in that."
She looked down, oblivious to the wardrobe choice. "If you say so. What look are we going for?"

Execution

I had gotten her clothing of every kind to see what else she liked. She had tried it all and rejected everything that covered too much skin. She didn't like the feeling of cloth on her body, maybe because of her heightened senses. I think if it were completely up to her she would have disregarded modesty altogether.

"Let's go with professional and casual," I said, pushing a bit of power to morph my own clothes into a pair of jeans and a sport coat.

"Mini-skirts are so constricting on my legs," she said.

"You have pants."

"Pants make me look like a male."

"Shorts are out," I said.

"I can choose what I wear," she said.

She was still playing with me over what I had said.

"Allie, we don't have time for games."

She stuck her tongue out at me. "Fine. I'll be right back."

She climbed into the window and vanished. I remained on the fire escape, looking up now instead of down. It was a clear night, though the city's pollution left counting stars a dicey proposition.

"Diuscrucis."

Abaddon's voice cut through me, and I stumbled forward, grabbing the railing before I found myself plummeting into more pain.

"Abaddon," I said internally. "What's happening?"

"I am not happy."

"Can you ease off a little?"

The pain subsided. Mostly.

"I don't blame you. Do you know where you are?"

"It is dark. Everything is dark. My power. They take it. It hurts. I do not like pain, diuscrucis."

"I'm working on it. It's only been a couple of hours."

"Hours? It feels like ages. You must free and destroy me, diuscrucis. Do not linger."

"Trust me, I'm not. Ending a demon like you isn't quite like making an omelet."

"I don't understand."

I should have known he wouldn't. At least now I knew he couldn't hear what I heard.

"It isn't easy. I've got a lead. I'll update you if it bears fruit."

"What does fruit have to do with my pain? Speak clearly."

"I'll tell you when I find a way. Except you told me you won't go without a fight."

"Yes. I cannot. I want to end, yet do not want to die."

It was an odd statement. At the same time, I knew exactly what he meant. "I've been there. I'm doing my best, I promise."

"Very well, diuscrucis. I will be waiting."

The sense of him shrank back once more. I heard a rustling behind me, and I turned around to see Alyx standing naked in front of me, holding a different outfit in each hand.

"Which one do you prefer?" she asked, a coy smile on her face.

Again, her actions were intentional. She could have put her underwear on to ask the question. My body reacted to the sight of her, and I stammered out an answer. "That one," I said, pointing at the tweed in her left hand.

She nodded. "I like that one, too."

She walked over to the sofa, put them both down, and began dressing. She did it slowly, deliberately, each motion smooth and languid. It was more comparable to a jaguar than a wolf, and I had to pull my eyes away from her.

Demons.

She joined me on the fire escape a minute later, leaning up to kiss me on the cheek. "I'm sorry," she said.

"No you aren't," I replied.

She laughed. "I'm trying to be what you call behaved, but you are my mate. We should be making pups. I can see how much your body wants mine."

"If that was the only criteria, we'd be on the floor together right now."

"We are mates. I am yours. That is the criteria." She took my hand, trying to pull me toward the window. I had to use my power to pull back and remain in place.

Execution

"Allie," I said, using my I-think-you're-adorable-but-no voice. She fake-pouted for a few seconds, dropping my hand.

"I had to try," she said.

I reached out with my power, using it to pull the window closed. Then I scanned the street for signs of Gervais. "Do you know where Gervais is?"

She lifted her head slightly to sniff for him. "An alley, four blocks east. Why?"

"I don't want him to see us leave. Come on."

I vaulted the railing and dropped, using my power to land gently on the ground. Alyx followed me down, her legs bending slightly as she hit the ground.

"Rose and Elyse are over at Cheng's."

Alyx wrapped her arm around mine. She looked great in the tweed miniskirt and short-sleeved blazer.

"What are we waiting for?" she asked.

9

We found Rose and Elyse in a fairly secluded corner booth. I half-expected that we would be interrupting a semi-public makeout session.

Instead, Elyse had her arm around Rose, and Rose was crying.

"What's going on?" I asked, sliding into the other side of the booth with Alyx.

"Where are you going?" Elyse asked, noting Alyx's outfit.

"You probably don't want to know," I said. "Rose, are you okay?"

Rose reached up and wiped at her tears. "Your timing sucks, Landon. You should have gotten here five minutes ago."

"Why?"

"That was before I asked Elyse what she had to do to become immune to the Divine."

I glared at Elyse. "I thought we weren't telling her yet?"

"It isn't her fault," Rose said, defending Elyse. "I wouldn't let it go. I should have, but you know how stubborn I am."

"Since the cat's out of the bag, what do you think?" I asked. It was insensitive, I know. I was in a hurry.

"About drinking the blood of angels?" Rose looked sick for saying it. "Forget it. If that's what it takes, I'm not doing it. I can hold down the fort, or do some investigative work for you, or just pull the trigger and pray. I won't desecrate God like that." The thought made her tears come harder.

"Rose, I know it's a bit of a shock, and that I'm going to sound like a total jerk here, but you've already helped me kill an archangel. It's a little late not to desecrate God. I told you when we met what knowing me meant."

"There's a difference between killing an angel and drinking their blood," she said. "Drinking something's blood is like being a demon. It's like being Gervais."

I softened my voice. "I know, Rose. And I'm sorry. I wish we could power you up another way. I used to be able to give over some of my power. I can't do that anymore. If you're against it, I respect that. It will increase your chances of dying young."

"I'd rather die young." She wiped her tears again. There was a half-eaten plate of sashimi in front of her. "Do you want it? I lost my appetite."

I passed. Alyx didn't. She grabbed the plate and starting eating.

"So, where are you going?" Rose asked.

"I already said-"

"That we probably don't want to know. I do want to know. I don't think anything you tell me could be worse than what I've already heard today."

"We're going to Hell."

Rose's face turned white. "What?"

"Hell," I repeated.

"The Hell?"

"It's the only one I know of. Yes. Elyse, I need you to keep tabs on Gervais for me. I know that can be hard to do, but I suspect he'll hang around and wait for me to come back. Rose, Dante is going to be trying to find an alternate means to assist with the Abaddon problem. I told him to contact you if he finds anything. Also, if you want to do some digging of your own, I'm sure it would help."

They both stared at me, dumbstruck.

"Okay," I said, breaking the silence. I reached into my pocket and grabbed the stone, holding it out toward Elyse.

"No," she said. "Keep it. You're going to need it."

"Elyse, the sword is yours."

"And I want you to keep it for now. Landon. Hell?"

"I know it sounds bad, but I'll have Alyx with me, and my power will work there. It's not like I'm going to be a defenseless soul. Besides, Abaddon is here, and that's a lot scarier than some fire and brimstone."

"Which is another good point. What if Hearst decides to set Abaddon free? Or what if he uses the demon's power against people instead of other demons?"

"Do you have your cell?"

Elyse dug it out of her pants pocket and handed it to me. I pulled out mine. "I'm putting Obi and Sarah's numbers in, along with Alichino's. If you need extra help, call Obi first and fill him in. If you're really desperate, call Sarah."

I didn't want to involve Sarah in anything having to do with fighting the Divine, but if it were a choice between that and Armageddon, it was worth the risk.

"I don't like this," Elyse said as I handed her phone back.

"I'm not in love with it either," I said. "It has to be done."

We all sat in the booth and stared at one another for an awkward moment. Elyse started sliding out of the seat at the same time I did.

"Be careful," she said, hugging me.

"Are you kidding? I have the easy part compared to you."

She forced the laugh for me.

Rose took Elyse's place a moment later. "Landon, I want you to know. I'm not giving up. I still want to be part of the fight. I just-"

"I understand," I said, interrupting. "To be honest, I wouldn't do it either."

She seemed surprised by that. "You wouldn't? Not even to save humankind from extinction?"

I was about to say I wouldn't. The extinction part gave me pause. "I cried the first time I killed an angel. If you were asking the same question to that version of me, I would say no without hesitation. Now? I've seen too much, done too much to rule out anything."

She smiled, offering a hug. I held her tight for a moment.

Execution

"Thank you, Landon."
"You said that like you aren't going to see me again."
"No. I know I will. Hell can't hold someone like you."
I broke the embrace, turning to Alyx.
"Are you ready?"
"Yes, darling."
"Let's go."
"Give 'em hell," Elyse said, her smile more honest this time.
"Funny," I replied, my smile equally sincere.

10

We were at the airport an hour later, waiting for a flight to Denver, Colorado. While I was as inconspicuous as they came, Alyx's power stood out like a sore thumb to any Divine that happened to be in the area.

There were always Divine stationed at airports, especially one as busy as JFK. We had barely made it through security when we picked up a tail in the form of a pair of angels. They were pretty good at following us, too, managing to stay behind without notice until we had reached the terminal.

That was when they got too close.

"There are two angels watching us," Alyx said, leaning in close and rubbing her face against my ear. "I can smell them."

"Where?" I asked.

"Behind us and to the left. In the food court."

"Are they moving in, or just sitting?"

"Sitting right now. Do you want me to kill them?"

I patted her hand. "Let's not be so quick to go for the throat. Wait here, I'm going to talk to them."

She growled softly, leaning back in her seat and pouting. I stood up, stretched, and began heading back toward the food court, scanning the people at the tables. I spotted them a moment later, a male and female, middle-aged. The male had a large stomach and a sour expression. The woman was as plain as plain could be.

They didn't notice me noticing them. Their eyes were tight on Alyx. Two angels wouldn't dare go after a Great Were on their own, and even if they did I wasn't worried about Alyx's safety. I was more interested in finding out if they knew about Abaddon.

At least, I was until I noticed that the terminal was beginning to clear out.

For no good reason.

I looked back at Alyx. Humans had a subconscious, uncanny ability always to clear out of areas where Divine were about to clash before the clash happened. If anyone was going to start a riot, I expected it would be her.

Except she was still sitting calmly in her chair, twirling a strand of hair and yawning.

I scanned the hallway further down toward the entrance. Ninety-nine point nine percent of the people were headed away from us.

Ten others were coming the wrong way.

Shit.

I reached into my pocket, finding the stone. I hadn't expected I would need the weapon so soon after leaving Rose and Elyse. By the show of force, I could only guess that the Heavenly Host had heard about Abaddon and had put their army on high alert.

Any time a Great Were showed up anywhere was a cause for high alert, and with things turning sour out there, I had a bad feeling they were going to turn sour in here.

I turned back to the first two angels. They were on their feet now, and they had noticed I wasn't abandoning ship like the rest of the rats.

"Call off the brute squad," I said to them. "She's with me."

"With you?" Plain Jane asked. She eyed me curiously. "You don't have an aura. Are you her plaything?"

"Not exactly," I replied. "We don't want any trouble."

I glanced back toward the oncoming squadron of angels. I was certain Alyx had noticed them though she continued to play with her hair like it was no big thing.

"A Great Were in an airport is always trouble," Sourpuss said.

It might have had to do with the fact that a demon like Alyx could board a plane, tear it to shreds at thirty-thousand feet, and survive the fall. Or it might have been tense nerves over Abaddon. There was only one way to find out.

"Don't you have bigger problems to deal with?" I asked.

"What do you know about it?" Jane replied.

"More than you, I would guess."

"So you're in league with Hearst?"

"I didn't say that."

The larger group had reached Alyx. They positioned themselves around her. The funny thing about angels was that they couldn't attack first. It was against their rules to be the instigator, and would cause whoever started it to fall.

"Who are you?" Sourpuss asked.

"You know who I am," I replied. "And I can tell you that now is not a good time for you to lose any more karma."

The two angels looked at one another, and then back at me, finally getting the hint.

"Diuscrucis," they said together.

I felt a wave of heat behind me. By the time I turned around the petite, adorable, sexy girl Alyx had been replaced with the massive, furry, massive were Alyx.

"Alyx, no," I said, trying to stop her before things got out of hand.

I was too late. With a snarl, she leaped onto one of the angels, using her claws to tear his sword arm off before he could draw his blade.

The other angels responded quickly, getting their swords in hand. It would only take one blessed blade breaking her skin to kill her. It was a good thing she had a tough hide.

The two angels blew past me, rushing to aid their brethren. I took hold of my power, reaching out and yanking them back. They fell on the ground ahead of me, confused by the sudden loss of momentum. I pushed off against the ground, leaping forward while summoning the spatha,

Execution

landing next to Alyx just in time to parry a particularly violent thrust.

"Alyx, what the hell?" I asked.

She had already downed the first angel and was reaching out for another.

"You didn't hear what that one said to me," she growled, wrapping her massive claw around the angel.

I sidestepped a lunge, bringing the spatha up and around, knocking the angel's blade away and slicing him with the scripted side. The wound would hurt, but it would heal.

"Don't kill any more of them," I said, pushing another back with my power.

"But, Landon-"

"No. Please, Alyx. I need you to help me, not hinder me."

The words cut into her more deeply than a blessed sword could. She shifted back into girl form, the action confusing the angels and breaking the flow of the fight.

"I'm sorry," she said, only slightly louder than a whisper. She had tears in her eyes.

"Hold up," I said to the assembly of seraphim. "Everybody just calm down."

"Who are you?" one of them asked. He was kneeling next to Alyx's initial victim and pouring holy water on the wound. He would be fine in a day or two.

"Diuscrucis," Plain Jane said. "Step aside. She attacked us. We have a right."

"She said that one was taunting her."

"It is allowed," Sourpuss said.

The statement reminded me of Adam. "Is that what this is coming to? Since when does Heaven care more about starting a fight than taking the higher ground? Since when is it acceptable to bend the rules to make them what you want them to be? She wasn't threatening you or anybody in this airport. If you were concerned about the flight, you could have bought a ticket."

"The demons have summoned one of their most powerful souls back to this world, diuscrucis," Jane said. "Surely, you of all people understand what that means for us."

"That's not an excuse for overreacting. What did you expect to happen here? You kill one Great Were and lose ten of your own in the process? How is that going to help your cause?"

None of the angels said anything.

"Besides that, you should know something like this would get me involved. I'm on the case, and I appreciate you not trying to kill my friends."

"We didn't know she was with you," Sourpuss said. "We didn't know you were you."

"If you had given me a minute, instead of insulting-"

"She's a demon," the instigator said, back on his feet. His lost arm was already beginning to heal. "A powerful one. It doesn't matter who she is with. She needs to die."

"Saul, be quiet," Jane said. "I'll speak to you about this later."

The angel glowered at Alyx. "I meant what I said."

She bared her teeth, taking a step toward him. I put my hand on her shoulder, and she stopped.

"Enough," I said. "You know Abaddon is back in this world. You can help me stop him from destroying the balance, or you can start fights with my people and force me to kill you."

Jane nodded, still glaring at Saul. "I'm not prepared to help you, diuscrucis. However, we won't stand in your way. Let's go."

She led the angels away, leaving us alone as the mortals began to return to the area as if nothing had ever happened.

"I'm sorry," Alyx said again, looking at me with big eyes.

"Forget about it," I replied. "They shouldn't have been pushing you. What did he say, anyway?"

"It doesn't matter now. I'll do better next time, I promise."

I smiled and gave her a hug. "I know you will."

11

The rest of the trip to Denver was relatively uneventful. Alyx slept most of the way, her head resting on my chest while she snored in a cute mini-growl. I spent the entire time awake, trying to get my mind right for the bigger and more important trip. It took a lot of effort to pep-talk myself into not freaking out about the idea of Hell. I had been trapped in the Box with the Beast, who was a bigger, badder version of Lucifer, and I had come out victorious. I shouldn't have been as nervous as I was.

It was the history, the fear ingrained since I was a child by my somewhat religious mother, that was psyching me out. Sure, the Box had been a scary place, but it had also been ever-changing, control of it usurped by the power of the Beast. Hell was static in comparison. Charis had been my first true love, but she had never been as well-suited to the environment of the Box as Alyx was to Hell. Great Weres were uncommon on any plane.

After we had landed, I rented a car and drove us downtown. The sleep had lifted Alyx's spirits, dampened somewhat after the altercation with the angels. She pointed at the buildings, made comments about the people she saw, and acted more like an enthusiastic tourist than a powerful demon.

"Where do we find Damien?" I asked as we cruised along Speer

Boulevard.

"His master owns a gentleman's club up in Westminster."

A gentleman's club. Of course. Demons tended to go for vice to fuel their own.

"His master? I thought he was his own fiend."

"No. He's a dealer for another fiend named Cabal. Cabal is about two steps below archfiend. Damien's two steps lower than that."

"So, do we talk to Damien directly or do I need to go through Cabal."

"We'll go to Damien. If he hasn't heard from Espanto, he won't know that I've left him. I can convince him I'm on a job."

"Did Espanto send you on a lot of jobs alone?"

"He was always nearby when he did. He never wanted to risk me being able to break his bond. He'd stay in a hotel and send me out on his errands."

"I'm surprised he didn't handle Damien himself."

"Because of the club? Espanto didn't want women who would sell their bodies like that. It was the power that turned him on. He loved having control over it."

"I don't need any more details," I said. She had already told me some of the things the demon had forced her to do. "What if Damien knows you left?"

"Since you didn't like my idea of payment, he'll probably make us go to Cabal. We'll negotiate with Cabal, and he'll send us on our way. Then he'll tell Espanto where I am and get paid again."

It was predictable demon behavior. "Which is why we'll find an alternate Rift to travel through and come out somewhere else," I said.

"Damien won't like that."

"I think you can convince him."

"I thought-"

"With your claws."

She laughed.

We made the trip up to Westminster. It was nine in the evening, and whatever action took place in the club would be in full swing. I was surprised to find a line outside the place, a decent sized building with no windows and a simple sign. A pair of large, human bouncers was controlling the crowd.

"I'm not used to seeing lines for a nudie bar," I said.

"Cabal gets some of the best talent from the industry," Alyx said. "He's got a lot of connections."

I parked the car, looking back at the assembled crowd and then at the two of us. The business casual would have to go. I reached out and put my hand on the Alyx's miniskirt at the top of her thigh. She put her hand on top of mine and held it while I morphed the tweed to something a little more slinky and moved on to her blouse and jacket.

I changed my clothes into a sharper, more expensive looking suit.

"You're up," I said as we climbed from the car.

She took my hand, leading me through the crowd to the front of the line. The bouncers wouldn't see her as Divine. To them, she was as human as anyone else in the cue, except that she was important.

"Is Damien here?" she asked. I could hear people on the line bitching about me getting to cut in because I had a "hot chick" with me.

"Alyx. It's been a while. Who's your friend?"

"This is Baylor. One of Espanto's newest acquisitions. He's just here to help me carry."

"Sure. Sure." The bouncer stepped aside. "Damien is backstage. If you'd come a couple of hours later, you would have missed him."

"Thanks, Ronnie," Alyx said, guiding me past the heavies. The other guests were still complaining, and I could hear Ronnie tell them to stuff it as we moved through a foyer and out into the club.

I wanted to ignore the fact that I was in a strip joint. I wanted to pretend I was somewhere a little more clandestine, like a library. It was tough to do when the girls were everywhere. Cleaning tables, carrying trays, tending the bar. They were all dressed in something slinky, and most of it was either topless or transparent. I could feel my face burning, embarrassed for being here.

Then there was the stage. There were three girls up on it, not even a thong to share between them. They were undulating and grinding against one another. I only spared them a two-second glance before I looked away.

Sometimes I really hated dealing with demons.

"How do we get backstage from here?" I asked, having to raise my voice over the din of dance music.

"Follow me," Alyx said. I expected her to be amused by my modesty. Instead, she seemed bothered that I was being subjected to the display. Was that progress?

We made our way off the left of the stage to a guarded and locked door. The guard recognized Alyx and slid his access key across the reader before we had even arrived. We went through without slowing.

I thought the floor of the club was bad. Behind it was even worse. There were private booths here, open out into the corridor we walked along, where patrons were receiving special attention from the dancers. I was sure most of it was illegal, and I did my best to ignore the sights, sounds and smells as we cleared that area and reached the offices behind.

"Are you okay?" Alyx asked.

I nodded. "I just hope Hell is nothing like this."

We kept walking until we reached a heavier steel door. Alyx pushed it open, and we descended some steps, heading down into a sub-basement below the place.

I could hear voices ahead of us as we entered a dingy, earthy corridor. Alyx came to stop.

"Cabal is in with Damien. Damn it."

"What do you want to do?"

"Did you come up with another way to pay for the trip?"

"Yeah." Elyse wasn't going to like it.

"Then let's get this done." She started forward again.

The voices gained in volume as we drew nearer to another door, this one made of stone and covered with demonic runes. One of the voices was a booming bass, the other equally loud and scratchy. The two demons were so busy yelling at one another that they didn't notice immediately when Alyx pulled the door open.

I didn't know which demon was which. They were both around six feet and thick with muscle, dressed in silk shirts and nice pants. They were arguing in the center of a ring of runed stones on a dirt floor. A Hell Rift.

Execution

"How many times I got to tell you to keep your hands off?" the deep-voiced one was saying to the other. "Girls start getting hurt in my club, they tell their friends, and before you know it I can't get any decent talent in here."

"She came on to me. What was I supposed to do?"

"You say every girl I bring in comes onto you."

"Well, they-" His eyes flicked over to Alyx, and he stopped talking. The other one noticed a moment later.

"Alyx," he said. "What a pleasant surprise."

"You're a terrible liar, Cabal," Alyx said, identifying the demons for me.

"Okay. Truth is you're the last thing I wanted to see in my joint. Your husband is looking for you."

"He isn't my husband," Alyx said.

"Whatever. I don't care about that stuff. I do care that he told me he would burn everything I own if you turned up and I let you walk."

"Like you could stop me?"

Cabal smiled. "Yeah, I didn't tell your husband that, not that he would have listened anyway. Just walk and I'll pretend I never saw you."

"Sorry, I can't. My new master wants to hire you."

His eyebrows raised at that statement. So did mine. How many times did I have to tell her not to call me master?

"Oh," he said, noticing me for the first time. "You aren't talking about this thing, are you? It isn't even strong enough to have an aura."

I didn't like the way he called me "it." I gathered my power, using it to throw him to the wall and pin him there. Damien tried to come to his master's defense, but Alyx stepped in front of him, turning one of her hands into a large claw.

"Have a little respect for the diuscrucis," she said.

His eyes widened, and he looked at me a little closer. "You're him?" he asked.

I let him go. "Yes."

"You have a knack for getting mixed up with interesting individuals," Damien said.

"Better him than Espanto," Alyx said. "That's why I'm not afraid of that asshole. I'm under Landon's protection. He's my true mate."

I could see the jealousy in Damien's eyes. Cabal just laughed. "How come Espanto didn't tell me you ran off with the diuscrucis?"

It was because he wouldn't have remembered how Alyx left. Only that she had.

"I need a ride, and a guide," I said.

"From me?" Cabal asked. "Where to?"

"You're standing in it."

He laughed again, harder. "You want to go to Hell?"

"Want? No. Need? Yes."

"Why would I help you get there?"

"I can pay."

"Oh? What do you have?"

I clenched my teeth while I removed the stone from my pocket and summoned the sword. "You can have this after we get back."

"Before you go," Cabal said, his eyes lighting up. "That thing is legendary."

"No. I might need it while I'm there."

"What if you don't come back?"

"I will."

He considered for a few seconds. "Deal. Damien was about to go out on a run. You can tag along. He'll get you where you need to go, and if you survive he'll bring you back."

"Fair enough. Don't even think about double-crossing me. I'm not an easy one to get rid of."

"Wouldn't dream of it," Cabal said. "I like my head attached to my neck. You want to seal it in blood?"

"Not necessary. I'll take your word."

"You have it. Damien, make sure the diuscrucis here comes back alive. I want that sword."

"Yes, master," Damien said.

"If Espanto comes back here, you haven't seen me," Alyx said.

"Of course not," Cabal replied. "Step aside and we'll get you on your way."

We cleared the circle. Damien vanished from the room while Cabal drew some additional runes on the wall by slicing open his hand with a knife and dipping his finger in the blood.

"What are those for?" I asked.

"I'm binding Alyx to this Rift," he said. "I can't have you deciding to take another path back here and getting away without giving up either her or the sword."

"Nobody said anything about this."

"You don't want to go; you don't have to."

"Give me a break, Cabal. We both know when we come back Espanto is going to be here waiting for us."

He shrugged. "Chance you got to take, diuscrucis. I thought you were a tough guy?"

I glared at him. Alyx squeezed my arm and leaned in to whisper to me. "It'll be okay."

"No, it won't be," I whispered back. "If we come back through that Rift, and Espanto is here, you'll be back under his control. I can't fight both of you alone."

"You can take a different path."

"And leave you with him? Not a chance."

"Won't you come to save me again?"

"Of course I would, but-"

"But what?"

My mind flashed back to the meat locker in China, to the sight of Espanto's brand and Alyx's story about how he used her. It wasn't an uncommon thing amongst demons, and I had become numb to it most of the time. Not with Alyx. I couldn't stand the thought of his hands on her body.

"If I don't do this, then I'm hindering you again," she said.

Damn. Why did my words always get me in trouble?

"Well?" Cabal asked.

Alyx pulled away from me before I could respond, using a claw to cut her other hand open. Cabal dipped a finger in it and finished the rune. It burst into flame, and I could feel the demonic energy pass between the circle and Alyx, binding her to it.

I suddenly felt guilty for not doing more to stop her.

"Even if you take another Rift, she'll be passed here through the Nether," Cabal said. "There's no way around it, so you can either come with or leave her behind. Either way I get paid."

Damien returned to the room, three more fiends trailing behind him. They arranged themselves around the circle with Cabal. Apparently, the fiend wasn't strong enough to activate the Hell Rift on his own.

"Damien, don't forget to make the pickup. This isn't just a sightseeing tour."

"Of course, Master," Damien replied.

The four fiends knelt, putting their hands on the stones and whispering. A moment later, a ring of fire enveloped the edge of the circle.

"Let's go, diuscrucis," Damien said. "Ladies first."

Alyx looked back at me, her eyes apologetic, before stepping into the Rift and vanishing.

A moment later, I did the same.

Execution

12

The trip between Earth and Hell was instant. One second I was in Cabal's subterranean lair, and the next I was much, much further down.

Of course, that wasn't an accurate description of where Hell existed. At all. It felt like an eternity since Josette had explained the physics to me. My version was that each realm was in its own plane, stacked together like a hamburger. Purgatory was the cheese melted on top of the mortal realm while Heaven and Hell were the buns. From what Cabal had said, I guess there was another layer called the Nether. That would be the mayo, or the mustard, depending on how they build burgers wherever you happened to be from.

In any case, we had arrived. I tested my power before I even considered looking around, not wholly convinced that it would translate.

It did.

"Are you okay?" Alyx asked, taking my arm again.

"I am right now. I'm not thrilled about what will happen when we're done here."

"I'm sorry, Landon. There was no other way. You need to do this."

"I wish I didn't."

I finally noticed our surroundings. If the walls of the room hadn't been darker and clear of runes, I wouldn't have known we had gone anywhere.

"I have to say, if this is Hell, I'm a little underwhelmed," I said.

"Please," Damien said. "You see one tiny little crap room, and you think you know anything?"

He smiled, showing a mouth full of sharp teeth that he didn't have topside.

Then he tried to hit me.

I was caught by surprise. Even so, I still managed to shift my feet, grab his punch, and keep going with his momentum, throwing him hard into the wall. He hit it with a grunt, and then turned and came at me again.

By then, I had the spatha out, and I summoned it just in time to leave the blade an inch from his chest.

"What the hell was that?" I asked.

"Just testing you out. You need to be quick to survive as a free soul out here."

I glanced over at Alyx, who hadn't moved a muscle. "You knew this was coming?"

She nodded. "I could smell his aggression. I knew you would be fine."

I let the spatha go back to the lettuce, or the tomato, or wherever it went when it wasn't in use. I pocketed the stone again.

"Lead the way," I said to Damien.

He headed for the exit, and we followed. We moved through dark corridors, up a flight of iron stairs, and back out into what was still a club. It resembled the club we had left somewhat, but it seemed as though it had been passed through a strangely distorted filter. It was still vice, but it had changed into something darker and more sinister.

There were girls up on the stage. They were still naked. They were still bumping and grinding. The music they moved to was discordant, off-tempo, like listening to the Beatles in reverse. They clawed and bit at one another, tearing into one another's flesh and drawing blood.

The patrons of the place had their eyes on them, but they didn't all seem to be watching. Most looked disheveled and downtrodden; their eyes glazed over with a look of utter hopelessness. There were a few demons in the club, a fiend and a pair of devils. They weren't like the kind that

Execution

existed on Earth. They were bigger and more imposing. I noticed them noticing us.

"It's depressing, but not much of a departure from what I'm used to," I said.

"Hell isn't for the free souls," Damien said. "Do you see those mortals at the front?"

I followed the dancers down to the front of the stage. Four men in ratty old suits were positioned there, heads drenched in the dancer's blood, eyes frozen on the display.

"What about them?"

"They're always there. In that spot. They can't leave." He laughed. "An eternity of being forced to watch, and covered in a reminder of their weakness. Those devils back there can come and go as they please. They like the show because they choose when to see it."

"You're saying the main torture of Hell is a lack of choice?"

"Bingo. Sure, you have some of the worse offenders who are also subjected to pain day in and day out, but they don't have a choice either. The lesser damned get stuck with their vice, be it lust, sloth, greed, whatever. They get the version of it that the Big Guy chooses, and they live it until they either become numb and lost or until they man up and break free."

"Break free? I thought Hell was eternal?"

"Where do you think the devils and all of the other free souls of Hell come from? Where do you think Lucifer gets his stock to send back to Earth? Some souls manage to break loose of their bonds and go on the run. When they do, if they can survive for a day without being captured or killed, then they get bumped up to a minor demon and can start earning more and more freedom."

"You did that?"

"Yup."

"How long were you down here?"

"Fifteen years." He shuddered visibly as he said it. "Then another ten working up to fiend and getting sent back to the mortal world. Most people think of Hell, and they think of chaos. There is a level of it, especially out here, but don't forget that Lucifer used to be an angel. He still keeps the underlying systems running like clockwork."

I was surprised by the information. I had always known that many of the demons on Earth originated in Hell and were sent back to sow chaos and destruction there. I had never learned how that process occurred.

"So how does a damned soul break loose of their bonds?"

"Usually it's because the torture doesn't work on them. Instead of growing weary and hopeless at the endlessness of it, they come to enjoy it instead. Even then, many will choose to remain for that reason, and Hell almost becomes Heaven to them. If Lucifer senses that and the soul doesn't try to claim free will, their punishment will be altered."

"Use it or lose it?"

"Pretty much."

Damien guided us to the exit. We were at the door out into the wilds of Hell when the two devils decided they had done enough watching. They took up a position in front of the doors, crossing their arms and trying to look more frightening. Each was over twelve feet in height and solidly built, their red, leathery skin bulging with strength.

"I don't recognize these two. Do you, Skalax?" one asked the other.

"Who are your new friends, Damien?" Skalax replied.

"Careful, Dilix," Damien said. "These two have business in the Pit. Let them pass or you may find yourselves starting over."

"Two creatures from the mortal realm are supposed to frighten us?" Dilix said.

Apparently, these two had never come across a Great Were before. Being born on the Earth plane, Alyx's kind probably didn't travel to Hell very often.

"Just let us go," I said. "I don't have time for your bullshit."

Dilix and Skalax glanced at each other. A moment later, massive swords appeared in both of their hands.

Damien backed away at once. I gathered my power while summoning the spatha to hand. It was a toothpick compared to their huge blades, but it was equally powerful, if not more so. The angelic scripture would lessen the brutality of any parry.

Execution

Alyx remained in human form, her eyes glued to the demons' every motion. She was keeping her demon form a secret. If they didn't know what she was, she wasn't going to tell them unless she had to.

"You're sure I'll be fine?" I asked.

She smiled and nodded at me, just before she slipped away from a falling blade.

I threw my power out at Skalax, hitting him hard enough to send him crashing into the wall and make a massive dent in it. At the same time, I scampered in toward Dilix, getting close before he could bring his blade around. It was a terrible weapon for this range. I pushed off, leaping up high and bringing the spatha around. His neck felt like soft butter as the sword eased through it.

I landed, spinning toward Skalax, who had regained his feet. He saw what had happened to Dilix, and his sword vanished.

"What manner of demon are you?" he asked.

"He's not a demon," Alyx said. "He is the diuscrucis."

"Diuscrucis?" Skalax didn't know the word or its meaning.

"It doesn't matter," I said. "Get out of the way or I'll take your head, too."

Skalax stepped aside. "Of course, Master," he said, bending into a subservient pose. "As you command."

We stepped through the pile of ash that had been Dilix only seconds before. Damien pushed open the door and held it for us.

Demons who were killed on Earth were sent back to Hell. What about demons killed in Hell? "What will happen to Dilix?"

"His soul will return to its original state as one of the damned. His torture will be greater for his failure. He may or may not ever become free again."

"It seems risky to start fights with consequences like that."

"We're the damned, diuscrucis. It's in our nature to cause conflict. You would have more luck teaching a pig to sing."

13

We moved from the club out onto the streets. There was a lot more to take in outside, from the constant, faint smell of sulfur to the red and black sky, where heavy clouds of smoke sent a constant dusting of ash falling across everything. It was already two inches deep in the streets.

The city was similar to New York, but it clearly wasn't the Big Apple. Everything was damaged to some extent. Broken windows, dented light poles, and cracked facades were everywhere, along with downtrodden pedestrians making endless loops barefoot through the streets, the glass from the windows slicing them up and leaving trails of blood in their wake. There were other damned souls here as well. Women that Damien said were adulterers were being chased through the streets by devils with massive, erect penises while their male counterparts were running from harpies carrying any one of an assortment of sharp instruments. Murderers were paraded on the back of slow-moving trucks as if part of a twisted Thanksgiving Day Parade, some in nooses, some in guillotines, some in the electric chair. They were killed, reformed, and killed again, over and over while we waited for them to meander past.

There were others, of course. So many others. This was Hell. It was also a city. A hundred different tortures prepared for all kinds of sinners and assholes.

I couldn't imagine how any of them could come to enjoy their fate and earn their freedom.

I also knew it had happened.

It only proved how twisted the person was to begin with, and it showed how deep Lucifer's hatred of his Father ran that these were the creatures he wanted to on Earth disrupting the balance.

Dante had warned me about the carnage. I was surprised to find that it was easy to become numb to, and even easier for me to recognize that these souls deserved it. Every one of them had done more harm than good in their lifetime, or they wouldn't have been there in the first place.

"How come the city doesn't get buried in the ash?" I asked, wiping some of it from my shoulders and hair.

"It all resets every day. We follow mortal time here though no-one in Hell sleeps. It makes it easier to synchronize with the efforts of the demons back home."

The demons who wanted to destroy humankind. It was easy to forget that, being here instead of there. I needed to get a move on, get the FOG and get back. Which reminded me...

"Abaddon," I said internally, seeking the demon.

I could still feel the link, but it had weakened considerably. He didn't answer.

"Where are you headed, anyways diuscrucis?" Damien asked. "You showed Cabal that sword of yours, and he didn't even remember to ask."

"Cain has something I need," I said.

A pedestrian with bare feet tried to walk between us. Damien grabbed him and threw him to the side, causing him to cry out in anguish. He didn't stop until he made it back to the broken glass on the sidewalk.

"Did you just say, Cain?"

"Yeah."

"As in, the son of Lucifer?"

"Yeah."

"Damn you, Cabal." Damien spat on the ground at my feet. It sizzled and burst into flame. "I never would have guessed you wanted to end down here."

"What would happen to my soul if I did?" I asked, regretting it as soon as the words had escaped me.

"That would be up to the Big Guy to decide."

Which is what I was afraid of. I doubted he was too happy with me stopping all of his evil plots to this point. Still, maybe he figured he would owe me one for getting rid of the Beast. It wasn't just humankind I had saved with that one. It was everything.

"Is Cain that dangerous?" Alyx said.

"He's the son of Satan. What do you think?"

"I don't want to confront him," I said. "I just want to take something of his."

"You want to steal from him."

"Technically."

"You do understand the definition of 'steal,' right?"

"Yes. He took this thing from the mortal realm. Since I'm the presiding Divine there, that means he stole it from me first. I'm just trying to get it back."

"Technically," Damien said.

"Yes."

He laughed. "Here's the deal, diuscrucis. I'm not going within a hundred miles of Cain without an invitation. No demon who wants to stay free does. I'll give you directions, and then I'm going to make my pickup. I'll wait for you back here. You have three days before I abandon you. Got it?"

"The deal I made with Cabal was for you to guide us," I said.

"I told you I'll give you directions."

"I can kill you myself."

"You could, but then I wouldn't be able to help you at all because I'd be back to walking the streets like these pathetic souls."

"What did they do, anyway?"

"Nothing. They did nothing. They squandered their lives without trying to live them."

"That's why you were down here?"

Execution

"Yeah. I was a sad sack of shit, wasn't I? I lived with my mom right up until the day I overdosed on crack. Never had a job, never had a girlfriend, never left home. Drug Addiction may be a disease. Lifelong ennui is the work of the Devil." He laughed at that. "So, take it or leave it."

I wasn't happy about losing my guide. I also didn't have much of a choice. I was happy to have Alyx with me, so I would at least still have a demonic companion. I glanced over at her. It was the first time I had ever had a thought like that.

"Fine. Tell me how to get there."

14

"Maybe we should have brought Damien along at swordpoint," I said.

Alyx laughed, an odd mix between a growl and a giggle that came across as disgustingly cute. "The directions he gave us are fine. See, there's the station up ahead."

We were still in the city part of Hell. I didn't know if it had a name, but I had taken to calling it 'The Kitchen,' in honor of the area in New York. We had been wandering through it for the last two hours or so, following the directions Damien had recited three times. There was nothing fun about it. I walked the streets, evading the sloths, turning my eyes away from the lustful and the adulterers, and trying to figure out the crimes of some of the even more twisted punishments we discovered along the way. Alyx kept her eyes forward, barking out every change in direction and leading me to our destination. I already knew she had keen senses. Her keen intellect was a pleasant surprise.

Damien's directions led us to the Terminal, a massive train station near the edge of the Kitchen. It was the main form of transportation from one area of Hell to another for any free soul who wasn't able to fly or wasn't big enough to walk quickly. That meant no fallen angels, devils, or harpies, to name a few. It did include fiends, succubi, incubi, and other

Execution

assorted wingless nasties.

Word of my identity had spread quickly, and, for the most part, the demons had left us alone on our journey, hiding in shadows and watching us pass. To be honest, the whole thing was strangely familiar and felt a little too normal to me for my liking. Was the inference that my life was already a sort of Hell? I hoped not.

The Terminal was crowded when we reached it, with all sorts of demons milling around, hissing and whispering and cursing at one another. They pushed and shoved whenever another of their kind got too close, but they didn't outright attack. It was obvious that the fear of going back to whatever they were before was strong enough to keep them mostly in line.

"Do we have to buy a ticket, do you think?" I asked as we slipped through the gates into the area. They were gnarled and twisted, with lots of pointy tips that a demon could get impaled on if they weren't careful.

"I don't think so," Alyx said. "I don't see anywhere to buy one."

I looked around. There was no counter, no help of any kind. We were surrounded by hundreds of demons on fenced-in grounds, a thin space in the center where the tracks crossed the only unoccupied area. I moved my eyes up, taking in the sight of a huge fire demon crossing the sky, on its way to who knows where. What did demons do in their spare time? Did demons even have spare time? Where were they all going that they needed a train to travel back and forth? Once more, I wanted Damien here so I could grill him on the finer points of culture in Hell.

"How about a timetable?" I asked.

Not that we had any idea what time it was. There was no sun, so the sky never really changed. It remained red and black. It continued raining ash. I was already sick of it.

"There's a lot of demons here. I bet it will come soon."

"What was the name of our stop again?"

"The Desolation."

"Sounds like a nice vacation spot."

She laughed again. I was going to have to up my game to keep her going. I was enjoying the sound, especially here.

"The son of Lucifer lives there. I doubt it's much of a vacation for anyone but him."

"Good point," I said.

We spent the next ten minutes or so standing around among the demons, staying shoulder-to-shoulder in the crowd. I was still on high alert, unconvinced that the denizens of the underworld wouldn't decide to gang up on us at some point, once enough of them realized who we were. I had noticed more and more of them casting their glances our way the longer we waited, and a soft murmur had risen in the background cacophony of hissing, whispering, and distant screaming.

"Hey," a small voice said from somewhere nearby.

I turned my head, seeking the speaker.

"Landon," Alyx said, squeezing my shoulder. I looked at her, and she directed my attention down.

"Yeah, here I am Burj Dubai."

It was a demon, of course. A two-foot-tall spike of dark brown leather, with a small snout and big, round eyes that bulged away from its skull.

"Are you talking to me?" I asked.

"Yes, I'm talking to you. Why do you think I'm standing on your foot?"

He was so light; I hadn't even noticed.

"Can we help you with something?" Alyx asked.

"You can help me with a lot of things," the demon replied. "Or maybe I can help you. I can see up your skirt from here." He stuck his tongue out suggestively.

"Disgusting," Alyx replied. "Tell me why I shouldn't kill you right now."

He scampered back behind my legs. "Oh. Whoa, whoa, whoa. I was just kidding. A little demon sexual humor, that's all. No, no, no. Zifah wants to be friends with the diuscrucis."

"Zifah? That's your name?" I asked.

"The short version." He came back around to stand between us. "I've been following you since you left the club. I wasn't sure who you were at first, but then I heard the others whispering. I think we can help one another."

A demon would never offer to do anything unless it wanted something

Execution

in return. While the diminutive demon didn't look like trouble, I knew better than to assume. I also remembered what Dante had said to me about being careful of offers down here.

"Not interested, thanks."

"What? You don't even want to hear my story?"

"Not really." I shook my foot, knocking him off. I had never seen such a small demon before that didn't have wings.

"Oh, come on, Landon," he said, dusting himself off. "I know, I know, don't trust demons, especially in Hell. I get that; I do. I even know where you got that advice. I met Dante, a long time ago. Did you know that?"

"Still not interested."

"I don't want much. Just a chance to escape. To level up, so to speak. I want to go to - look out behind you!"

I didn't turn around. I wasn't dumb enough to fall for that trick. The demon had probably heard about the sword and was going to try to steal the stone from my pocket the moment my attention was diverted.

Something hit me in the back of the head. Hard. It sent me reeling forward into Alyx, who reached out and caught me. We were both off-balance, and we fell in a tangle together.

"Not now," Alyx said. "We're in public."

"Funny," I replied, using my power to push myself up and twirl around at the same time.

A demon was standing a few feet away, staring at me with death in its eyes. He was eight feet tall, with a bad overbite from the size of his teeth, and wrinkled, thick skin. I had never encountered a creature like him before.

"They say you free soul from the mortal world. They say you tough. They say Jazir should fear diuscrucis. Jazir fear nothing."

I reached into my pocket and withdrew the stone, summoning the spatha. It seemed the demons wanted to test me and had sent a brute to do it.

"Come on," I said, dropping into a crouch.

A circle grew around us. Alyx moved back with it, and I noticed Zifah was beside her, his eyes shifting between me and her legs. I made a mental note to deal with him when this was over.

The demon pounced at me, his agility defying his size. I stepped back, raising the point of the sword and holding it out to let him impale himself on it.

It hit his flesh and slid up and to the side, not even leaving a scratch. His fist hit me in the jaw, and I flew back into Alyx a second time.

I pushed my power into healing, keeping an eye on the demon. He waited for me in the center of the circle, giving me a chance to understand how he worked instead of taking advantage. Now I knew that his skin was tough enough to stop the obsidian spatha.

That was bad.

"I can kill him for you," Alyx said as I pulled myself away.

"And leave me looking weak? Not unless he's about to kill me."

"Okay."

I approached the demon again, discarding the spatha and putting the stone back in my pocket. He was smiling now, a toothy grin of superiority.

"Come on," I said a second time.

He rushed forward again, repeating his first move. I planted my feet, surrounding myself with my power, holding it tight against me like a second skin.

His fist came at my face. I pushed out against it, catching the force of it and leaving him standing with his weight forward, into his suddenly ineffective punch. I returned his smile as he adjusted himself and backed away.

"You tougher than you look," he said. He lifted his head slightly. "Train coming. I break you now."

He didn't hesitate this time, rushing toward me at ridiculous speed. I stepped out of the way of his first punch, ducked under the second, and steered myself around to his side. I threw a couple of ineffective punches of my own before dancing away again. I could hear the train in the background now, a growing howl like it was powered by a million tortured souls, and it probably was.

Jazir growled in frustration as I moved away from two more strikes, and then jumped forward and punched him in the face. He didn't even

Execution

flinch, and I barely escaped his grasp before he crushed me.

"Stop moving," he said. "You like little piss demon, flying around and being annoying."

A harsh light appeared over the mass of demons, the lights of the approaching train. It was time to end this game.

I gathered my power, pulling it in and bunching it into a tight ball. I stepped back away from Jazir, putting a few feet of distance between us.

"Give up now," I said.

Jazir wasn't the only one who laughed. A hundred demons laughed with him.

He tried to hit me again. I pushed my power out, wrapping him in it and lifting, throwing him up and over the crowd.

He howled as he arced through the air and landed right in front of the train. His skin might have been impervious to a blade. His bones weren't immune to being crushed. The train didn't notice his howling, or when it stopped.

The laughter stopped with it. All eyes fell everywhere but where I was standing, and the demons began assembling to climb onto the train.

Alyx grabbed my arm and kissed my cheek. "Well done, my love," she said.

"Yeah, nice work, diuscrucis," Zifah said, still hovering under Alyx's leg.

"I saw you looking," I said.

He backed up a few steps. "Heh. I am a demon, you know. Damn mortal prudes. Look, I saved your life-"

"How did you save my life? I would have had to fight him whether he got that sucker punch in or not."

He shrugged. "At least I tried. How many demons down here would go that far?"

"I'm still not interested."

He growled softly and spat on the ground in front of me. "Fine. Have it your way. One more word of advice: you should be more careful who you make enemies with. Or at least, who you refuse to make friends with. See you later, Landon."

He scampered off into the crowd, vanishing in a sea of legs.

"Do you think I should have listened to him?" I asked Alyx.

"No. Take your chances with what you can see in front of you, not intangible threats and promises."

I nodded before leaning in and kissing her on the cheek for once.

It was good advice.

Execution

15

The train was a distorted replica of the Orient Express, a steam locomotive powered by the Damned, who were chopped and fed like coals into a massive furnace. The interior was mahogany and red, the seats plush and relatively comfortable, and filled with demons. They acted almost civilized, choosing a seat and sitting quietly while the locomotive made its travels.

Alyx and I found a seat near the back. As with the Terminal, none of the demons on the train would look at me, turning their heads away the moment I came anywhere near them. It was odd how it made me feel more out of place than being the only non-demon in an entire plane full of them did. Even though it was a sign of respectful fear, it was easy for my formerly human ego to take it as rejection.

"How far to the Desolation?" I asked.

"According to Damien, it's the third stop. He said about an hour."

"I still can't believe this is Hell."

"Me neither."

"Really? You're a demon."

She looked hurt by the statement, true or not. "I'm a Were. A child of Lucifer, yes. Does that make me nothing but a demon to you?"

I swallowed a sudden lump in my throat. My mind wandered back further than it had in a long time. All the way back to Rebecca. She had been the first demon I met, and I thought she had been able to change. Maybe she did in the end, but not before she screwed me a few times for believing in her.

I reminded myself that Alyx was not Rebecca. Not in any way I could discern. Was it true that she could be completely playing me with the sweet, naive Great Were act? Of course. Demons were good at that. Rebecca had been. I was more experienced now. I hoped I was wiser. I didn't see anything in Alyx that I had seen in Rebecca. She had decided I was her mate because Ulnyx had been the Alpha of her pack, and I had absorbed the Great Were's powers at one point. It made sense from a Divine perspective, and it was the simplest reason anyone could have given for anything.

Simple was always more believable.

"You're more than a demon to me," I said. "You know I don't choose my friends by their affiliation to good or evil. That's not my way." I couldn't afford to be that narrow-minded.

"Do you love me?"

"Alyx, how many times are you going to ask?"

"Until you say yes."

"What if I never say yes?"

"Then I'll keep asking."

Simple.

"What if I did say yes?"

"Then we should mate. I will make you happy."

My heart was pounding by now. I was starting to feel like every time she asked I was getting closer to saying yes, despite every intention not to.

"You make me happy as a friend," I said.

"I'll make you happier as a lover." She paused, looking down at her lap. Her voice softened. "Landon?"

It was odd behavior from her. "What is it?" I asked, concerned.

"I knew that I loved you because I was intended to be one of Ulnyx's mates, and you were once the Alpha of my pack. But-"

Execution

Her voice trailed away. She looked uncomfortable, and vulnerable in a way I hadn't seen and could barely imagine.

"But what?" I asked.

"I have other... feelings. From here." She put a hand on her heart. "And from here." She put her hand on her gut, where I believed the soul rested. "Not just obligation and a desire to mate with you. Something more. We've been together for the last three weeks, and when I think of being parted from you, I don't like it."

I stared at her, my heart ready to thump right through my chest. Was she telling me that she really loved me? Not only in the way she had believed love was but for real? I knew demons were capable of real love. Izak had loved Josette and Sarah.

"What does it mean?" she asked when I remained silent for too long.

"It means you're more than a demon. A lot more."

16

The two stops before the Desolation were the Spikes and the Pit.

The Spikes were a series of sharp mountain peaks where the torments of the damned echoed from the spires, the actual torture generated deep within the mountains. I didn't know what kind of souls were sent there, but I could hear the difference in their screams from those of the Kitchen, and from those fueling the train. Judging by that, they were not in a happy place. Not. At. All.

The Pit was the more classic representation of Hell. It was where the fire and brimstone hit it hard. The train paused at a station there to take on more passengers, who seemed to pick up on their counterpart's attitudes and instinctively know not to look at me. From my position near the window, I could see the massive pit in the ground, and the cliff faces where damned souls were chained and screaming out as fire licked at their bodies. I had wondered as we began moving again how those souls ever got free to become demons. They didn't have use of their hands or feet to get themselves out of the chains. Did they call out to their keepers? Or were the eternally trapped? Maybe that was what happened to the demons who died?

The Desolation made me cry.

Execution

I did it silently, and I tried to hide it from Alyx. I didn't want to cry. I didn't want to look weak. I was glad none of the demons would notice anyway.

"What's wrong?" Alyx asked me, noticing the tears.

I pointed out the window. "I've been here before."

"In Hell?"

"It wasn't in Hell, but it looked just like this."

It was inside the Box. A broken Earth. A post-apocalyptic, destroyed world. Buildings turned to slag and scrap, corpses everywhere. It was the Beast's world. The one that he had destroyed with his power. Or at least, it was a reproduction of it. I had defeated the Beast, but I had lost Charis. I had lost Clara. I had almost lost myself.

It hurt to see it again.

"It isn't the same place. Whatever hurt you there, I won't let it hurt you here."

I reached out and took her hand without thinking. I squeezed it, and she squeezed back.

"It will be well, my love," she said.

"Thanks," I replied.

The train slowed to a stop. Most of the demons were getting on the train. Only a minority departed with us.

"Damien said Cain's palace is near the center. He said you can't miss it."

It was going to be the Freedom Tower. I just knew that it was. It would make the entire nightmare complete. Dante had said Lucifer wouldn't bother with me, but I couldn't help thinking that he was watching, and he had done this to torment me as best he could. A joke only he could make.

I took her hand again, and we started walking, picking our way over the corpses and through the destruction. We hadn't gone too far when I realized that the corpses weren't dead, per se. They were more of the damned, souls left to hunger and thirst for all of eternity. The gluttonous, I assumed.

We covered a lot of ground in two hours, but the broken city seemed to stretch forever. Turning in circles revealed more of the same as far as we could see, as true a desolation as I could have ever imagined.

"If Cain's palace is too far away, we won't make it back to Damien in time," I said.

"We have lots of time left. We can move a lot faster than we have been if I change."

"I'm worried a Great Were running across this landscape is going to attract the wrong kind of attention. I don't want Cain to know we're coming."

"You don't think two people walking across the Desolation will attract attention? There's nothing else out here but the damned, and they aren't upright."

"My plan hinged around sneaking into Cain's palace." I knew it wasn't much of a plan. But then, how could I plan anything when I had no idea what we were walking into.

"I think we need to change the plan. We've been walking for two hours, and I don't see anything. How do we even know we're going in the right direction?" She gave me that mischievous smile again. "Besides, it's the only way I can get you on my back."

I could feel the heat on my face, and it wasn't from being in Hell. I stood silently for a minute, looking around and thinking.

"Okay. You're right. We only have three days, and I don't want to waste them all walking through this."

She leaned in, nuzzling my neck. One second, I could feel the softness of her skin against mine. The next, I felt the rougher fur of a massive muzzle.

Our eyes met. I could still see Alyx behind them, but it was an understatement to say her demon form was nowhere near as attractive as her human form. At the same time, I could still feel our growing connection there.

"Get on," she growled, her voice rougher.

She dropped to all fours, dipping lower so I could climb onto her back. I used my power to plant me to her, and we were off.

Alyx bounded across the landscape with ease, leaping over shorter walls and debris and pushing aside burned out cars and other garbage.

Execution

Within minutes, we had pushed our past location beyond the horizon, and within an hour we had traveled nearly fifty miles. I knew Alyx was enjoying the run, and having me riding her. Part of me didn't want to be having a good time in Hell, but I was a balance of good and evil. I did enjoy it, and I leaned down and wrapped my arms around Alyx's thick neck, holding on tight.

We covered another twenty miles. We saw nothing but more of the same. There had to be a million souls or more out here, laying among the ruin, barely able to move. It was horrible to see them, knowing there was a semblance of life in the withered frames. I had to remind myself over and over that they had been gluttonous enough in the mortal world that they had been delivered to this one. Was it fair to torture them for all of eternity? I never expected anything to be fair.

"This isn't getting us anywhere," I said, growing frustrated by out lack of progress.

Alyx came to a stop, and I slid off her back. She changed back to human form, looking sweaty and maybe even a little tired. I didn't think Great Weres could get tired.

"Damien didn't tell us which way to go," she said. "Maybe he wanted us to get lost?"

"And piss off Cabal by not bringing us back with the sword?"

"Good point."

"In any case, I think we need to start over. Head back the way we came until we get to the station. We can try a new direction, or maybe ask one of the demons which way to go."

She nodded. "I think that's the best option."

"Do you need to rest?"

She was hesitant to tell me she did, but I could see it in her posture.

"It's okay if you do."

"I don't know what it is. Back home I can run for a day without tiring. I know it's hot here, but I'm not used to this."

"Have you fed recently?"

Weres were like any of Lucifer's children. They needed human blood at least occasionally to survive.

"Not since you freed me from Espanto."

"That was almost a month ago."

"I know. I have gone longer. I feel like being in this place is draining me when it should be energizing me."

"You're still a creature of the mortal plane, even if you're Hell-made."

"You aren't tired."

"I'm technically not alive. In fact, I've technically died twice already. We can rest a while." I pointed over at a low wall that used to belong to an apartment building or something. It was clear of the damned. "We can sit there. You can feed."

I said it without thinking. Alyx's expression changed to one of shocked pleasure.

"Are you sure?" she asked, noticing my sudden discomfort.

I had let Rebecca feed on me when she was tired. That hadn't worked out well. Alyx wasn't Rebecca.

"Yes. I'll heal as fast as you can drink, and it should give you your energy back. You're going to need it."

We walked over to the wall, and I sat down against it. She was going to sit next to me, but I reached out and pulled her into my lap.

"You pick strange times to be interested, Mast-Landon."

"It will be easier for you to reach my neck."

"I'm not a vampire. I don't need your neck."

"It's easier to reach."

One of her fingers extended into a razor claw. "You're sure?" she asked again. Her face was close to mine, and I could smell her sweat mixed with her normal scent.

"Yes," I said, taking her hand and putting the finger on my neck. I felt a light sting as she cut me, and then her mouth was against my flesh, drawing out my blood.

She murmured softly as she drew it out, her hands wrapping around me so she could hold me tight against her. The murmur changed into a pleased growl that was almost a purr.

I focused on restoring myself, pushing my energy into my body to heal as fast as she fed. She was thirstier than she had admitted, and I soon

Execution

found myself closing my eyes and relaxing into it. I put my attention on the feel of her weight in my lap, her lips against my skin, her bottom against my thighs.

I opened my eyes. She had stopped drinking and was leaning back, looking at me while she rocked gently on top of me. Of course, I had gotten aroused.

"Alyx," I said softly, lost for breath.

She responded by leaning in and pressing her lips to mine. Half of me begged to push her away, feeling guilty for the sudden rage of emotions I was feeling and telling me I was dishonoring Charis' memory. The other half was a demon in Hell, and it returned the affection with an equal and opposite response, gripping her tighter and opening my mouth to accept her tongue.

What was I doing? Why was I doing it? Lust? Love? Something in between? Or was it the atmosphere of the place, driving me mad?

I didn't know, and for precious minutes I didn't care. I held Alyx tight against me, returning her kisses with equal passion. It felt wrong. It felt wonderful. I hated myself for it, and yet I didn't want to stop.

I should have known that nothing so perfectly flawed was meant to last.

I heard the demon before I saw it, and I broke off our latest kiss in a too-late effort to defend. Large hands grabbed Alyx by the shoulders, pulling her from my lap and throwing her across the wasteland. She went fifty feet at least until she crashed into a dilapidated car, hitting it hard enough to roll it over and bend the frame.

I pushed out with my power with all the force I had. The demon standing in front of me didn't even flinch, and I felt his power peeling mine aside like it was nothing more than a nuisance.

"Diuscrucis, I presume?" the demon said. As powerful as he was, he had to be an archfiend. He was six feet tall, with dark, chunky hair, narrow features that would have made him a great runway model, and an overly pleasant smile. He wore a dark purple leather duster on top of a neatly worn suit.

There was only one demon this could be.

"Cain, I presume?"

Execution

17

"How did you find us?" I asked.

We were riding in the back of a carriage that had followed the son of Lucifer out into the city. Alyx was beside me, dazed but unharmed by the throw while Cain sat opposite us, his posture that of supreme confidence. And why not? He had made my power look like a water pistol instead of an assault rifle.

"This is my realm, diuscrucis. How would I not find you?"

He smiled disarmingly, casting his eyes over at Alyx. He had made it clear that he thought she was something special when he had helped her back to her feet, apologizing for being so rough and dropping to a knee to kiss her hand.

Of course, Lucifer's son was handsome. Lucifer was supposed to be doubly so. Alyx seemed oblivious to it, and her expression didn't change when his gaze fell on her.

"My apologies again, Alyx. I needed to make a statement to your companion."

Alyx didn't respond.

"I know you wouldn't have come all the way to Hell without reason," he said, putting his attention back on me. "And since you decided to grace the Desolation with your treasure, I assume that reason has something to do with me."

He had the look of a man who knew.

"Go on," I said.

"There's only one reason I can think that you might have gone through the trouble to come to Hell and seek me out, despite the fact that you must have been warned that your power is a pittance compared to mine. Here, at least." He smiled again. "Abaddon's soul has been ripped from his realm and returned to yours while I have captured the so-called Fist of God, an interesting mashup of mortal technology and Divine energy that may be the only thing that can contain Abaddon indefinitely."

I tried not to look surprised. "What do you mean, indefinitely?"

"Of course, you didn't know, did you?" he asked, pleased with himself. "The prison the demons have constructed to keep him will not keep him forever. He is more powerful than they realize. He is almost more powerful than me."

That was bad news, and Cain was giving it freely. I didn't like anything about that.

"But the Fist of God definitely can?" I asked.

"It can now. We took the damaged shell and managed to get it reconditioned, and then we added our special sauce to the mix. Demonic runes, allowing it to be controlled by the mind. All you need is a pendant like this one."

He reached under his shirt and produced a metal disc with runes scratched all over it. I think it had been taken from the FOG.

"You made it work?" I asked, almost impressed.

He shook his head. "Not quite yet. I was waiting for the right soul to put in it. I had been hoping maybe for an archangel." His smile changed, and I realized I was right to be worried about how much he was divulging. "I think your arrival has been most timely, don't you?"

"You can't put me in the Fist of God," I said, fighting to keep my exterior appearance calm.

"No? Why not?"

"My power isn't Divine. It came from the Beast."

Execution

"His smile lessened, and he rubbed at his chin. "Hmm, interesting. That would make for quite an experiment."

"I won't let you hurt him," Alyx said, pouncing toward Cain, her hands shifting to claws.

He didn't even flinch. Without moving a single muscle, she was thrown back against the seat of the carriage and held.

"Feisty. I like that."

I stared at Cain. Dante had warned me, and I had rushed ahead with the plan anyway. At least now I knew the mortal world was screwed if I didn't make it back with the FOG. Abaddon would escape, and his power would pull the life out of everything he crossed until there was nothing left.

How the heck was I going to get the armor away from Cain when Cain was completely owning me? I couldn't fight him. I couldn't hurt him. We were stuck. Totally stuck.

Damn.

"So now what?" I asked.

"I'm taking you back to the palace," Cain replied. "You'll be chained up while I discuss the potential of using you in the armor with my team. If they don't think it's possible as you claimed, I may simply mount you as a trophy. Or I might gift you to my father."

"I don't suppose we can bargain for the Fist instead?"

"Out of the question," he replied. He looked at Alyx again. "As for you, I think you're rather exotic, and I admire your spirit. You'll be brought to my harem and prepared as one of my concubines. I should like a taste of you."

"Forget it," I said before I realized how stupid it sounded.

"I don't think you're in a position to argue," Cain said, patronizing me.

Alyx was trying to move, and to shift. Her muscles were bulging from her arms, and her face was wrinkled from the effort. She paused for a moment, her eyes sadder than anything I had ever seen. I couldn't imagine what it would feel like to be made prisoner to a demon again after finally managing to get free.

"Next time, you should be a little more prepared before you plan to visit the son of Lucifer," Cain said, still patronizing.

I glared at him in angry silence for the rest of the trip. I wasn't going to let Alyx be a prisoner again. I was going to find my way out of this, and I was going to destroy Cain.

Somehow.

18

Cain's palace was pretty much what I expected. Think Taj Mahal, with a bit more gaudiness, iron spikes, and ugly statues. It was a massive place, and probably the only location in Hell that had a pool. Or was it a moat? As the carriage rode over the bridge crossing it, and I looked down, it was hard to tell.

It separated the palace from the rest of the desolation. It also had some succubi and incubi in it, splashing, swimming, and being frisky with one another. It was like crossing over to the Playboy Mansion; orgy included.

"I can let you go for a swim before I string you up if you like?" Cain said.

"No thanks," I replied.

It had taken twenty minutes or so to arrive from the time Cain had pinned Alyx to her seat. She had alternated between complete calm and total struggle a few times, fighting hard to break free of the demon's hold. It was no use, even with all her power and her recent feeding. Cain was just that strong. The more interesting part was that we had gone back in the direction Alyx and I had come. Either Cain had hidden the palace from us, or it had moved.

In other words, we would never have found it until Cain wanted us to.

Whether I had concocted a good plan beforehand or not, that was the bottom line.

It made me feel a little better about being caught. Not much, but a little. If I hadn't been so preoccupied with Alyx, I would have seen him coming. Maybe. At the same time, now I knew that this mess could be the only way to have even a slim chance at grabbing the FOG.

The carriage crossed the pool and entered a large courtyard. A pair of demons met us there, opening the door for Cain and dropping to their knees so he could climb down their backs. They did the same for Alyx before leaving me to my own devices.

Cain didn't try to keep me from running. He knew I wouldn't leave Alyx behind, and he was still manipulating her like a marionette. She walked stiffly beside him as he strolled across the open area to a marble archway, through the archway and into a large foyer. I followed him, unsure what else to do.

Then Cain clapped his hands. Immediately, a dozen female souls in gossamer fabrics filed out and to him, surrounding him and looking at him with adoring eyes. They were all wearing a gold bracelet with demonic runes etched around them. Cain took an extra from the hands of one of the women and slipped it onto Alyx's wrist. Then he whispered something; it flamed on for a few seconds, and he visibly relaxed, no longer having to hold her with his will.

She fell into line with the others.

"I thought you liked her feisty," I said, doing my best to stay calm about the whole thing. It wouldn't help either of us to be stupid.

"I will release her when needed. Right now, I want her docile so that I can show you around."

"Show me around?"

"Yes. I want you to see the work I've been doing."

"Why bother?"

"Because I'm surrounded by peons, diuscrucis. Pathetic demons who don't know what true power is. You do. I can talk to you on an almost even level."

"Your power is much stronger than mine."

Execution

"Only here. If we were in your realm, it would be different."

He was humble enough to admit it. That wasn't a common quality in a demon.

Or maybe he was just placating me.

He led me out of the foyer through a series of corridors that I tried to memorize as we passed. I had no way of knowing if the demon would change the layout behind us. I figured if he could move the entire palace, he could shift a few walls. He spoke casually while we walked as if we were old friends.

"I visited the mortal realm once. Did you know that, diuscrucis?"

"You can call me Landon. No, I wasn't aware."

"It was before your time, of course. Though I believe the other one may have been getting started then. What was that one's name again?"

"Charis," I said, wondering if he was trying to get under my skin.

"Right. Yes. That was it. British. I've always loved the British. So proper. So much class. Stiff upper lip, and all that rot." He feigned a proper British accent. "They crumble to nothing when their souls find their way down here. The Germans, though." He laughed but didn't finish the sentence. "Where is she these days?"

He was trying to get under my skin. There was no other reason for him to be mentioning Charis. I should have guessed Lucifer's son couldn't be anything but a bastard, in every sense of the word.

"She's one with the universe," I said. "Her soul is free from all of this crap. Forever."

He seemed confused by the statement. "Free?" I had totally thrown him off his game, and I hadn't even done it on purpose. "Forever? How?"

"I had the power of the Beast inside me. You know the Beast was almost a God in his own right?"

"Can you still do it?"

I didn't think so. But to be honest, I didn't know. Demons had the ability to try to transfer their souls into another host before they went back down to Hell. Did I have the ability to set those souls loose into the aether? I couldn't rule it out completely.

"Maybe, but I doubt it," I said.

He looked at me for a few seconds, and we continued the rest of the walk in silence until we finally reached his laboratory.

"There it is," he said, pushing aside a curtain of spiked beads and leading me into the room.

The Fist of God was hanging above an altar in the center, its shape much less clean than it had been before I crushed it. It had small dents and ripples throughout, and the demonic runes had been etched on the outside, not the inside like the scripture. It was a trap within a trap.

The rest of the room was filled out with some fiends and devils of all sizes, sitting at computers and typing out algorithms and code, and 3D modeling runes. It was as high-tech an operation as I had ever seen, and it felt surreal to be witnessing it in Hell.

Then again, everything about my life was surreal.

"What do you think?" Cain asked, steering me over to it.

"I don't recognize any of the runes."

"That's because they're new. All of them. It had never occurred to us that we could generate unique capabilities by altering the age old glyphs. Not until we saw how the seraphim had done it."

"It never occurred to you? In thousands of years?"

"Such thinking isn't limited to humankind, Landon. We kept it the way it was because that was the way it had always been."

It reminded me of a Youtube video I had seen once about an experiment with monkeys, bananas at the top of a ladder, and electric shocks. The point was to prove how easy it was to create that kind of thinking.

"Master," one of the fiends said, approaching us. He was slender and a little bent, with a ring of wispy white hair circling his scalp. He looked like a scientist.

"Ah, Wilson. Just the fiend I wanted to see." Cain put his arm over the older demon's shoulder. "I want you to meet my friend, Landon. He is the diuscrucis."

Wilson looked me over like I was a lab rat. "Interesting," was all he said.

"I want to put him in the armor, to trap his soul and his power and see what happens. Can it be done?"

It bothered me that he said it with me there.

Wilson stared at me again. "I don't know, Master. We will need to measure his energy and see if we can calculate the wavelengths."

"Wavelengths?" I asked.

"Yes," Cain said. "All power in existence is measurable if you have the right tools. Wavelengths are as good a word to describe it as any other. The ingenuity of humanity has helped provide us with those tools." He paused before he sighed. "Sometimes I wish we could stop the fighting for a while and let your kind be. I am always curious to see what new things you would devise to kill one another with, and the tools you would create to devise them."

"Me, too," I said.

"Can you measure it?" Cain asked.

"We'll need some time to create a new idolastat," Wilson replied.

"How long?"

"Three days."

"Very well."

Wilson bowed below Cain's arm and wandered off, barking orders to a few of the smaller devils in the lab. Cain shifted his arm to my shoulders.

"Just think about it, Landon. You will be part of the greatest change ever made in Hell. If we can perfect the armor, we will be able to claim the other planes once and for all."

"Lucky me."

He laughed. It was a smooth, charismatic laugh. Part of me felt like he honestly believed he was doing me a favor.

"Come, Landon. Three days is plenty of time to get some nice torture in."

I cringed on the inside. I wasn't going to give him the satisfaction.

"I'm looking forward to it."

19

Cain kept his word. He brought me to a dungeon, a pit in the ground that raged with flames and stunk of sulfur, a smaller version of the Pit we had passed by train. He had me stripped naked, and then he shackled my arms and legs and hoisted me up against the hot side of the exposed earth. It would have burned my skin in an instant if I didn't wrap my power around me to protect myself.

"My minions will care for you from here," Cain said. "I'm going to pay a visit to your companion."

"If you lay a hand on her, I will kill you," I said. It was more bravado that I couldn't cash in on, but it escaped me without hesitation.

"I'll keep that in mind while I'm playing with her. Thank you again for stopping by, Landon. You've made me a very happy demon."

He bowed to me and then took his leave.

I struggled against the shackles, pushing my power out beneath them. They were covered in demonic runes that made them extra, extra strong, and they didn't break. I had guessed Cain knew what he was doing, and wouldn't have made it that easy.

A demon fluttered down to eye level on leather wings. In my anger, I gripped him in my power and threw him into the pit.

Execution

"Stay away from me," I shouted.

All I got for the effort was laughter from the other devils. Assholes.

I tried to relax. To calm my mind and think. I didn't know if my innate power to be forgotten would work on Cain. He had been able to find me out in the Desolation, after all. If it did, either I would eventually escape, or I would hang here for the rest of eternity. At least, until he re-discovered me.

Unless I figured out how to escape my bonds.

I had three days.

I was dangling for a few hours when the first visitor arrived. She was an ugly thing, with a rough face and distorted limbs. She had the legs of a goat, the torso of a female weightlifter, and a pair of thorny wings that sat cockeyed on her back.

"A new prisoner," she said. "What fun."

She produced a serrated whip from somewhere, holding up so I could see it. "Master says not to hurt it too much." Her eyes fell to my midsection. "Maybe I won't hurt it at all."

There was no way I was going to let that happen. I threw some of my power out at her. Just enough to shove her away.

"Oh. It has power. More fun." She unrolled the whip, drawing it back. "Hit me again, you get pain over pleasure."

I hit her again, shoving her back hard enough that she needed to use her wings to keep from falling into the pit.

"Have it that way," she said.

She came at me, and I threw my power out once more. She didn't react to it this time. In fact, it seemed almost as though it entered her, traveled through her arm, and extended out into the whip. The end smacked against my chest with enough force that I was shoved back into the rock hard enough that it broke my spine.

I tried not to make a sound. I couldn't help it. The pain was intense, and I cried out, even as I worked to heal myself. The demon began laughing.

"It could have had pleasure," she said.

This was one of those times when pleasure was worse than pain. I was still happy with the choice I had made.

"Go to-" I started to say. That vulgarity didn't mean anything down here.

The whip hit me again. And again. I winced each time but didn't scream. I healed the wounds as quickly as she made them, causing her to increase the pace.

We kept going like that for some time. I refused to let her break me or destroy my spirit, and she refused to stop. I don't know how many times I was struck, at least, a thousand. I don't know how much time was passing. We settled into a persistent rhythm of whip and heal, whip and heal.

After a while, I became numb to the pain.

After a while, the whole thing just became tedious.

And then boring.

And then, it truly became hell.

It was like someone poking you in the arm over and over again. Tolerable for a while, until it became the most annoying, frustrating thing imaginable. This was just like that. I went from boredom to true anguish. Not physical. Mental.

And the damn demon knew it.

She knew it was going to go like that. From experience, I guess. She gained this sick, smug grin, and she wore it proudly while she drew back and threw the whip forward one, two, a hundred more times. There was nothing I could do.

I was stuck.

I closed my eyes, unable to bear the sight of her anymore. I felt each strike like a slap on the skin, and I wished it would just stop, even if only for a moment. I knew it wouldn't though. It would continue for hours. She wouldn't get tired because she knew how much I hated it. Even though I tried not to show it, I knew that she knew.

Hours passed. Or maybe it was minutes. When you're in the state of being tortured, it becomes impossible to know. The only thing I felt certain of was that it would never, ever stop.

Until it did.

Execution

20

I opened my eyes slowly.

The demon that had been whipping me was on the ground at my feet, a pool of blood spreading below her.

Zifah was standing on top of the corpse, looking up at me.

"I decided to give you another chance," he said.

"What?"

I was a little bit dazed, and a lot confused. How had that tiny demon cut down the harpy without her even making a sound?

"I said, I decided to give you another chance. The truth is, I need to get out of this place, and you're the only one who would even remotely be willing to help me do it. I know you don't trust me, diuscrucis, but you will. I'll make sure of that."

"How did you find me? How did you even remember me?"

"Sorry bub, you've got too many demons down here talking about you for them to forget. I mean, nobody remembers seeing you, but you've already become like a legend down here. Plus, I got off the train when you did. I couldn't remember why I got off, but I figured the reason was in the Desolation, and if it was in the Desolation, that meant Cain. So I came to the palace and started poking around until I saw you, and then I remembered that was why I was here. Where's your hot girlfriend?"

"Cain took her. How did you get in here?"

"Look at me. Nobody gives a poop about a demon like me."

Did he just say poop?

"Are you going to help me down?"

"Heh. Deal first, down after."

"Whatever you want, you've got. Just get me down."

"I want to come back to the mortal realm with you."

"Okay."

"I want to have sex with your girlfriend."

Was that all demons thought about?

"No."

"You just said anything."

I reached out with my power, squeezing it against him.

"Hey. Oh, come on, diuscrucis. That hurts. Fine. No sex. Just take me with you."

I let him go, and he leaned over like he couldn't breathe.

"How do you know I'm going to get out of here alive?" I asked.

"Because now you've got Zifah. Big things come in small packages."

I hoped he was right. "Fine. We have a deal. I'll swear it in blood once you let me down."

"No need. I believe you. We have a deal. There's only one problem."

"Which is?"

"I can't get you down."

"What?"

"I have some power, but it's not enough to break Cain's runes. You have to get yourself down."

"What happened to big things in small packages?"

"I'm not Son of Lucifer big."

Great. So my torturer was dead, but I was still trapped. And Zifah thought I was going to get out of this alive?

"Alyx," I said. "You need to find Alyx and set her free. She's in Cain's harem. He put a bracelet on her."

"Cain?"

Execution

"Yes." I groaned. He couldn't open that one either.

He stood there, tapping his foot on top of the harpy's chest as it turned to ash. "What if you pull the rock out that the shackles are connected to? You would still be confined, but you'd be able to move."

"The moment Cain sees me I'll be back up here. Unless he dies of laughter first."

"There has to be a way."

I had tried being hopeful. I was starting to lose it. "I'm sorry you came, Zifah. There isn't."

"Cain's power isn't absolute."

"I can't break the bonds. I tried."

"What if brute force isn't the answer?"

Brute force. Pushing and pulling. I closed my eyes again.

"Diuscrucis?" Zifah said, concerned.

"I'm thinking," I replied.

And I was. I had taken the smallest morsel of the Beast's power. A god's power. I had let it enter inside of me, and used it to remake myself. I had taken on many new traits in my experience of it, but Zifah was right. In all of this time, I had always taken a brute force approach to its use. Push it out, pull it back. There were a million applications of the same idea, and even so the concept of it was limiting me.

The Beast's power had been enough to challenge both God and Lucifer, and I had a sliver of that inside my soul. I had used it to set Charis free, to cast her energy and light out into the universe and set it loose from the cycle of the Divine. It had been a simple act, born of love and sadness. It had hardly taken any effort at all.

I had taken the Divine power and turned it into something else. Something simple and beautiful. I hadn't created or destroyed. I had only transformed it.

Neutralized it.

Balanced it.

I opened my eyes. "Zifah, you're a genius."

He returned a toothy grin. "I know."

I felt the shackles on my wrists and ankles. I felt Cain's runes burning into me. I sensed the power there.

I reached out with my own. Calmly. Gently. I laid it on top of the demonic energy. I didn't push. I didn't pull. I let it be. I felt Cain's power beneath it, and I asked it to change.

Almost at once, the shackles shattered.

I fell to the ground, landing on my feet.

"Holy poop," Zifah said.

"I can't believe that worked," I replied, smiling.

All this time I thought I knew myself.

I still didn't know myself at all.

21

"We need to find Alyx," I said, bending down and retrieving the dead demon's whip from the ash.

"You need some clothes," Zifah said.

I looked down at my naked self. I couldn't create clothes out of nothing. "That would help."

"This way." Zifah scampered off toward the door to the dungeon.

I followed behind him, noting the other smaller piles of ash as I went. He had killed the other demons down here, too.

The dungeon fed out into a small chamber. My clothes were thrown in the corner, and I picked them up and put them on. Of course, the stone was missing from my pocket. It was safe to bet that Cain had claimed it.

"Where is the harem?" I asked.

"I can take you."

We made our way up a long staircase and out into the palace proper, where limestone and brimstone were exchanged for marble and gold. A fiend was coming out of a small room across from the exit as we were coming through.

I didn't have time to react before Zifah had leaped impossibly high, jabbing a small, dark needle in the demon's neck.

"Help me get him inside before he crumbles," Zifah said.

I used my power to shove the fiend back into the room.

"What did you stab him with?"

Zifah held up the needle. It was transparent now. He stuck it in his arm and withdrew some of his blood, turning it dark once more.

"My blood is poisonous to the Divine. All of the Divine. I'm one of the Father's experiments that didn't make the cut."

"Lucifer made you himself?"

"Yep. I'm the only one of my kind. It sounds like it shouldn't be a bad gig, but it is. Especially being so small. The only reason the others tolerate me at all is because they think I'm a joke."

"It's not easy being green," I said.

"Shut up," he replied. "I don't need you to mock me, too."

"I'm sorry, Zifah."

He nodded. "Don't worry about it. It has its perks."

"We need to hurry."

Zifah ran back to the door, scanning the hallway before dashing out. I followed behind him at a walk, easily keeping pace.

"Up the stairs," he said, pointing to a wide staircase. "Don't be seen."

He started his way across. He paused halfway, pressing himself against a red marble column. Immediately, his skin tone changed to match it. Whatever the other demons thought, that was no joke.

A pair of devils wandered across the hall without noticing Zifah. He finished the evasion, reaching the steps and then waving me forward. I crossed without incident, and we hurried up the stairs to the second level.

The palace was huge, but Zifah navigated it with ease, as though he had been here many times before. We crossed the length of the structure, staying hidden from passing demons and making our way toward the harem. Each step was leaving me more impatient and agitated. I wanted to get Alyx, get the FOG, and get the hell out of Hell.

"It's through there," Zifah said, pointing across one last open hallway to a pair of gold-plated doors. A large demon stood on either side of them, each resting a large ax between the floor and their elbows. "Those are Cain's personal guards. I can get past them, but you can't."

Execution

"You've done this before, haven't you?" I asked.

Zifah nodded enthusiastically. "A room full of damned female souls under Cain's control and the ability to blend in? I'm a demon; I'm not dead."

"Do you have any idea where Cain is?"

"Most likely in his lab. He hasn't spent much time in the harem in the last hundred years or so though his new addition may spark his libido again."

"That's what I'm afraid of."

I was worried enough about it that I didn't even consider being sly about getting past the guards. Instead, I started walking right toward them.

"What the heck are you doing?" Zifah asked, scampering along behind me and pulling at my pant leg. "Maybe you can beat them, but Cain will know something's up."

"Good," I said.

My patience was out, and the discovery of a third way of using my power had made me bold. Let Cain try me again. He wouldn't find me so weak the second time.

The guards caught sight of me a moment later. I spared a glance back at Zifah, who had changed color to blend in. Then I threw my hands out, bringing them back in and using my power as a pair of massive claws. It slammed into the sides of the two demons, picking them up and bashing them into one another. Bones shattered, and they fell to the ground, stunned.

Zifah was on the first in a flash, jamming his needle into an arm and bouncing away before the devil could grab him. I ran at the other one, meeting him as he rose to his feet. I put out my hands, leading with my power and shoving him back again. He went airborne before smashing into the gold doors with enough force to push them open.

The demon got back up, a snarl crossing his snout. I reached forward and then back, pulling him to me and hitting him hard in the gut with an extra-strong fist. He hit the wall to the left of me, cracking the marble and fell to the floor again. Zifah jumped on him, stabbing him with the needle.

"You're pretty handy with that thing," I said.

"It's the only defense I have. It ain't easy being green." His smile was sharp and crooked.

I turned back to the now open doors, hurrying inside. The harem was what I expected it to be. A room of pillows and mattresses, with a large bath in the center. The girls were arranged around it, lounging, bathing, sleeping, and in a few instances pleasing one another. I didn't know how much of their activity was under their own control and how much Cain was making them do. They looked pretty content in their chosen activity.

The other thing I noticed was that there were a lot more of them than I had expected. The souls who had taken Alyx away were only a small fraction of his concubines. There were at least a hundred of them here, all wearing the same gold bracelet.

"Alyx," I said, calling her name and picking through the obstacles in search of her.

"She won't respond to you even if she's here," Zifah said. "These souls are prisoners to Cain's whims."

If she wasn't here, that meant she was with Cain. I could feel my face burning at the rising tide of anger. "Where is his room?"

"Diuscrucis, it's one thing to bully a couple of devils. Cain is something else entirely. He's the son of Lucifer for jeebers sakes."

"The only way we get out of here is through him. Where is his room?"

Zifah didn't look happy as he pointed back the way we had come. "Follow me."

Execution

22

My heart was thundering, and my blood was boiling by the time we reached Cain's apartment on the top floor of the palace. I had already dispatched more demons than I could count on the way up, and to be honest, I was surprised that my activities hadn't drawn him out.

Was he that distracted by Alyx?

The thought made me sick.

I had told myself I didn't and couldn't love her. I had only known her for a few weeks, and there was still that twinge of guilt every time I thought that maybe there was potential there. What about Charis and Clara? What about those feelings? I knew she would never be mad at me for having an afterlife beyond her. We had settled our love when I set her free.

So what was the problem?

The biggest problem was the fact that she was a demon. In some other part of me it felt shameful to have an interest in one of Lucifer's creations over one of God's. But then, God had created Lucifer, so that still made her one of His, didn't it? And anyway, she had shown me her heart was innocent enough that she didn't have to be straight evil. Not that evil was always permanent. Mephistopheles had been full demon before he met

Josette, and she had changed him.

The other problem was that she was a Great Were. There were positive qualities about it, like her extreme loyalty and protectiveness, as well as her incredible hearing and sense of smell. There were negatives, too. Like the need to feed on human flesh, and the fact that despite everything, I couldn't wonder about falling in love with a girl who could change into the big, bad, wolf.

On the flip side was the way she said, "I love you."

Who wouldn't fall for that?

So maybe I did love her? I didn't know. I wasn't sure. What I did know was that the idea of Cain touching her and forcing her to touch him was enough to drive me over the edge of reason. The thought of anyone or anything hurting her was a sharp knife in my gut. I didn't need to worry about it most times because she was more than able to take care of herself.

Most times.

I wasn't going to let it happen. If it had already happened, I was going to make sure whoever did it regret the decision. It sounded corny and cliche, but it was true.

"Remember brute force?" Zifah said as I approached Cain's door.

I could hear a soft growl on the other side. It was Alyx for sure, in beast mode. She didn't sound happy.

"I remember," I said, gathering my power and throwing it out at the door. It exploded from the brute force, shattering into a thousand splinters.

I walked through the ruined door a man on fire, burning with anger and ready to throw down with Cain. I scanned his apartment. Beyond the door was a large living space with plush sofas and all of that garbage. Past that was a columned archway.

Alyx had fallen silent from the other side of it.

I kept moving, not too fast, not too slow. Zifah had disappeared. He was hiding from Cain, and I was okay with that.

I reached the second room. A massive bed sat in the center of it. Cain was sitting on it, propped up against some pillows and watching my grand entrance with a casual dismissal. Where was Alyx?

I turned my head. He had forced her to change and chained her to the

Execution

wall. She was struggling against the bonds, as unable to break them as I had been. The gold bracelet was gone.

"Cain," I rumbled softly.

He answered with a half smile. "Now, how did you get out of my pit?"

"I'm resourceful like that," I replied.

"Ah, I bet you are, Landon. But no, someone released my shackles from you. Who was it?" He made a face like he was thinking, and then he shrugged. "No matter, I'll return you there shortly. Do you like what I've done with your companion. It's been so long since a Great Were came down to Hell, I decided I would rather have a trophy like this than another concubine."

I glanced over at Alyx again. Her eyes were morose, and it broke my heart.

"I'm going to end you," I said.

He laughed. "Still trying to be a champion for the underdog," he said, laughing harder. "Underdog. Get it, Landon?"

He flicked his wrist. I felt his power coming at me, and instead of pushing against it with my own, I relaxed, letting it wash over me. It burned against my skin, and I let it. I urged it to transform and be set free. The burning turned into a tingle, and the tingle of exhilaration.

Cain's eyes narrowed at the reaction, and he threw his hand out. A gout of hellfire spewed from it, heading right toward me, while a second force tried to hold me in place. I negated that force, stepping aside from the hellfire and knowing that it would melt the wall behind me to nothing.

"I learned a new trick, thanks to you," I said.

His pretty face twisted in rage, and he sprang from the bed. As he did, the black spatha appeared in his hand. I knew he had taken it.

I braced myself against him, catching his first sword strike with my power, pushing back and shoving him away. He threw his power at me again, and I balanced it once more, sidestepping a thrust and hitting him hard in the jaw with my fist. His head snapped to the side, and when he looked back at me his eyes were red, and small horns had grown from his forehead.

"You want to fight me, diuscrucis?" he said. "Fight the real me."

And then he grew. Ten feet. Twenty feet. His entire body muscled up while the horns on his head grew up and out. The spatha fell from his hand, too small to hold.

"Fight all of me," he shouted, his voice echoing across the Desolation as the palace vanished from below my feet. "I am the Son of the Morningstar. This is my world. You can't defeat me here."

I bent down and picked up the spatha from the scorched Earth. I guess he didn't feel like he needed it anymore. I looked back at Alyx. She was still chained to a steel girder that was embedded deep into the ground.

I wondered if Zifah's poison blood would work on Cain?

That was the last thought I had time for. The demon came for me with incredible speed, his large hands sweeping where I was standing, trying to scoop me up. I power-jumped backward, avoiding the grab, and then reversed course, rocketing at him and slipping the spatha against his leg.

It skidded uselessly off his mottled red skin.

I hated boss battles.

Cain charged again, one claw sweeping from the left, the other from the right. I pushed myself up, scaling over them both. Something big and heavy hit me hard in the chest, throwing me away. I hadn't seen that Cain had grown a tail.

I hit the girder above Alyx, leaving a dent, breaking half the bones in my body, and tumbling down. She caught me before I hit the ground, a moment of incredible tenderness as I frantically knitted myself back together.

"I love you," I said, trying it on for size. It felt crazy and good at the same time.

"I love you," she replied, her monster voice deeper but still carrying the same sweet innocence.

I kissed the side of her muzzle, at the same time putting my hand on her collar. It fell to dust.

"Now let's kick his ass," I said.

She snarled in agreement, and I held on while she pounced forward, her own form large enough to even the odds. She knocked his arms aside, digging her hinds into his chest and pushing him back, her jaws seeking

Execution

his neck. Cain's power swirled around us, attempting to crush us into pulp. I kept my grip on Alyx's back and eased the demon's attack, preventing it from harming her.

"This is my realm," Cain said again, clearly on the defensive. He spun around, trying to shake Alyx loose. She kept her claws dug into him, holding tight.

"You should have made a deal," I said. I used my power to keep my balance, coming to a crouch on Alyx's back before sending myself forward in a leap. I reached up and grabbed one of Cain's horns, using it as leverage while I stabbed him in the eye.

He howled in pain, stumbling back and falling over. Alyx was relentless, her teeth tearing chunks of his throat away, her claws cutting his chest to ribbons. He was healing from those wounds, but the spatha was another story. His eye steamed and hissed, the angelic scripture active on his flesh.

"No," he shouted, gathering himself. He grabbed Alyx but the shoulders, lifting her and throwing her back. She flew through the air, landing hard on the ground, yelping as she did.

She didn't get up.

I rushed Cain as he tried to get back to his knees, his throat closing up, his body healing. I came at him with everything I had, using my power to knock him off balance while leaping back at him with the sword. I jammed it into his neck. Once. Twice. Three times. The wounds all steamed, but he was more powerful than that. He was in Hell, and he was able to overcome the poison.

"I've got this."

I had heard Zifah before I saw him. He appeared on top of Cain, right next to his ear, his tiny needle in hand.

"Maybe they'll stop laughing now," he said, jamming the small point of it into the demon's cheek.

"Zifah?" Cain said, even as his ear dissolved to nothing. "You?" His eyes grew wide with fear, his face beginning to crumble.

"My apologies, brother," Zifah said. "But you had this coming for a long time. You should have been more careful who you made enemies with. Or at least, who you refused to make friends with."

Cain tried to say something else, but his lips turned to dust. His head was gone a few seconds later, and I started running toward Alyx before I saw the rest of him die.

His power gone, the palace reappeared below my feet. Alyx was crumpled in the corner, having changed back to her human form.

"Alyx," I said, kneeling down next to her.

She was breathing shallow, but she was awake. "Did we win?" she asked.

"Yes."

She smiled. "Good. Did you mean what you said?"

I looked at her. I had never been happier than I was to see she was going to be okay. "Yes."

Her smile grew larger. "Does that mean we can mate now?"

"Not now. Maybe once we've saved the mortal world from Abaddon."

"Will you kiss me at least?"

I leaned in, putting my lips to hers. She tasted of salt and sweat and blood. She returned the kiss eagerly.

"Ahem," Zifah said, appearing at my side. We both looked at him. "Got any of that action left for the one who actually destroyed Cain?"

"Come here," Alyx said.

I started to protest, but she put her hand to my lips. Then she leaned forward and kissed Zifah on the cheek.

"Thank you."

I had never seen a demon blush before.

"You called Cain, brother," I said.

"Yeah, because we have the same father. Beyond that, it's complicated. The point is that I never liked that asshole."

"What will happen to him?"

"Lucifer will give him a new form and he'll be bad as new in a few days. I recommend getting out of here."

"I couldn't agree with you more. Let's grab the FOG and go."

I reached out and helped Alyx to her feet. Then I returned to the pile of ash that was Cain and retrieved the pendant he had said could control the

Execution

armor. We left the bedroom and headed for the laboratory.
　The Fist was mine. Alyx was mine.
　It had been a pretty good day.

23

We made our way from Cain's bedroom down to the laboratory. The demons had known the moment we destroyed Cain, and they scattered out of our way as we entered, abandoning the Fist of God.

I approached it with a measure of disgust. Adam's creation had caused more trouble in the last few weeks than I had been weighed down by in years.

Of course, it had also led me to Alyx, so it wasn't all bad.

I couldn't use my power on it directly. Instead, I enhanced my strength, climbing onto the table and lifting it from its hooks. I lowered myself gently, holding the large machine over my head. It had to weigh at least a thousand pounds. Probably more.

"Let's go," I said, taking the lead from the room.

I carried the FOG through the corridors and out to the large foyer. We only saw a few demons en route, and they were all fleeing from us as fast as they were able.

"Do you think Lucifer is going to be pissed at me?" I asked.

Zifah had taken a seat on Alyx's shoulder. He shook his head. "No. He probably thinks Cain deserved to be cut down a notch. He's been plotting to murder Lucifer for years."

"He probably thought he could with the help of the Fist," Alyx said. "Especially if he had managed to get you inside of it."

"Yes," Zifah agreed. "Or if you had put Abaddon into it for him."

I tripped a little bit on my next step, my Divine spider-sense going off at the comment.

"You know about that?"

Zifah could tell he had made me wary. He laughed it off. "I told you, Landon. I can go anywhere without being noticed. I heard you talking to Cain about it in the lab."

"You told me you found me in the dungeon, not that you followed me."

Zifah's laughter faded. "Okay, so I lied a little bit."

Alyx reached up, grabbing the demon in a suddenly larger, sharper hand so that only his head stuck out beyond her fingers.

"Why?" she asked. I could almost feel her protective instinct.

"I didn't want you to know that I knew. Oh, but I messed that up. I helped you beat Cain, doesn't that earn me any credit?"

"Not enough," I said, growing warier. "Are you working with Gervais?"

"Who?"

"Don't tell me you don't know Gervais. He isn't exactly an unknown quantity around here."

Zifah was silent until Alyx squeezed him a little tighter.

"I can smell your fear, little demon," she said.

"You're crushing me to death. Why wouldn't I be afraid? Fine. I know Gervais. And yes, I've seen him recently. He offered to bring me out of Hell if I helped him find a way to get the armor from Cain. I was the one who suggested sending you down here. But I didn't do it for him, I did it for me. I want out of this place; you know that. I don't want to work with him, though. There isn't a demon in the universe that trusts him."

"So you were using me?"

"We all use each other. That's how all this poop works. Especially down here."

He had a point. And I couldn't ignore the fact that he did help me escape, and he was the one who had killed Cain. Sure, he had ulterior motives. Didn't they always? The only thing that was bothering me was that Zifah knew Gervais. More than that, they had discussed the very thing I had just done before I ever knew about it.

Which meant the demon knew someone had been summoning Abaddon while he was still here in Hell.

"Who summoned Abaddon?" I asked.

"What?"

"You heard me, Zifah."

"Randolph Hearst. I'm sure you already knew that."

"I do. I also know he had help. What I don't know is who helped him?"

"Why do you think I know?"

"Because Gervais told you what was going down before it went down. Gervais said he doesn't know who the other player is, but he doesn't have your ability to sneak around down here where the action is. Summoning Abaddon from Hell without inside help? I don't buy it."

Zifah released a long, low sigh. "Okay. Yep. I know who his partner is. No, I'm not telling you until you bring me to your plane. If I do, I've got no leverage to prevent you from leaving me here."

"Does Gervais know this mystery demon?"

"No. Like you said, he doesn't have much clout down here. He's persona non grata since he sided with the Beast. That's why he keeps going back to you. Any demon with any self-respect doesn't want anything to do with him."

"So you're saying you have no self-respect?"

"I'm saying I'm desperate. I can't tell you how much I hate it here, and I've been stuck here for almost four hundred years."

"Are you saying I have no self-respect?"

"I'm not judging you, but if I were in your shoes, I would stick that sword of yours in his heart as soon as possible."

"I'd love to, but he's already indicated Lucifer will just send him back up. Do you know the saying, 'keep your friends close and your enemies closer?' I'm better off knowing where and who he is."

"I can't argue that. So, are we good?"

Execution

"As good as we're going to be. I still don't trust you."

"I wouldn't expect you to. Say, can you let me go now?"

Alyx looked over at me, and I nodded. She opened her hand, and he landed gracefully on the floor. We were nearing the front doors of the palace, and I could see the Desolation spreading out beyond it.

"I hope you know how to get back to the train from here."

24

Zifah did know how to get back to the train. He explained the entire process while we walked, but I was tired and didn't pay much attention.

Alyx was kind enough to change to demon form once we had left the palace, and she carried everything on her back across the broken landscape without complaint. I took a position up near her head, stroking her fur and being affectionate. I had admitted to what I felt almost from the day we met, and it felt liberating.

Yeah, she was a monster. But she was my monster.

We arrived back at the train in plenty of time. Many of the demons who had fled the palace had wound up here, and they scattered once more at our approach. I used Zifah to tell them I wouldn't hurt them as long as they didn't try to hurt me, and we somehow wound up managing to blend into the mix by the time the transportation arrived. Sure, we looked strange carrying the Fist of God up onto the train, but none of the demons were about to comment on that. I was sure the word was spreading in a hurry about what I had done to Cain. I had earned their respect and fear, and I liked it.

The return trip to the Kitchen was going to take two hours. I decided to use the time to rest, putting my arm around Alyx while she nestled her head against my chest. Zifah wandered off at some point, leaving us alone with the FOG spread across the seat in front of us. We didn't need to talk. Not right now. It was enough to have her near.

I closed my eyes. Immediately, I saw Charis in my mind. We were back in the Box, and she was telling me how tired she was of being part of the war between Good and Evil. I could see it like it was still happening, and while I was tempted to release myself from the memory, I decided to remain. Old emotions swelled up again. It was love, but it was a different kind of love than I was feeling for Alyx. It felt old and comfortable, as though it had been pre-ordained. Maybe it had been. We were two of a kind, and shouldn't like attract like? To forgive a pun, Alyx was more of a youthful puppy love. An infectious love like we were a pair of newlyweds. It was different from what I had known, and I was drinking of it without reservation.

I had earned that much, hadn't I?

I held her close and told her I loved her. I brought her from the Box with me, and I released her to the stars. If you love something, you have to let it go. So I did. It was hard not to feel like I was betraying her to love someone else. I didn't want to, but there it was.

"Are you okay?" Alyx asked me, somehow noticing my distress. Was it my heartbeat? A smell of salty tears?

"I was thinking about Charis."

"Was she your mate?"

"Kind of. She had died before we were ever close like that, but I loved her, too."

"Why does that make you sad?"

"I feel guilty."

"Why? It is not improper for an alpha to have multiple mates. It is only natural that the strongest will produce the best offspring."

She wasn't human, so I understood why she didn't understand. Who was to say her perspective wasn't the better one? It would save me a lot of negative emotion.

"Maybe having you makes me miss her more."

"She must have been a fine mate."

I leaned down and kissed her head. "Yes, she was."
"I'm sorry I didn't get to meet her."
"Me, too," I said.
Strangely enough, I meant it.

Execution

25

It felt good to get back to the Kitchen though I was surprised to discover that an entire Earth day had passed since we had arrived in Hell.

Time flies when you're having fun, I guess.

Alyx carried the Fist of God while I walked alongside her with Zifah on my shoulder. The damned still crowded the city, but it seemed as though my new reputation had reached their subconscious as well. Instead of forcing us to navigate around them, they steered clear of us. The adulterers ran big circles to avoid us, while the sloths simply stopped moving, standing barefoot in the broken glass and waiting for us to pass.

We returned to the club to wait for Damien to open the rift and take us back. We still had another day before he showed up again. I could only hope nobody knew we were with him, and that he would make it back in one piece. I didn't know what his business in Hell was, other than retrieving artifacts to bring back to the mortal realm. He had done it plenty of times before without issue, so I knew I shouldn't have been too worried. Still, I was feeling pretty lucky to have beaten Cain and gotten the armor back.

It was only a matter of time before my luck ran out.

Zifah stayed at the front of the club. He said it was to give Alyx and me a little private time, but I wondered if he wanted to watch the action on stage. He was an odd demon; that was for certain. It wasn't only his diminutive size and green skin, but also his apparent refusal or inability to curse, and his overwhelming desire to leave Hell. It was understandable for fiends and former humans to want to go back. It was rare for a demon made in Hell, no matter what their circumstances were.

Alyx and I entered the small room where the Hell Rift was resting. It was too small for her demon-form in there, so I was carrying the Fist. I dropped it over in the corner and heaved a content sigh, happy to finally be able to put it down.

"What a day," I said, turning to face Alyx.

I wasn't even all the way around when her lips found mine and her body pressed into me, shoving me back against the wall. My heart jumped into my throat as I struggled to keep up with her sudden passion, my own kisses barely able to match hers. She was on fire. Ferocious. An animal. I could feel the heat of her, smell the desire on her skin and taste it in her mouth. I'd never experienced anything like it before.

"Alyx," I said, turning my head to speak. Her kisses continued, from my cheek to my ear, to my neck. Her hands ran over my chest. "Alyx."

"I want you," she said in reply.

"I know," I said. I wanted her, too. More than I had ever wanted anything.

That was the problem.

"Alyx. Please stop," I said. I wasn't sure how I got the words out. It was only the smallest sliver of my soul that wanted her to. The rest wanted to tear her clothes off, pull her to the ground, and... I stopped the thought before I finished it.

Alyx didn't wait for me to ask again. She took a step back, her eyes sad. "I thought you loved me?"

"I do. That's why we can't do this like this. Being here is bringing out the evil side of me. I don't know how, but I know it is. I don't know if you understand, but I've never been with anyone before. Not even Charis. I don't want the first time to be on the floor in Hell. You're special to me, and being with you deserves to be special. Not like the adulterers out

Execution

there."

She stared at me for a few seconds, and I felt myself growing tense. Would she cry? Would she yell? Would she leave? I didn't want to hurt her feelings.

Finally, her sad eyes turned into the softest, most loving eyes I had ever seen. She did start to cry, but a smile spread across her face at the same time. "Thank you, Landon," she said. "Espanto never made anything special for me. He never treated me like I was special, other than in the ways I could hunt for him. You make me feel like more than a thing and more than a demon."

I moved forward, taking her in my arms. At the moment, she seemed so small. So defenseless. Hardly.

"We'll have time later. I promise."

"Okay."

"There is something else I can do for you before we go back. If Cabal did tip Espanto, they'll both be in for a surprise."

She tilted her head in confusion.

"You need to pull your pants down."

She laughed. "You just said-"

"I know. Not for that."

She grabbed the band of the light pants Cain had left her in, sliding them past her thighs. I looked down at her, fighting against my darker self to avoid the patch of hair in the center and focus on the spot next to it instead.

The spot where Espanto's brand was etched into her skin.

I put my hand on it. She twitched slightly at my touch and then remained still as I traced my finger along the brand. Izaak had been marked by Gervais, and he had managed to remove it by cutting it out of his flesh. We had tried that a couple of times already, and both times the runes had healed back with the skin. Whatever Espanto had done, however he had done it, he had made the brand permanent.

This time would be different. I was smarter now. I had learned something new. I didn't need to heal the brand. I could transform it.

"This might hurt," I said. "I don't know."

"It's okay. It will be worth it."

I closed my eyes, shifting my hand to rest across it. I could feel the heat of the demon's power in the runes. I focused on it, asking it to change. It burned against me, flaring up as if in anger at the effort. Alyx cried out in pain, leaning back against the wall, trying to pull herself away. I reached back and put my hand on her rear to keep her in place, holding her tight and at the same time working to remain calm. I couldn't force the energy to neutralize. I had to be passive. Delicate.

"Landon," Alyx said, her voice strained with hurt. The flames were burning her legs, moving in a direct line toward her genitals like some kind of crazy safety measure.

"It's okay," I said.

Was it? I wasn't sure. Every part of me was being tempted to push back, to fight fire with fire. I couldn't. I knew that was the wrong thing to do. I stayed the course, keeping pressure on the mark but not forcing any of my power into it. It was a crude, slow negotiation, and the flames continued to move their way downward. I could smell her burning pubic hair, and she whimpered and shook against my grip.

"Landon," she said again, growing panicked.

"It will be okay," I repeated, keeping my voice calm.

It would be. It had to be. I relaxed further, feeling the heat against my palm begin to cool, the power beginning to morph.

The flames lowered in intensity before reaching her sex. My hand was growing ever cooler, sucking every bit of demonic energy from the scar and turning it into something raw. Alyx began to relax in my grip, breathing heavily.

Within a minute, the flames were out. The brand on her skin would never heal, but the power held within it was gone.

She was free.

She leaned back against the wall, sobbing. I stood up, wrapping my arms around her and holding her tight while she buried her head in my neck. There was such an odd contrast between this tiny, vulnerable thing in my arms and the creature she could become.

"It's okay now," I said, kissing her head.

Execution

"Yes," she replied. "I know. I'm not crying because I'm afraid or hurt. I'm crying because I'm happy. The last time I felt like this was the night before Espanto came and took me away, when I felt warm and safe in bed with my brothers and sisters."

"He can't take you away from me again," I said.

She moved back away from me, a feral smile creasing her lips. "I'd love to see him try."

I nodded, and then reached out and pulled her pants back up.

"Are you sure?" she asked playfully.

"Yes," I replied with a laugh. "We can sit together. We can talk. I'd love to hear more about your life before Espanto."

"Okay."

I was positioning myself to sit with my back to the wall when I heard a commotion from the club.

"What is it?" I asked, knowing Alyx could smell and hear whatever was happening out there.

"I'm not sure. I don't see how this can be possible."

"How can what be possible?"

She opened her mouth to respond. At the same time, a bruised and bloody Gervais swept into the room.

26

"Gervais?" I said, completely confused and off-guard. "What the hell are you doing here?"

Zifah appeared a moment later, racing along after the fiend.

"Landon," Gervais said, his expression and voice more serious than I had ever seen it. "We have a problem."

That was the second or third time I had heard that in the last twenty-four hours. It didn't make me happy.

"Where is Elyse?" I asked.

"That is the problem. She's dead. So is your sweet flower by any other name."

I instantly lost all ability to move, or to think or to breathe. My entire body fell to mush, and I opened my mouth to try to express something, anything.

It was impossible.

"I don't believe you," I said. "This is just another one of your bullshit games."

My mind was reeling, my entire body was numb. I was too shocked to cry. I felt Alyx's hands on my shoulders, supporting me.

"I don't blame you for being doubtful diuscrucis. That doesn't make it

Execution

any less true. Look at me. Not only am I here, but I am beaten and bloody. They killed me, too."

I heard the words like an echo across time. I tried to look at the demon, but my eyes refused to focus. This wasn't real. This couldn't be real. It was a trick. Lucifer was having fun with me, hurting me in the most productive way he could.

"How?" I heard Alyx say behind me. Her voice was ice.

"Elyse followed me into the deli. She didn't think I saw her, but I did. I see everything, you know. She was shot in the head by the clerk. He had a pistol hidden behind his counter. Rose was with her. She killed the clerk, but then one of the shoppers attacked her and hit her over the head with a bottle. I tried to protect her. I knocked the shopper down, but before I knew it, I was jumped by a man who came into the deli from the street. He didn't say a word to me, just hopped on my back and dragged me down."

"You're telling me some unarmed mortal killed you?" I said, my voice angry. There was no part of this that was making sense. I knew the clerk at the deli. His name was Ahmed, and he had a wife and three kids. He knew Elyse, too. I had brought her in with me more than once.

"No. Not that one. I broke his neck. By the time I got to my feet, two vampires had grabbed me, and Randolph Hearst walked in. He said, 'I told Landon not to interfere. Does he think I'm stupid? Finding another way to steal Abaddon still counts as interfering.' Then he cut my throat with a cursed dagger, the son of a whore."

"He knew who you were?"

"He's been stalking us the entire time, mon frère. Somehow, he heard everything I said to you."

Shit.

I closed my eyes as if it would drown me out from existence. I was in Hell, but the true hell was back home. Elyse, dead? Rose, dead? Just like that? No fight? No fanfare? Just gone? Hearst was bolder than I had given him credit for. It meant he had a lot of confidence in the power he was stealing for Abaddon. Either that or he was going to fulfill his promise to set the demon free.

"This is all my fault," I said, my jaw clenching in uncontrolled anger.

"Yes, it is," Gervais replied.

"Shut up," Alyx said. "It is not. Landon, you can't watch everything all the time."

"I have to," I shouted, pulling away from her. "That's my job. To watch everything. To stop everything before it gets out of hand. This is getting out of hand." I turned and threw my fist into the stone wall. Mortar exploded from it, coating me with a layer of dust. "Son of a bitch. I'm going to kill that worm."

"And I would be happy to assist you," Gervais said. "I lost months of gathering my power to that little shit. Oh, and the way Lucifer laughed at me for it. He sent me back out here, naked and unarmed. I only found you because every demon down here is talking about how you killed Cain. Which is impressive, by the way."

"He didn't do it alone," Zifah said.

Gervais noticed the demon for the first time. "You?" he said, surprised.

"Yes, me. I'm going back with Landon. We have a deal."

Gervais looked at me. "Landon, don't tell me you made a deal with this little pissant?"

"I did," I said, still trying to straighten my head. "He helped me defeat Cain and get the Fist. I owe him."

"But, you can't," Gervais said.

"Why not?" I snapped.

"Zifah is a worse trouble-maker than I am. Mark my words, diuscrucis. If you bring him to the mortal realm, you will regret it."

"But I won't regret it if I bring you?"

"I don't need you to bring me. I've been banished."

"He's full of poop, Landon," Zifah said. "I told you; nobody down here will listen to a thing he says. I don't want to make trouble. I just want to go somewhere that I won't be treated like dirt."

"I'm not the one who is full of it. Landon, I know we have had our differences, but I am telling you the truth."

"Will both of you shut up?" I said. The two demons fell silent. I opened my eyes, glaring at them both. "I don't care about either one of you right now. You can both stay in Hell, or you can both come with me. At this moment the only thing I want to do is find Randolph Hearst and rip his head off."

They were both silent. A dozen quick heartbeats passed.

"Landon, can I say one thing?" Zifah said.

"I don't know. Is it useful?"

"It might be. It's about your friends."

"What about them?" My voice was still full of venom. I couldn't help myself.

"I know what killed them. Or who killed them. Whatever. It was Hearst's partner."

"You know who that is?" Gervais said.

"Yeah. I was going to wait until we got out of Hell, but seeing as how we're all here together like this, and you've already kinda been primed for bad news-"

"Who?" I said impatiently.

"What do you know about ghosts?" Zifah asked.

"That they aren't real. Who, Zifah?"

"They are real, Landon. Very real. And they can possess any mortal they want to. They can control their bodies and make them do anything they want them to. Like shoot someone, for example."

Gervais' expression changed. "You know this for a fact?"

"Yeah. I do. I got wind of it through Cain. She's been making deals with demons left and right, and promising them all a bit of Abaddon's power."

"Damn it, Zifah," I shouted. "Who?"

"It's Rebecca, Landon," Gervais said. "He's talking about Rebecca."

27

"What?" I said my voice a harsh whisper of disbelief.

The last time I had seen Rebecca was in the Box. She had helped me defeat the Beast. She had told me she was trying to change.

I had told her to be good.

This was being good?

"How do you know it's her?" I said.

"There's only one ghost I know of with the pedigree to get a demon to do anything for them," Gervais said. "And that is Rebecca."

"The word down here is that she thought she was going to go to Heaven after she saved you from the Box," Zifah said. "She figured that saving God from the Beast was a pretty strong item to put on her resume. I wasn't there, and this is all rumor, hearsay, and gossip, but apparently she went to ask God about letting her in, and He basically told her no.

"You would think that would have driven her to try a little harder, and for a while it did. She set about saving kittens from trees and stopping people from being raped and all that poop. She went back a second time, and He said no a second time. She got pissed about being denied, and here we are."

I shook my head. "No. That can't be. She was stabbed with the

Redeemer. Her soul became good."

"Souls can change, Landon," Alyx said. "You know that better than anyone."

"This was different. The sword changed her."

"There is no difference," Gervais said. "She was given a new start, but she still had the choice. She's angry at God for denying her. That is the only thing that makes sense."

"Because she didn't earn it," I said. I knew that was how Josette would have responded. "You can't just buy your way into Heaven with good deeds. It takes time and patience to prove your worthiness. Patience never was one of her strengths."

First she had saved me, and then she had betrayed me. Then she had saved me again. And now she had killed at least one of my closest friends and was making another massive power play.

Everything was coming full-circle.

I didn't like it.

"We need to get back, now. I need to find Rose, and then I'm going to pay another visit to Hearst."

"You need to be careful, Landon," Gervais said. "Hearst is not the same as when you left."

"I've only been gone a day."

"No. You've been gone a week."

It had only felt like a day to me.

"Time is similar between Hell and Earth, but different," Zifah said, noticing how confused I was. "There isn't really a parallel. Sometimes a day is a day; sometimes it isn't. Lucifer controls all of that."

"He controls time?"

"Down here? Yes. God cast him down to this realm and gave him full power over it."

"And he thought it would be fun to mess with your sense of things," Gervais said. "He enjoys watching you."

"Great. I'll have to put that on my marketing material. When you say Hearst isn't the same, you mean what, exactly?"

"He's been taking in Abaddon's power," Gervais said. "Him and his top flunkies. They're stronger than a regular vampire, and their touch kills instantly."

That didn't sound good. "What about Rebecca?"

"A ghost can't take in power," Zifah said. "They're in between worlds. She won't be able to level up through Abaddon."

"How is being a ghost different from being in Purgatory? Also, if she's always only a ghost, why would Hearst keep working with her now that he's über?"

"Purgatory is for two kinds of people," Gervais said. "There are the ones who are serving penance for lighter sins, who work off their penance there for a few hundred years before going to Heaven. Then there are the ones that neither Heaven or Hell wants. Ghosts are stuck in the mortal world because they have unfinished business that will direct them to Heaven or Hell."

"So Rebecca got stuck when the Beast killed her? Why?"

"I would say it was because she felt responsible for freeing the Beast. This would have been much easier if you had let him destroy everything. Or if you had let me take his power."

"So you could destroy everything?"

"I wouldn't have destroyed it. I would have used it as my personal playground."

Like that was so much better. "Okay, fine. Rebecca is stuck as a ghost, and now she's back to being a super-bitch. Why would Hearst keep her around?"

"She's immune to Abaddon's power, for one," Zifah said. "She's immune to pretty much everything. You can't kill a ghost. You can exorcise them, banish them, which sends them a few thousand miles away. You can't end them. For another, she can control any mortal who isn't protected."

"Think of what you can do with that, diuscrucis," Gervais said. "President. General. Deli clerk."

"The perfect assassin," I said.

"On both sides," Gervais agreed. "She can kill Hearst if he isn't

Execution

compliant unless he never wants to leave his house again."

"There has to be a way to spot them. A P.K.E meter or something."

"There are ways, but they are only open to mortals. I've heard the Nicht Creidem know a way. It may be that you can see them. I don't know."

"I've never seen one before."

"Despite the television shows to the contrary, ghosts are incredibly rare. It may be that you have simply never crossed paths with one."

"Or it may be that Rebecca has been watching us since I visited Hearst and I didn't know it."

"That is also possible."

I really, really didn't like this. Things had been calm for almost two years, and now it seemed like the entire universe was blowing up in my face again.

"What are your intentions, Gervais?" I asked, staring at the fop-haired demon.

He put a hand to his chest as if offended. "My intentions? Why Landon, you wound me. My intentions are to help you put a stop to this. Of course, I still want to take over the mortal realm and kill you, but I can't do that if someone else takes it first. We are allies, for now, though I don't know what use I can be to you."

I wasn't sure what use he could be either, but it was like I told Zifah. I needed him close to keep an eye on him.

"What about you, Zifah? I'll bring you back. What then?"

"After I get tired of internet porn?" he asked, laughing until he saw no one else was. "I'd be happy to hang out with you and help, but if I think I'm going to die, I'm out of there. Sorry, Landon, but I waited too long to get away from Hell to come back that easy."

"What if I promise to come back to get you?" I asked.

He wrinkled his snout. "Mmmmm... Maybe we can work something out."

"Good enough. Gervais, let's go."

"What about Damien?" Alyx asked.

"I don't think he'll care that we left without him."

Gervais knelt in front of the stones, putting his hands on them. He whispered something, and they burst into flames.

"Ladies first," he said, motioning for me to step in. Instead, I shoved him from behind, pushing him into the Rift.

I lifted the Fist of God with my power and followed him through.

28

We came out of the Rift in Cabal's underground compound, just like I knew we would. The fiend wasn't present, but one of his mortal followers was. She jumped at our sudden appearance, taking three steps toward the door before regaining her composure.

"Where is Damien?" she asked.

"Don't know, don't care," I replied. I needed to find Rose, not waste time on this. "Where is Cabal?"

"Up in the club."

I kept my grip on the armor, carrying it out into the underground passages.

"Do you smell Espanto?" I asked.

"No, but the odor of sex and blood is strong down here. It is hiding other scents."

"Landon? Where are we going?" Gervais said. "Why did we come out here? We should have arrived in Central Park."

"The Rift was bound to this location," I replied. "I made a deal with Cabal for the trip down. I'm going to deliver the payment and get him to send us to New York."

"Cabal? That weak-willed snot? I'm disappointed in the class of demons you're throwing in with nowadays, Landon." Gervais shot a glance over at Zifah, who flipped him the bird.

"It's your fault for lowering my standards so much," I replied, getting a chuckle from Zifah.

We emptied out into the club. The music was thumping, and I expected to be greeted with a full house and a partial view of a breast or ass, or any combination of the same.

The stage was empty.

The tables and chairs had almost all been removed.

There was one left front and center. Cabal was sitting at it, leaning back in his seat with his arms crossed behind his head, looking like he didn't have a care in the world.

Espanto was sitting next to him.

Over a hundred demons, weres, and vampires waited on the outskirts.

I don't know if we had just walked into a trap because I was expecting something like it and that would indicate I was caught completely-off guard. It didn't matter. He was here, and from the looks of things he had brought a veritable army to bring me down.

My eyes flicked over to Alyx. She hadn't been able to spot him past the other scents, which I had no doubt had been planted for that very reason. Now she stared at him, her eyes big, her face stone.

"There you are," Espanto said, putting his attention on Alyx. He pushed his seat back and got to his feet. "Come here, my darling. I've missed you."

I felt my heart begin to thud in excited anticipation at his confusion and then fear when Alyx didn't respond to him.

Instead, I was confused when she began walking forward.

"Alyx?" I said.

She didn't seem to hear me. She went over to Espanto, and he put his arms around her and wrapped her in a solid embrace.

I didn't know what was happening. I was sure that I had drawn the power from the brand. She wasn't under his control anymore. She couldn't have been. Then why had she gone to him?

"Alyx," I said again, louder this time. There was no reaction.

Execution

"She isn't yours, diuscrucis," Espanto said, looking at me over her shoulder. "She's mine. You had no right to take my wife from me."

I felt my heart sinking. I had neutralized the brand. I knew I had. The only other explanation was that she had been playing me the entire time. That she was being the demon and lying to me, just like Rebecca.

"I'm so happy to see you again," Espanto said, running his hand over her rear. She nuzzled his neck, growling softly.

I watched them, feeling stupid and jealous. How could I have fallen for that again? How could I be so dumb? I was supposed to know better than this by now.

I swallowed my heart and shook it off. No. I wasn't being dumb. Alyx's loyalty was real. Her love was real. Maybe she could fake the sexual interest. She couldn't fake the way she had protected me. The fury. The strength. It was the doubt that was stupid.

I loved her. Foolish or not, demon or not, I trusted her.

"I see you've brought me something," Espanto said. "A Fist of God. That's what they call it, yes? I appreciate the gift." His eyes shifted to Gervais. "And you? I owe you."

He kissed Alyx on the cheek, and then gently turned her around to face us.

"Alyx. Kill them all."

"Yes, Master," she said. She began to grow and change, shifting into her demon form.

"Landon, remember what I said about dying?" Zifah said, vanishing from sight.

Alyx stood in front of us, huge and frightening. She bared her teeth, snarling viciously.

I didn't reach for the stone to summon the sword.

I didn't gather my power.

Instead, I stood before her and smiled.

"I love you," I said, showing her that I believed in her.

She smiled back as best she could in that form. Then she turned on Espanto, scooping him up in a massive claw.

"You don't own me anymore," she growled.

Espanto's eyes widened, clearly confused. "I do own you. I branded you."

"Your brand is powerless."

"That isn't possible."

"No? How do you explain this?"

She grabbed his head with her other claw and tore it from his body. Then she dropped both to the floor.

Cabal finally got to his feet. He had betrayed me to Espanto as expected, and now he was faced with a very angry Great Were.

"Kill them," he shouted to the assembled demons, his voice heavy with fear. He drew a dagger, holding it in front of himself as if it would be worth anything against Alyx.

The other demons started forward, but it was obvious they didn't really want to get involved. I considered letting it happen anyway. A hundred dead demons would help the balance overall. I was in a hurry. I needed to know what had happened to Rose. If she was in trouble, I needed to help her.

"Cabal, wait," I said. "I don't want to fight you."

I dug my hand into my pocket and pulled out the stone. I rubbed in between my fingers, for a moment hesitant to give it to him. It had belonged to Elyse, and now she was dead. It was all I had left of her. That, and memories.

I tossed the stone to the fiend. The memories would have to do.

"Take it. I need to get back to New York. The business with Espanto is over. Alyx is her own demon, and I don't think you want to suggest otherwise."

Cabal caught the stone. He eyed it for a second and then put up his hand. "Very well. Consider the deal complete. I don't want a fight with you, diuscrucis. I like to pick battles I know I can win."

"You can get us to New York?" I asked.

He nodded. "I have a Rift. I will open it for you."

Alyx changed back to human form. She had a large smile on her face, and she seemed as though a massive weight had been lifted from her.

Cabal glanced over at her with terror in his eyes. A free Great Were

Execution

was always something to fear.

"I had no choice," he said. "He would have killed me if he knew I had seen you and didn't tell him."

"I know," Alyx said. "Don't cross me again, and we'll have no problem with each other."

"Of course," Cabal replied, his eyes shifting to the pile of ash where Espanto's head had been. "Will you be claiming his territories and assets?"

"It's her right," I said.

"As long as she can defend it," Cabal said. "And I believe she can. As you know, I have served under Espanto for a number of years. I would be pleased to continue my service under the new mistress."

Alyx looked surprised and confused. "Me? Mistress? Landon, what should I do?"

"She accepts," I said. "She also demands a show of allegiance in the form of a gift."

Alyx and Cabal both looked at me with unknowing faces. I could hear Gervais snickering behind me.

"Well played, diuscrucis," he whispered.

I hadn't planned it that way, but it worked out.

"What kind of gift?" Cabal asked, growing uncomfortable.

Alyx glanced over at me, and then flashed a smile, finally catching on. "I'll take the sword," she said.

"What? But-"

"It's your choice, Cabal. The sword or your life. I'm sure I can put this operation to good use."

For a second, I thought he was going to give the attack order again. I knew he didn't want to. It was all to not look weak in the eyes of his subordinates.

Except they all looked weak in front of Alyx and me.

"Fine," he said at last, flipping the stone to Alyx. She caught it and tossed it back to me.

"I want you to go to Espanto's home in Spain," Alyx said to Cabal. "First, set all of his slaves free. Then figure out what his assets are and prepare a report. I expect it to be complete, and I will likely audit the results, so don't even think of cheating me."

"Yes, Mistress."

"Also, if you have any slaves of your own, they are to be freed at once."

Cabal's face blanched. "But, Mistress, I'll be ruined."

"Offer them pay for their work. Some will stay."

He bowed his head. "Yes, Mistress."

I was impressed. Alyx was taking to her new status like she was born for it. In the back of my mind, I hoped the power wouldn't go right to her head. She had been a Great Were for some time, and it hadn't, but this was her first true taste of freedom.

"Now, show us to the rift. We have business in New York. I'll return here when it is done to check on your progress." She held out her hand, allowing it to grow into a large claw. "Do not disappoint me, Cabal."

The fiend was shaking visibly. His lackeys had also shied away, trying to vanish in the dark corners.

"As you wish, Mistress."

Execution

29

Cabal's rift transported us instantly to Central Park, to a small circle of stones hidden inside Belvedere Castle.

"We can throw the Fist in Turtle Pond," I said. "We can get it when we need it."

"A fine idea," Gervais said.

I focused my power, reaching out toward the armor to lift it from the ground.

"Diuscrucis!"

Abaddon's voice filled my head, a shout so loud I raised my hands to my head without thinking, groaning and stumbling.

It was Gervais who caught me this time, getting his arms under mine and holding me up.

"Where have you been?" Abaddon demanded.

"Hell," I replied. "Finding a way to stop this."

"They take my power. It is mine. Release me."

"I'm working on it. I told you-"

"You take too long, diuscrucis! I grow impatient. I grow weary. I will not wait much longer."

I could feel the blood running out of my nose and ears. I could taste it in my mouth.

"You're going to kill me," I said.

"A warning only, diuscrucis. I can kill you, and I will if you delay any longer."

"Then you'll never be free."

"Neither will you."

His power vanished from my soul as quickly as it came. I pushed myself away from Gervais and spat blood onto the ground.

"Landon?" Alyx asked, concerned.

"I'm okay, Allie. Abaddon is getting restless, thanks to the week it took me to get in and out of Hell. He said he won't wait much longer."

"What does that mean?" Zifah asked.

"It means he will break himself out of his prison, and he will eat the world," Gervais said.

"You think he can get out on his own?" I asked.

"By now? Yes. He is waiting."

"Why?"

"I do not know. Why don't you ask him?"

I wasn't about to invite him in again. Instead, I wrapped my power around the Fist and lifted it, carrying it out of the castle and dropping it over the center of the small pond. It was late, but there were still people in the park, and they turned to see what splashed in the water. They were too late to actually see it.

"Alyx, we need to find Rose. Can you pick up her scent?"

"I will try. We should go back to where she was last seen."

I looked at Gervais. "Lead the way, mop-top."

He made a face at me before taking off at an inhuman speed. Alyx shifted beside me, and I climbed onto her back while Zifah rode my shoulder. It reminded me of that homeless man I had seen that had a rat who rode a cat who rode a dog.

The universe was crazy that way.

We got back to my place with fifteen minutes. I dismounted from Alyx, and she returned to human form. Then we made our way over to the deli.

Execution

There was police tape across the entrance, and it had been shuttered and locked down. I broke the tape and pulled the metal gate away with my power, and we made our way inside.

"Anything?" I asked Alyx.

"So many smells," she replied. "She was here. She was afraid. Very afraid. She went this way."

We followed her through the store. There were broken bottles and cans laying on the floor, and the police had drawn a chalk outline around where Elyse had fallen. I stared at it as we passed, feeling a wave of sadness and regret wash over me. She was so young, and her involvement with me had gotten her killed.

It had gotten a lot of people killed.

We went to the storage room in the back of the location, through an emergency exit and out into the back of an alley. Alyx stopped when she reached it, shaking her head.

"I don't know. It's been too long."

I turned to Gervais. "How long ago did this happen?"

"Three days."

"What? Why didn't you tell me that beforehand?"

Gervais shrugged. "It slipped my mind, in the middle of being tortured and beaten by the demons in Hell."

Three days was forever right now.

Rose was gone.

"How are we going to find her?" Alyx asked.

"I don't know," I replied, feeling sick. "I just don't know."

"I can find her," Zifah said. "Do you have something that belongs to her?"

"Not here. I do back at my place. How are you going to find her with that?"

"A spell. A demonic spell. Witchcraft, actually. I can bind the object to her, and it will grow hotter the closer we get to her location."

"Will it work if she's dead?" I asked.

"Not unless she's in Hell. But that's the only way it won't work."

"Since when did you become a witch?" Gervais asked.

"The proper term for a male is Warlock," Zifah said.

"Since when did you become a witch?" Gervais repeated.

"I've had years to practice. Unlike yourself, who failed miserably at every scheme you concocted and wound up banished from Hell for it."

"Can both of you shut up?" I said, stopping them before they could get going. They both fell in line in an instant. "Alyx, can you take these two back to the apartment and give Zifah one of Rose's t-shirts?"

"Panties would be better," Zifah said.

"T-shirts," I said again. "If either of them give you any trouble, you have my permission to send them back to Hell."

"Of course," Alyx said. "What are you going to do?"

"The Nicht Creidem know how to see ghosts, and I don't. I need to change that." I stepped over to her and kissed her. "I'll be back soon."

She rubbed her face against my neck for a second, suggesting that her freedom hadn't changed her in any bad ways. "Be careful."

"Don't worry," I said. "I'm too pissed to get killed."

Execution

30

I had to hail a dozen cabs before I got the one that was being driven by Joey Lincoln. Half of them were plain old ordinary mortal driven while the rest were a mix of the Touched and the Turned. I didn't tell any of them who I was, and they had no idea on their own. They drove me the short distance I requested an dropped me off without any trouble. I wasn't looking for trouble from cabbies.

Only from Rebecca.

I still couldn't believe that she had done this. Well, there was a part of me that definitely could believe it. After all, I had fallen for her with little to no background information on who she was or what most demons were like. She just happened to be the first thing I had bumped into during my sojourn into defending humankind, and I had been an easy mark.

The ghost thing? That was something else entirely. She had been stabbed by the Redeemer. Her soul had been cleansed, and God had given her a second chance. She had done well to help save me, and to help save the universe, and yeah, maybe God should have given her a little more credit for that. But maybe He had also seen inside of her, to the true depths of her being where that resident evil still lurked. I wasn't pretending to be good while at the same time thinking evil. I wasn't pretending to be either.

I had my strengths and my faults, my benefits and my vices. I got mad when I didn't get what I wanted, too, but I didn't plot the end of the world in retaliation.

"Joey," I said, sliding into the back seat.

He turned his head to look at me, surprised. "Do I know you?"

"Yes, but you wouldn't remember. My name is Landon."

He kept looking at me. It still wasn't registering. "Okay. What can I help you with, Landon?"

"I need to see your boss."

"What boss?"

I didn't have time to play the game. I decided to be blunt.

"You're Nicht Creidem. I'm the diuscrucis. Take me to your leader."

His eyes grew wide, and he stammered out an affirmation. "Uh... oh... okay."

We pulled away from the curb. He was a little erratic at first, struggling to contain his anxiety and keep the cab within the lines.

"Relax," I said. "I'm not going to hurt you. To be honest, I need your help."

"You do?"

"What do you know about ghosts?"

"You mean spirits? Or, like, Slimer?"

"More like spirits."

"Not much. I know they're real, but ninety-five percent of people who say they've seen one haven't."

"Have you ever seen one?"

He laughed. "Me? No. I heard there's one that's been spotted around the city a few times in the last couple of weeks." He paused. "I probably shouldn't be telling you this."

He had already told me enough. That ghost had to be Rebecca. "Who spotted it?"

He didn't say anything.

"Joey, I can either listen to you answer my questions, or I can kill you right now."

His face paled. "Don't you need me to take you to my boss?"

Execution

"I have other ways to find people. I thought this would be faster, and I'm in an awful hurry. This ghost that you said has been spotted? She killed one of my best friends three days ago."

"Are you kidding?"

"Do I look like I'm kidding? Have the Nicht Creidem figured out that Abaddon is back in play yet?"

"I had heard some rumors about something like that."

"They aren't rumors. He's here, right now, and the ghost knows where he is."

"Shit."

"You can say that again."

"Shit. I hope I don't get busted back to bicycle messenger for this. We've got a guy. His name is Bradford. He's got these sigils on his forehead. He calls them his third eye. Said he initially lifted it from a tattoo mag because he thought it looked cool, not because it let him see ghosts."

"Where is Bradford?"

"I'm taking you to him. He's not the boss man, but he's been a Nicht for a long time, and he's pretty badass. I'm sure Bianca will let you talk to him, once you tell her what you told me."

A tattoo on the forehead. Elyse had once had something similar, until her father burned it off her, along with all her hair.

"How long will it take to get there?"

"We have to head over to Jersey City. You're lucky it's late, or it would take forever."

"Just get us there as fast as you can, unless you want to watch everything in the city die."

"My city? No way." His foot dropped further on the accelerator, and we raced ahead.

"Hey, do you have a cell I can borrow?" I asked, pulling mine from my pocket. It hadn't survived Hell.

He leaned forward, opened the glove compartment, and pulled out an old candy bar cell. He tossed it back at me. "It's a prepaid. I keep it for situations just like this." He laughed. "Not like this, exactly. For normal riders who need to make a call and have a dead phone."

I leaned back in the seat and closed my eyes, trying to remember Alichino's number. Once I had it, I gave him a call.

"Yeah, what do you want?" The checkered demon's voice was raspy and tired.

"Alichino. It's Landon."

"Who?"

"Landon Hamilton."

I waited a few seconds for the name to resonate. "Oh, hey Landon. It's been a long time since-" He paused. "No, wait. Just checked my log. It hasn't been that long. What can I do for you?"

"Is Dante there?"

"Nope. I haven't seen him in three days."

I felt a stream of cold rush through me. The timing couldn't be a coincidence.

"I have a feeling he might be in trouble," I said.

"Dante? How is that even possible?"

"I don't know. What were you two working on the last time you saw him?"

"He wanted me to see if I could find a way to destroy Abaddon. I guess he's back in town?"

"Unfortunately."

"Tell me about it. Yeah, so I've been doing a ton of research. I'm talking, comb the entire internet, hack into a few intranets, and scan the darknet research. Not specifically about Abaddon, but how to destroy the soul of a demon completely enough that it can never return."

"What did you find?"

"As far as I can tell, it can't be done. I mean, there was the Redeemer that could turn the demon good, but that's not the same thing."

"And the Redeemer is gone."

"There is that. I haven't found any other way."

It wasn't what I wanted to hear. At least I had the Fist to try to trap Abaddon.

"Alichino, do me a favor and see what you can dig up on ghosts. From what I've heard, they can't be destroyed, only banished. That's not good enough for me."

I didn't like the idea of ending Rebecca, even now. She wasn't leaving me with much of a choice.

"You all like to keep asking me to do the impossible, don't you?" the demon said. "Why don't you just ask me how to solve the freaking Hodge conjecture?" He hissed into the phone. "Fine. I'll see what I can do. You're going to find Dante, right?"

I had a feeling I knew where Dante was. The same place Rose was. Maybe the same place Rebecca and Abaddon were.

The question was whether he was a prisoner or not. He couldn't stay out of Purgatory long without losing his power, so I was very much hoping for not.

"I'm going to try," I said.

31

Joey drove the cab through a roll-up and down a ramp, into a garage full of other cabs. The place was dingy and ugly and smelled like motor oil and urine. I was glad Alyx wasn't here. I could only imagine how she would react to the smell.

The hood on one of the other cabs was open, and someone in overalls was leaning in, working on something. Joey gave the horn a quick burst to get their attention, and they straightened up and looked our way.

A pixie-haired, narrow woman who could have been easily mistaken for a junkie or a bulimic stared through the windshield at us. Joey stopped the cab a few feet away from her.

"That's Bianca," he said.

"She's the head of this Chapter?"

"Yes."

"And she's fixing cars?"

"She says it relaxes her."

I opened the door to the cab and climbed out. Getting a closer look at Bianca, I could see the slight resemblance to Elyse. The Nicht Creidem had spent hundreds of years building their immunity to the Divine, and limited inbreeding were only one of the ways they had achieved it.

Execution

"Joey," she said. She didn't look happy that he had brought a passenger. "What is this?"

"This is the diuscrucis," I said, walking toward her. "Landon Hamilton. It's a pleasure." I put out my hand. It was a flippant way to introduce myself, but I wanted to see how she would react.

She reacted by making a blessed dagger appear from somewhere and using it to slice a neat line across my outstretched palm.

"Ouch," I said, closing my hand to keep the blood from dripping on the floor. I healed the wound and opened my hand again. "I'm not a demon, and if I were an angel, I'd be able to attack you right now."

She dropped the dagger on the floor. "It really is you."

"Yes."

"Why are you here?"

"He wants to talk to Bradford," Joey said.

"Bradford?"

"I'm hunting a ghost," I said.

She nodded. "Funny. So are we."

Sometimes it was a good thing when my goals aligned with the Nicht Creidem's. Sometimes it wasn't.

"Why do you want her?"

"How do you know it's a female?" By her reaction, I would guess she hadn't.

"I know a lot of things. It's my job."

"It's my job, too," Bianca said. "And if the diuscrucis is involved, I want to know. Who is she?"

"You give me something, I give you something," I said.

"I figured as much." She picked up a rag sitting on the fender and wiped off her hands. Then she slammed the hood closed and gestured for me to follow her. "I'm sure you already know about Abaddon?"

"Yes."

"And you know Randolph Hearst is involved," She said it as a statement of fact.

"I made a deal with him not to interfere. Then I interfered. He didn't like that. He and the ghost killed my friend. You might have known her.

She used to be one of yours. Joe's daughter, Elyse."

She nodded while she opened the door to the offices behind the garage. "I knew her. We met a couple of times while she was hunting for relics. I heard she got shot by a deli clerk. I was suspicious, but now it makes sense."

We moved past the offices, to a locked door in the back. She knocked a beat out on it, and it opened a moment later.

"It's okay, Rudy," she said as we walked past the guard, a big guy who reminded me of Obi. "He's with me."

We began to descend a stairwell.

"What's your play in this, diuscrucis?" she asked.

"The usual. Stop Hearst, get rid of Abaddon, avenge my friend. There have been a few complications, but I'm managing."

"Are you?"

I shrugged. "I'm trying to. That's why I'm here."

"You can't see ghosts, and you can't fight something you can't see."

"Exactly."

We kept going down for a hundred feet or so. There was another guard stationed at the bottom of the steps, and he knocked another pattern on the door to have a third guard open it.

"You've got a lot of security in here," I said. "Expecting trouble?"

"We're always expecting trouble."

I called her on it with a sidelong glance that told her I knew she was lying.

"Fine. We're worried about how Hearst is going to move. This is a power grab unlike anything I've seen before, and even HQ is worried about the fallout. Now you're telling me Hearst bought you off-"

"He didn't buy me off. I bought myself some time. At least, I thought I did." That move hadn't worked out. At all.

"Well, you knew what he was doing, and you didn't stop him-"

I interrupted her a second time. "You don't think I would have if I could? Like I said, there have been some complications."

We were in a long corridor with doors on either side. Bianca stopped at one of them and knocked.

Execution

"Now you're here because you need our help," she said. "And I'm inclined to help you because neither one of us wants the world to end. At least not if it isn't on our terms."

Nobody answered the door. She knocked again.

"Come on, Bradford," she shouted.

We waited another ten seconds. Finally, she took a step back and kicked the door. It bent off the hinges, collapsing inside.

"Whoa. Shit. What the hell?"

Bradford was in the room, laying on his bed, headphones over his ears and a comic book in his hand. He was naked, sort of. He had no hair and wasn't wearing any clothes, but he had so many tats and scars that there was no way to tell where the flesh was below it.

He shifted and sat up, pulling the headphones off. "Geez, B. You almost made me piss myself. And I was laying down, so that would have been messy." He grabbed a pair of boxers from the floor and slid them on. "What's so important you busted my door in?"

"The ghost we've been tracking," she said.

"What about it?" He looked at me and put out his hand. "Hey, Bradford Smith. How you doing, bro?"

I shook his hand. "I've been better."

"This is Landon Hamilton," Bianca said.

"No shit? I knew things were getting nasty out there, but to have you paying us a visit means it's worse than I thought."

"It is worse," I said. "I need you to teach me how to see ghosts."

He laughed. "You can't teach it, bro. It's all right here." He tapped his forehead. "The third eye. Only way you can do it."

"Then I need a third eye," I said.

"Hmmm, yeah, about that. I don't think it works on non-mortals. There are relics, though. Rings and pendants with the third eye on them. Those should work."

"Fine. I'll take it."

He laughed again. "Dude, we don't have any here. That's why I had to mark up my noggin."

Great. Rebecca was out there using mortals to kill people, and there was nothing I could do to stop her. Well, not nothing.

"I need to borrow him," I said to Bianca. "And I need you to teach me how to do an exorcism."

"What?" Bradford said. "Borrow? What do I look like, bro? A freaking sheep?"

"You look like my only chance to spot a ghost. Bianca, you just said you're worried. I'm trying to stop this, but I need your help. What do you say?"

"I have to contact HQ."

"There's no time," I said. "Hearst is getting ready for war. Oh, and if you didn't know this nugget already, Abaddon is just about ready to break out of his prison."

"How do you know that?" Bianca asked.

"The complication. I made a deal with Abaddon way back when, and now we've got a link between our souls. He can talk to me, and I can talk to him. Not that I want to, because it hurts like a bitch."

"That sounds like a shit deal," Bradford said.

"It is. Look, I told you my story. Is the Nicht Creidem in or out?"

"We're not supposed to work with you," Bianca said. "Especially after what happened with the Beast. I really should get in touch with the home base."

I bit my tongue. I wasn't going to start the argument about Elyse's father's plans to use the Box to create his own brand of Armageddon. All it would serve to do would be to drive them away, and right now I needed their help. Or at least, I needed Bradford's.

He seemed a little more empathetic and free-spirited than Bianca, so I targeted him directly.

"I already said, there's no time. I'm not asking for a lot. All you have to do is come with me and tell me if you spot her. You don't have to fight or get involved in any other way, and you could be saving the world."

Bradford bit his lip and glanced over at Bianca. He wanted to help. His body language made that obvious.

"B," he said, pleading.

She looked torn. She didn't want to get in trouble with the elders, and I understood that. They would be hard on her, as in death penalty hard, if things turned out badly.

"Nobody has to know," Bradford said. "Tell them I'm out on my usual hunt. If anything happens, it's on me."

She growled softly. "Fine. Go. Don't tell any of the others about this. Just forget I ever saw you, Landon."

"I won't forget you, but you'll forget me. I'll make sure of it."

"You can do that?"

"How else do you think I say anonymous when every angel, demon, and Nicht Creidem on the planet wants to keep tabs on me? Thirty seconds after I'm gone, you'll forget I was ever here. You'll remember Bradford left, but you'll just assume it was to go on the hunt. Of course, you won't remember me telling you this, either."

"That is one awesome superpower, bro," Bradford said.

"It comes in handy. It doesn't seem to work that well in Hell, though."

He laughed. "What? Are you serious?"

"Completely. Put on some pants, and let's go."

32

"So, what's it like, being the diuscrucis?" Bradford asked.

We were in Joey's cab, on our way back to my place. I was leaning against the window, staring out into the night. I was starting to get the feeling that I should never have come back after I defeated the Beast. My best intentions seemed to be getting me nowhere fast while the war between Heaven and Hell was escalating at an increasing pace.

"It kind of sucks most of the time," I said. "I thought by changing the rules a bit I could make it easier, and for a while it was. But when I evolved, everything seemed to evolve with me."

"I don't get what that means, but I still get you. I thought joining the Nicht Creidem would make things better, but in a lot of ways, they're worse than ever."

"What do you mean?"

"I could see them. The angels and the demons. My whole life."

"You were born Awake?" I had never, ever heard of that before.

"Yeah. Can you imagine that? When I was a kid, people thought I had this incredible imagination." He changed his voice, making it high-pitched and scratchy. "Oh, he's so cute the way he makes up stories. They're so vivid, too. He should become a screenwriter, or a novelist, or something."

Execution

He shook his head. "Yeah, right. When I got older, and by older I mean ten, I saw a vampire feeding. Then I saw a winged something or other tear someone's insides out. I had a breakdown. PTSD. My mom committed me. The Nicht Creidem got me out."

"The Nicht Creidem don't usually visit asylums to recruit inmates," I said. "Most Awake wind up homeless."

"I know. They found me, though. They said I was different. Whatever my lineage is, they told me I was immune to Divine power. Not resistant like they are. Completely immune."

The statement gave me pause. Matthias Zheng had been immune by being completely oblivious to the Divine; not only Sleeping, but Sleeping so strongly that nothing could wake him. Now here was Bradford as his polar opposite.

"Do you mind if I test something?" I asked.

"You want to hit me with your best shot?" he said. "Fire away."

I threw my power out at him. Not too hard, but hard enough.

"Did you do it yet?" he asked.

I stared at him in astonishment. My power wasn't like Heaven or Hell's. It seemed he was immune to everything. "Yeah. Did you feel anything?"

"Nope. I got bit by a vampire once. The teeth couldn't break my skin. Hey, what do you think of this one? The Nicht Creidem used me as a stud for ten years. I think I have like four hundred kids out there or something. I'm glad they don't make me pay child support." He laughed and clapped me on the shoulder like we were old friends.

"Did it work? Breeding you?"

"It worked for me," he said, still laughing. "I did three at one time once. Dude, I slept so good that night."

"I mean the kids."

"Ha-ha. Yeah, I think so. They said some of them were more resistant. None of them are immune. I think more than a few might have had impairments. Like you either get the gift, or you have problems."

"Do you have any contact with them?"

"No. Don't ask, don't tell, you know what I mean, bro?"

I wasn't going to be the one to tell him what the Nicht Creidem did to unhealthy offspring. At least not unless I needed leverage.

"So how come you aren't a stud anymore?" I asked. "And, what are you doing in New York? I would think you'd be a higher value somewhere else."

"I went sterile. I spent three months in the same cycle, and not one pregnancy. Don't know how or why, but it is what it is, you know what I mean? The reason I'm in the Big Apple should be pretty obvious."

"I've never seen you around."

"I've never seen you either. Your power doesn't work on me so I would remember. There's lots of people in this city, and while I stand out in a crowd, no offense, but you don't."

"That's the idea."

"I hear you, bro. But yeah, I'm a tracker. I find Divine, and then we call in the hunters to kill them. They never asked me to track you. I don't think they think it's worth the risk unless it's really important. The mucky-mucks don't like you, but I think you're cool. We're fighting the same fight; you know what I mean?"

"It's nice to know at least one of you gets it," I said.

"More than just me. There are others who are rooting for you."

"So, since I can't make you forget me, will you keep quiet to Bianca."

"Ha-ha. I'll tell her the truth if she asks."

Which she wouldn't.

"Thanks, Bradford."

"No problem, dude."

We chatted about normal mortal interests for the rest of the trip. The weather, the Yankees, stuff like that. It was nice to have a guy conversation for a change. I'd spent the last three weeks with three females, and while I was all for gender equality it wasn't quite the same. Obi had been overseas for a while, and I missed it.

"Yeah, I saw that one," Bradford said. "It was - Joey, stop the car!"

Joey slammed on the brakes while Bradford turned his head to look at a homeless woman who was wandering by.

"Shit, Landon. That's her."

33

I threw open the door to the cab, sliding out and looking back at the woman. She stopped walking, turning around slowly to face us.

There was no hint of Rebecca in the woman's appearance, but I could sense her in the posture, and in the way she stared at me.

Then she started walking toward us.

Bradford produced a knife, while Joey climbed out of the driver's side.

"Wait here," I said, pushing his knife hand down as I walked past.

I was calmer than I would have expected to be, my lingering anger over Elyse keeping me cold and focused.

I had never expected it to be this easy.

"Landon," she said, her voice the voice of the homeless woman, soft and weathered. "I figured it was only a matter of time before you caught up."

"What do you think you're doing, Rebecca?" I asked, my anger oozing out.

My venom knocked her off-guard. "What do you mean?"

"What do I mean? Do you remember Elyse? You used her body for a while a couple of years ago to do something that wasn't completely selfish."

She pursed her lips, but didn't speak right away.

"Be good. Do you remember that? Do you even know what that means?"

She recovered in a hurry, her posture changing. She stepped toward me. "Don't you dare judge me, Landon. Don't even pretend to think that you can. You have no idea."

"Seriously? Are you kidding me?"

"I saved you from the Beast. I saved this entire miserable world from complete destruction. Damn it, Landon, I saved God. Did that get me anywhere? No."

"Bullshit. It would have gotten you there in time."

"In time? How much time? We're immortal. It could take centuries. Sorry, but I'm not spending centuries pulling kittens from trees to get a pass. Not after what I did."

"So the other alternative is to go back to evil? To kill someone who trusted you?"

"I'm not playing for Lucifer's team. I took a page from your story. I'm on my own side, working toward my own end."

"And what end is that?"

"I'm consolidating the power of the demons here on Earth. Once we're strong enough, I'm going to start the chaos and the killing. Not to end the world. To force Him into submission. To make Him take me. I didn't want to kill Elyse, but you forced my hand. I tried to keep you out of this, Landon. I wanted to skirt around you, to leave you be. I know my plans mean disrupting the balance, but it would only be temporary."

I stared at her, dumbfounded. Whatever she had been before, she had gone completely insane.

"You think God is going to negotiate with you? Have you lost your mind? He didn't do anything to stop the Beast."

"That's not true. The Inquisitors helped you. Adam helped you. Do you think they would have if He didn't want it to happen? He won't negotiate directly. Someone will come in His name. They'll listen to reason."

"Does Hearst know about this plan of yours? Don't you think he'll have a small problem with it?"

Execution

"Hearst is an idiot. He thinks he's in control of this operation, and I'm working for him to restore myself to the head of the Solen family. He's already forgotten how much I hated my father and my lineage."

"And you intend to overthrow him how? You're stuck in the bodies of mortals, and he has Abaddon's power."

She laughed at that comment. "I've got Abaddon's power, too."

That was news to me. It was supposed to be impossible.

"I can see you weren't expecting me to say that. That's right, Landon, I've absorbed some of the demon's power for myself. I'm not limited to mortals anymore. Abaddon's power allows me to break down the mental barriers of the Divine. If the mind is weak enough, I can take it. Trust me when I say that Hearst's mind is weak. I've already been inside of it a couple of times. I know exactly what he thinks of me, and of himself. I know what he thinks of you, too."

"So you're using him the way you used me with the Grail? You haven't changed at all. After everything you went through, you're the same selfish demon you always were. The world isn't your playground. It isn't yours to destroy so that you get what you want."

"You're wrong, Landon. I have changed. I know better now than to expect anything to be given to me. Whatever I want, I have to take. And I will get what I want. I don't want to have to destroy you to do it. I still love you."

I had thought her other statements were crazy. That one blew me away.

"No, you don't," I said.

"I do," she insisted.

"Do you even hear yourself speak?"

"I paid my price. I earned my way. I'm only trying to get what I deserve."

"By killing thousands of people?"

"Millions if I have to. It is worth that much to me. I'll do anything. We'll see how much it's worth to Him to keep me out."

"I can't let you go through with this," I said.

"You can't stop me, Landon. I know you want to, and I know you'll try. It doesn't matter that you retrieved the Fist. It doesn't matter if you take

Abaddon, or send him back to Hell. You're too late. The wheels are in motion, and all of your power isn't enough to stop them. That's why I stayed to talk to you. You can't hurt me. You can't even touch me." Her angry tirade faded, and her vessel's face softened. "Besides, I wanted to see you again with real eyes. I wanted to hear your voice again with real ears. It isn't the same as a spirit."

I stared at her, my own anger a bright ember in my soul. It was mixed with a crushing sadness. A lamentation for what could have been.

Even if I somehow managed to get Abaddon under control, one of us was going to destroy the other. For everything that had happened, I still didn't want it to come to that.

There was no other way.

"What about Rose?" I asked.

"Who?"

"Rose. My friend. She's this tall, brown hair, big chest."

"I saw her at the deli. She ran away. Is she missing? I didn't take her. It may have been Hearst's people."

There was no real reason to believe her, other than the fact that there was no reason for her to lie. That was good enough.

I reached a hand out toward her. She stared at it for a moment before reaching out as well. What did she have to be afraid of? I couldn't hurt her.

"It doesn't have to be this way," I said.

"Yes, it does," she replied.

We both knew that was true.

I took her vessel's hand in mine. "I'm sorry," I said, squeezing it.

"I'm not," she said, squeezing back.

It was a goodbye. We both knew the next time we met, however, it happened; we'd be trying to kill one another.

I wasn't going to wait that long.

Calmly, gently, I reached out toward her, the real her, with my power, using what I had learned in Hell. Immediately, I felt a sense of her at the edge of my energy, a mass of Divine power, unlike anything I had ever experienced.

I asked it to rest. To calm and sleep and give in to the universe. I didn't

Execution

focus, I didn't force, I didn't push. I did the opposite, letting her power mingle with mine.

It began to change.

Her eyes widened in front of me, and she screamed in agony, wrenching her hand from mine. I stepped forward to grab her, to hold her and keep going until she was done with this existence.

I didn't get the chance. Her mortal vessel collapsed in a heap, and I didn't need Bradford to know she had fled it.

"She's gone," he said anyway. "What was that all about?"

"She's not as immune as she thought she was. Come on, we need to get back to my place. This is going to get ugly, fast."

34

We weren't that far from my apartment, and Joey's extra haste got us there inside of ten minutes. Bradford and I exited the cab, and I sent Joey back to tell Bianca to get ready for anything. Now that Rebecca knew that I could affect her existence, she was sure to at least be considering moving up her timetable.

And I still didn't know where Rose was.

We hurried up the steps and into my place. Alyx was standing near the door when we entered, and she threw her arms around me the moment I entered, planting her lips on mine. I returned her affection, giving her a quick hug.

"Landon," Gervais said. "You're back. It is about time."

He was on the couch watching television again. Zifah was sitting next to him, eating popcorn.

"The world is cracking at the seams, and you're eating popcorn?" I asked.

"They don't have this downstairs," Zifah said. "It's delicious." He eyed Bradford. "What? You've never seen a demon before?"

Bradford was staring. My guess was that he hadn't ever seen a demon before. At least, not one like Zifah.

Execution

"Bradford is Nicht Creidem," I said. "He's helping me find Rebecca. Actually, we already found Rebecca. I had a nice chat with her."

"You spoke to her?" Gervais asked. "What did she say?"

"She wants to hold the world hostage so that God will let her into Heaven."

Zifah's laugh was a rocky cackle. "She's out of her mind."

"Unfortunately. She's got Hearst under her thumb though I don't think he knows it yet. She's also absorbed some of Abaddon's power. She can possess Divine. Or at least, she says she can. Anyway, we need to find Rose and hopefully Dante, and then we need to grab Abaddon and stick him in the Fist. If we get a chance to take out Hearst or Rebecca in the meantime, even better. Zifah, have you made any progress?"

"I gave him one of Rose's bras," Alyx said.

I raised my eyebrow at that.

"It was a compromise," she added.

"Everything is ready to go," Zifah said. "We were waiting for you to come back."

"Let's not waste any time. Quick introductions. Bradford, this is Alyx, Gervais, and Zifah. You probably already know they're all demons, but that's how I roll."

Bradford laughed. "Yeah, dude. Not surprised. Nice to meet you all."

"You might not think so once you get to know us," Zifah said.

"Sorry to stare. I haven't seen a demon your size or color before."

"Get used to hearing that one," Gervais said.

"Shut up," Zifah snapped at the fiend. "Forget about it. Landon, everything is up on the rooftop."

We made our way to the window, out to the fire escape, and up to the roof. Zifah had laid out a circle of small stones there, each of them etched with demonic runes. Rose's bra was in the center, with more runes painted onto it in Zifah's blood.

"I hope I get to meet this friend of yours, bro," Bradford said, his eyes on the bra.

"Me too," I replied.

Zifah entered the circle and stood next to the bra. He held his hands out over it and whispered something. I could feel his Divine power rising out of him and pouring into the clothes. The runes on it began to burn, sending wisps of dark smoke into the night sky.

A few seconds later, he lowered his hands. "It's ready to go."

"You're sure?" I asked.

"Who do I look like, David Copperfield? This is real warlock poop, not a crap illusion."

"Toss it over to Alyx," I said. Zifah picked it up with both hands and threw it to her.

"What does it do?" Bradford asked.

"It's like a Divining Rod for big boobs," Zifah said. "It'll help you find Rose."

"You? Don't you mean us?" I asked.

"Nope. I'm staying here. It sounds like it's going to get dangerous, and I wasn't done with my popcorn."

I was tempted to argue with him and try to get him to come along. He would only vanish once things got hairy anyway.

"Suit yourself. Gervais, do you have anything to make yourself useful with? You can't even change form anymore."

Gervais glared at me, clearly unhappy with his currently weakened position. It was kind of fun having him around when he was so pathetic.

"Give me a blade, diuscrucis. I still know how to fight."

"Here, bro," Bradford said, producing a dagger. "You can take one of mine." He held it out, handle first.

Gervais walked over and took it, growing angrier as he did. "Thank you," he said through clenched teeth. Bradford seemed oblivious to it.

"Alyx, are you getting anything?"

She held the bra in her hand and turned in a full circle. After a full rotation, she started turning more slowly, stopping when she was facing roughly south.

"That way," she said.

"Then that's the way we're going," I replied.

"Good luck," Zifah said. "If you need me, you know where to find me."

Execution

We headed back to the fire escape, taking it down to the street. Alyx took point, leading us through the city on foot. It was slow going, and she had to pause often to recalibrate our bearings since we couldn't take a direct path. It would have been easier if any of us could fly.

"Hey, Landon," Bradford said, coming up next to me.

"What's up?" I asked.

"You and Alyx. Are you, you know? Together?"

"Yeah, why?"

"Ha. Don't get the wrong idea. I was just wondering, since she's a were, you know? What it's like?"

"Love is love."

"Nah, bro. I don't mean that either. I mean, what it's like."

He made a face that told me exactly what he was referring to. I could feel myself getting embarrassed.

"That's private, don't you think?"

He seemed confused by that. "Oh. I was just curious. I've always fantasized about it; you know what I mean? Yeah, I'm supposed to take demons out, not get excited about them, but it's just so kinky."

"She can hear you; you know," I said, hoping it would end the conversation.

It didn't. "Have you ever been to a comic-con?"

"No, why?"

"So, I went to this convention once. You know there's people out there that like to dress up as characters."

"I've heard of cosplay."

"Yeah, bro. It's something like that, but not quite. Some people like to dress up like animals and have sex with each other."

I wasn't sure what to say to that. I'd never heard of it. "Okay."

"Ha. Seriously, dude. I mean in full suits, you know, kind of like sports mascots, except with little cutouts for-"

"Is there a point to this story?" I asked.

"You know, I've never done it or anything, but it's kind of hot, and when you think about it, it's like a cheap version of the real thing, right?"

He shifted his head toward Alyx. I noticed Alyx glance back at me, a small smirk on the edge of her lips. She was enjoying the discourse a lot more than I was.

"I liked you better five minutes ago," I said.

The comment didn't dissuade him. It tended to be a problem when a person was too comfortable with who they were.

"Oh, come on, Landon. I'm just saying, bro. Maybe it's messed up, but I never said I was healthy. I did spend time in an institution, you know?"

"You haven't seen her change yet. It's not what you think."

"Then I guess I have something to look forward to."

He was silent for a few seconds before putting his attention on Gervais. The fiend was walking a few feet behind me, whistling softly and using the dagger to scratch the sides of cars as we passed. He just couldn't stop himself from being an asshole.

"So, what's your story?" Bradford asked.

Gervais stopped whistling. There was a long, silent pause. "Do you really want to know?"

"Yeah, dude."

"Then ask Landon." He sneered slightly and went back to whistling.

Bradford shrugged and came back my way. His mouth opened to speak, and I put up my hand.

"I don't want to talk about it."

"Okay. Whatever, bro. Do you mind if I go talk to your girlfriend?"

"It's not my decision to make," I said.

He slapped me on the shoulder and approached Alyx. He had just reached her side when she grabbed him by the arm and threw him roughly to the ground.

"Alyx?" I said, confused.

She stood over the Nicht Creidem and shifted, only halfway through the process when the first of the vampires arrived.

Execution

35

It wasn't immediately clear how Alyx didn't smell them or hear them coming, or why the mortals around us didn't evacuate the area before the fighting began.

One second, we were walking along the sidewalk on our way across the city, and the next we were under full-scale attack.

The first of them hit Alyx hard mid-shift, knocking her back and away before she could get her legs under her. She slammed hard into a car, knocking it over and almost crushing a few pedestrians below it. They screamed at the sudden chaos and began scrambling away.

In that split-second, I wondered what they thought was happening.

A dozen more vampires followed behind the first. They were special ops types dressed in black and armed with swords. They knew who the most dangerous target was, and they headed right for her.

Or at least, they tried to. I threw my power out in front of them, using it as a wall. The bulk of them slammed against it, losing their momentum and hitting the ground. They were on their feet in seconds, but seconds were all Alyx needed.

She finished her change, reaching out with a monster claw to grab the original assailant. At the same time, Bradford had regained his feet, and he jumped on the back of one of the vamps, digging a blessed knife into its neck. It howled and collapsed under his weight.

"Well, don't just stand there," I said to Gervais, who was stationary beside me. I pushed myself forward, bringing the obsidian spatha to hand, ready to enter the fray.

Then I heard Alyx cry out. I looked over and saw the vampire had bit her hand, and it was turning black and dead as he held onto it. My stomach churned at the sight. I had seen something like it before, the way the skin shriveled and died beneath the bite.

That was Abaddon's power.

I tried to change direction and head her way to help. A sharp hiss to my left forced me to pause, and I ducked and brought my blade up just in time to avoid decapitation. The vampire bared his teeth at me, showing me dark fangs that oozed a black saliva. They had all been imbued with the demon's energy.

"Get off me, bro," I heard Bradford say. His fist bashed into one of the vampires, knocking it back with tattoo-enhanced strength. A second got its teeth onto his arm, and he used it to pull the surprised vampire into his dagger.

I sidestepped a claw-swipe from my opponent, noting the darkened fingernails with moisture at the tips, and then cast out my power at him, throwing him thirty feet and through a window. I turned back to Alyx, who had managed to dislodge the first of the vampires but was coming under attack by four more.

I glanced back at Gervais. He was still standing there, watching everything unfold. Because of course he was.

I charged toward Alyx, at the same time she leaped, getting herself out of the fracas. The four vampires turned to follow, and I hit them with my power, pushing them back and into the opposite wall. They bounced off and charged me, swords flashing under the streetlights.

I dropped into one of Josette's fighting stances, turning to keep them all in view as they organized themselves for the attack.

"All of that power and this is the best you can do?" I said, taunting them.

Execution

"Ask the were what the best we can do is," one of them said.

Ask the were? I glanced back to find Alyx. She had joined Bradford behind me and had pinned one of the vampires to the ground.

Her left arm dangled at her side, still useless. It hadn't healed.

"Oh no," I whispered, the anger exploding inside of me.

The vampires used the distraction to charge, and I pulled my power back in, wrapping it around me like a shield. As they reached it, I threw it back out as a wall of spikes, the energy piercing them and throwing them back once more. They grunted in pain that turned to laughter at my rage.

"Rebecca sends her regards," the same one said right before I cut his head off.

I threw myself toward Alyx even as their bodies collapsed and turned to ash. She and Bradford were holding their own, the Nicht Creidem's immunity giving him a firm advantage in the fight. As long as he avoided getting skewered, there was nothing the vampires could do to hurt him.

Gervais was still observing. No. He wasn't. He had disappeared.

I reached Bradford and Alyx, stabbing one of the vampires in the back. A second tried one more time to cut Bradford with its claws, and then it too was taken down by the blessed knife.

And then it was over. There were no more vampires to fight. Only piles of ash. I turned my attention to Alyx, who shifted back to human form. Her arm was still black and dead at her side.

"Landon," she said, upset at the wound.

I knelt down beside her and reached out for the arm. "Tell me if this hurts."

She nodded. I had never seen a great were so afraid of anything.

I lightly touched my fingertips to the wound. I immediately felt a wave of pain flow into them, and my fingernails began to turn black. I drew my hand away, more worried than I was before.

This was bad. Very bad.

I held my fingers up in front of my face. Whatever Abaddon's power had done when mingled with the vampires, it was contagious. I pushed my power into the wound, trying to heal it like I would any other. There was no effect.

"Landon?" Alyx said again, her voice small. She had tears in her eyes. It broke my heart to see her like that.

"Oh shit, bro," Bradford said.

"It'll be okay," I said.

To calm Alyx or me? I closed my eyes, letting my power flow forward and envelope the damage. I didn't push it, and instead, put my attention on relaxing. I felt a tingle in my fingers, and the wound began to heal.

I opened my eyes. The damage was gone.

"I can fix it," I said.

She smiled pensively. I reached for her arm again, keeping my hand slightly above the ruined flesh. I could feel the power below it, and I forced myself to calm while I worked to transform the poisonous demonic energy.

I smiled as the wound began to heal, the black skin fading and first turning pink, and then red, and then returning to the color of healthy flesh. It spread from her elbow down to her fingertips, until finally she was whole again. She wiggled her fingers and then dropped down to embrace me.

"Thank you, Master," she said, forgetting herself in the emotion of the moment. I was so happy that I forgot myself, too, bringing her lips to mine and kissing her intensely.

"Nice, bro," Bradford said behind us.

I broke off the kiss, stood up, and helped Alyx back to her feet. "I can fix it, but it isn't easy or fast. If these vampires start infecting other demons like this, or if they infect mortals, it's going to be an epic disaster."

"We have to find Abaddon," Alyx said. "We have to stop them before they can give any more of their number the same abilities."

"It might already be too late," I said. "Bradford, did you happen to see where Gervais went?"

"No. Sorry, dude. I was a little busy."

I scanned the street. I could hear sirens in the distance, drawing closer. They might not know what had occurred, but the damage was still done. Fortunately, we didn't hurt anybody.

"As soon as things go south, he disappears," Alyx said. "At least Zifah

Execution

was honest about his cowardice."

"Hmph. Cowardice."

The fiend appeared behind the broken glass of the window I had thrown the vampire through. His face was coated in blood, his hair a mess.

"The things I do for you, diuscrucis."

For me? I doubted it. "What did you do?"

He reached down and lifted the vampire where I could see him. He was in one piece, which meant he was still alive. His pants were around his ankles, and his genitals were knitting back together as I watched. It was a disgusting display.

"I thought that didn't work on the Divine," I said.

"True. Very true. But then I remembered what you said about Rebecca, and how Abaddon's power allowed her to enter the Divine. So, I figured I would take a shot. He had Abaddon's power, and now I have eaten some of it. It is embarrassing and distasteful, but I do what I must."

The vampire began to come around. Gervais threw him at me with more force than he should have been able. Then the fiend changed shape, into an exact replica of the demon.

"It appears to work quite well. Surprisingly so. Perhaps no demon can wield the sheer volume of power Abaddon has except for Abaddon, but in smaller bites?" He laughed at his stupid pun. "It is effective."

"Wow," I heard Bradford say behind me.

That wasn't the word I would use. A Gervais who could feed on demons and take their form and their power?

Things were getting worse by the minute.

I lifted the original vampire up with my power, bringing the obsidian spatha to his neck. His eyes rolled open slowly, and he looked at me with bleary eyes.

"Where is Rose?" I asked.

"He doesn't know," Gervais said. "Or I should say, I don't know, which means the same thing."

If Rebecca had sent them, it meant that there was, at least, one thing she hadn't lied about.

"You haven't seen her, have you, Bradford?" I asked.

"Who? The ghost? No. Sorry, bro."

I pushed the spatha against the vampire's neck, threatening to break the skin. "Do you have anything useful that you do know?"

"He doesn't know anything useful, Landon," Gervais said. "Kill him and let us be done with it."

I was hesitant to do anything Gervais recommended, and if the vampire hadn't been carrying Abaddon's poison, I might have let him survive. He was no good to me if he didn't know anything.

I pushed the blade through his neck with my power, killing him in an instant. Then I scanned the street for Rose's bra. Alyx had dropped it near the banged-up car, and I went over and retrieved it. I could feel the tingle of the power the moment I touched it, and the difference in the feeling as I turned. I was pissed about what had happened to Alyx. I was pissed because Gervais had leveled up, and I was pissed because Elyse was dead. I was also sure there was more and would be more to be pissed about soon enough.

I didn't say anything to the others. I just started walking in the direction the enchanted lingerie indicated. Alyx was at my side a moment later, while Bradford and Gervais followed close behind.

"We'll find her," Alyx said. "You'll save her. That's what you do."

"I didn't save Elyse."

She flinched at my pessimism, and then took my hand in hers.

"You'll save her," she repeated.

Execution

36

"That has to be it," I said, pointing out over the bay.

The Statue of Liberty was looming in the background, a symbol of freedom for many, a personal symbol of sacrifice for me. It was where my afterlife adventure had started, where I had met Rebecca, and where I had made the original deal with Abaddon. Whatever the reason was, it always seemed to be turning up whenever something major was about to happen.

That didn't make me feel better.

At least it wasn't Lady Liberty herself that I was pointing at. Instead, I was looking at a massive container ship sitting to the immediate left of the Grand Dame. Rose's bra was facing in its direction, and it was tingling my hand hard enough to make it itchy and numb.

"I guess we need a boat," Bradford said. "It figures. I can't swim."

"Do you want to wait here?" I asked. Alyx didn't look happy either. Weres hated water.

"And miss the action? No way, bro."

"Do you see any boats around here, diuscrucis?" Gervais asked. "Because I don't."

"There's the ferry coming right now, dude," Bradford said.

"Do you think they will be kind enough to head over to that ship for us?" Gervais snapped. "Dude?"

Bradford shrugged. "I think they'll do whatever we want them to, if it comes to it."

He wasn't wrong. We could easily commandeer the ferry and drive it over to the ship, and the idea of it was tempting. I had a feeling whoever was on the ship would notice that.

"The sea approach isn't going to work," I said.

"There's a heliport a little bit east of here," Gervais said. "I know how to fly a helicopter, though I'm not eager to be removed from the fight."

I gave him a look.

"What?" he asked.

"When I wanted to take a chopper in China you didn't volunteer to fly it."

He shrugged. "I wasn't in the mood. I'm feeling more peppy today."

It was so Gervais that I dropped the subject entirely. There was no point.

"Fine. We'll fly over. Unless anyone wants to swim?"

Alyx and Bradford both looked terrified at the thought. It was cute and amusing how she was afraid of water, especially when she would be fine with jumping out of a helicopter and onto a hard surface from a few hundred feet up.

We hurried over to the heliport. There was a single helicopter waiting there, a privately owned, sleek, black thing with a slowly spinning rotor that was ready to jump into action. A pair of men in dark suits waited on either side of it for its passenger to return.

They were both mortal, and they watched us approach with a trained look of cautious disinterest though I could see their hands shifting to a better position to reach the concealed weapons I was certain they were carrying.

"Can we help you with something?" one of them asked. We were surely an interesting bunch to them. Interesting, and barely threatening.

If only they knew.

"Do you do sightseeing tours?" I asked, pointing at the helicopter.

"Do we look like we do sightseeing tours, jackass?" the man said. It

Execution

was typical New Yorker.

"Oh. That's a shame because I really need a ride."

"Get lost."

I didn't want to use my power on them. If I weren't careful, they would wind up Awake, and their lives would be ruined.

Of course, demons had no problem causing stuff like that to happen. Gervais kept walking up to them, a smile on his face.

"He said we need a ride," Gervais said.

"Just stop right there," the man replied, drawing his gun.

"Or what? Will you shoot me? Ah, I don't look threatening do I? One moment." He had the knife tucked into the back of his pants. He pulled it out and held it toward the men. "There you are. Shoot me, and I'll kill you."

"Gervais," I said. Too late.

Both men shot him, one bullet in the leg each. He fell to his knees without a sound.

"Damn it, Gervais," I said, moving forward to stop him before he made good on his word.

Two bullets hit my legs as well. I stumbled slightly before pushing my power to them. They had healed before I fell.

Gervais sprang up from his position, knife heading toward the first man's neck. I threw out my power, snapping the knife out of Gervais' grip, and then pulling it back into him and knocking him on his ass. The guards were rightfully frightened at this point, and they backed away as I approached.

"Whatever the hell is going on, we don't want any trouble," the first said.

"Yeah. You want the chopper? Take it."

What I wanted was to cut Gervais' stupid head off. I couldn't do it without losing our pilot.

"Get in the helicopter," I said, following behind him. The pilot hadn't seen or heard the commotion, but he bailed out quickly when Bradford brandished his knife at him.

"Now, let me see," Gervais said, taking the pilots seat and looking at the dashboard. "It's been a long time since I flew one of these things. I did a few days in Vietnam flying for the Americans. Have you ever heard of the Mỹ Lai Massacre?"

"That was infantry, bro," Bradford said.

"Oh, yes, you're right. Hmm... Have I ever flown a helicopter before?" He chuckled softly, hitting a few switches and getting the rotors going for real. "You should hold on tight, just in case."

The chopper lurched forward into the sky, made a tight rotation, and started going back to where the two guards and the pilot were standing and watching the proceedings.

"Gervais," I shouted, knowing he was heading for them on purpose.

"Oh, Landon. You have no sense of humor."

He twitched the stick, and the helicopter leapt over the frightened men and up into the sky.

Execution

37

"Go in high on the first pass, so we don't look suspicious," I said.

"Don't tell me how to do this thing, diuscrucis. I wasn't born yesterday," Gervais replied.

"Technically-"

"Don't technically me, either."

The helicopter kept climbing as we headed out over the bay. I picked up a pair of earphones and put them on, listening to air traffic control as they were apparently trying to contact us.

"I think you should answer them," I said.

"Perhaps you are right." He smiled at me. I hated when he made that face. "Go to hell," he said to air traffic control.

"You're going to get us shot down," I said.

"Oh please."

I shook my head and stared down at the water below, and then at the container ship as we passed over it. It was about half-loaded, with containers of a dozen different colors and lengths stacked one on top of the other. I could see sailors walking the perimeter and moving in a pattern that was hardly random.

"Demons," Alyx said, putting her face right next to mine. "I can smell them from up here. Weres, mainly. A few vampires."

"Do they have Abaddon's power?"

"No. I wouldn't smell them if they did. It kills their odor."

"It may be the only thing that can," Gervais said. "A miracle in itself."

"We'll circle and come back lower to get one more look," I said.

"Uh, Landon?" Bradford shouted from the back of the chopper.

"What is is?" I asked, turning back to look at him. His eyes were down, staying on the ship as we passed by.

"Your ghost lady is down there."

"On the ship?"

"No. Not yet. Out over the water. I think she may have followed us."

Had Rebecca followed us? Damn. Not only did that mean she hadn't known where Rose was, but it may have also meant that she didn't know where Abaddon was. But how could that be if she had taken some of his power? I considered it for a minute. What if Hearst was trying to make a run for it with Abaddon? What if he had figured out that Rebecca was playing him for a fool?

Just like she had played me. Our meeting was no accident, and by asking her about Rose I had told her what my priorities were, and where I was going. The attack back on the street was a diversion. A misdirection.

"Okay, forget the second pass. Gervais, get us in position to jump."

"Very well, Landon," Gervais said. "Try not to break your neck on the way down. I want to be the one to do it."

"I'll do my best."

The chopper swung in a tight circle. As it did, I could see another helicopter incoming. NYPD. Damn Gervais.

"I told you not to be an asshole," I said, pointing out the company. Mortals may not have noticed the Divine under ordinary circumstances, but there were only a limited number of things they could think about a stolen helicopter.

"I'll handle it. You jump."

I had no idea how he was going to handle it. "Bradford, you ready?"

"I'm not immune to gravity, bro," he said.

"I'll help you down. Alyx, are you good?"

Execution

She smiled, her teeth growing pointed as she did. "Of course, my love."

I moved past her to the back of the helicopter, leaning over Bradford and throwing the door open.

"Trust me," I said, wrapping my arm around his shoulders.

He was too frightened to speak. I looked out the open door at the ship approaching in a hurry. I could see that the guards had noticed us now, and were pointing and shouting.

"Ready," I said for Bradford's sake. "Get set." I lifted him slightly from the seat, keeping him low so we would clear the landing pads.

I was just about to shout, "Go," when I saw something hit one of the guards, and he fell over with steam pouring out of a wound. Then Rose appeared, running out from behind one of the containers to grab the knife she had used to drop the vampire. Dante was close behind her.

What the hell?

"Go, diuscrucis," Gervais said.

He dipped the side of the helicopter, catching me off-guard and sending Bradford and me both tumbling out. I felt an initial moment of panic and then pushed out with my power, spreading it below us and using it to slow our descent. Bradford was silent and terrified beside me though he began to calm as he saw we weren't going to splat onto the deck.

The NYPD chopper was growing near, and it hovered a few hundred feet from Gervais, no doubt trying to contact him over the radio. I saw Alyx leap from the helicopter a moment later, changing and growing as she fell.

Then we had reached the container ship. I pushed out my power even harder, using it like a jet engine to stop our fall. We landed fairly gracefully on our feet, and I let Bradford go.

"Oh wow, bro," he said, breathless. "That was awesome!"

"Good. Now help me with these guards."

I took the spatha from my pocket while Bradford produced his knife. Four vampires were bearing down on us, guns in hand.

"I'm not immune to bullets, either," Bradford said.

Divine didn't carry guns unless they were planning on fighting mortals, the Nicht Creidem, or me. It meant they were expecting me. Or maybe they were a defense against Rebecca?

The vamps opened fire. I threw my power out around us, using it as a shield. Bradford shied away, expecting to be shot. When he wasn't, he straightened up.

"Dude, I need to bring you everywhere with me," he said.

I dropped the shield, leaping at two of the guards, pushing their weapons aside and making one neat cut that dug into both of their chests. I heard a grunt behind me, and I spun around, ready to fight the other two.

Bradford had them in hand, getting too close for their rifles to be effective and shaking off their clawed attacks. The surprise of his immunity allowed him to stab them both in the neck.

"I saw Rose before we jumped," I said. "She has to be here somewhere."

I scanned the area for Alyx. I hadn't seen her land.

I heard a roar, and a body passed overhead. She was close.

Where were Rose and Dante?

And what were they doing?

Neither one of them looked like a prisoner to me.

"Keep an eye out for Rebecca," I said. I didn't know what her game was, but I was sure it wasn't meant to come out well for me.

"Doing it," Bradford replied.

We made our way along the side of the ship, heading in the direction I had seen Rose. I could hear more growls, roars, and screams echoing in the night, and when I looked up for Gervais, I saw that he had allowed the NYPD to guide his helicopter away. I had a bad feeling about his goals, but there was nothing I could do about that now.

The echo of gunfire pierced the night up ahead. I knew they weren't shooting at Alyx, what would be the point? It meant Rose had to be close. I grabbed Bradford again and pushed off with my power, leaping high into the air and bringing us down on one of the containers. I could see the muzzle flashes down below, deep within the maze of boxes. I didn't see the target.

"Wait here," I said, not waiting for a response before I jumped down on top of the shooter. I stabbed him with the spatha. "Rose," I called, not too loudly.

I waited a few seconds.

"Rose," I said again.

Her face appeared from around the corner. "Landon?" She smiled. "Hey."

"What the hell is going on?" I asked, getting closer to her. She came out into full view, with Dante trailing behind.

"I'm working the case," she said.

"What?"

"I've been following Hearst for the last three days," she said. "I tracked him and Abaddon back here."

Dante coughed behind her.

"With a little help."

"You've been tracking Hearst? I thought you were taken."

"No. It's a long story, and I can tell you later. Right now, we have our chance to get Abaddon. He's here. On this boat."

"Hearst?"

"Him too, but we need to be careful. He's not the same vampire he used to be."

I already knew that much.

"Elyse is dead," I said.

I saw a momentary flash of remorse. "I know. All the more reason for me to help you with this. You promised Hearst you wouldn't get involved, and he killed Elyse for it. I never made that promise, so I got involved."

"So did I," Dante said.

"So you know how to trap him without the Fist of God?" I asked.

"No, signore. I believe there is no other way."

"I knew you would come looking for me," Rose said. "I wanted to be wherever Abaddon was when you showed up. His prison is still intact. If we can bring it to the Fist-"

"Is it small enough to carry?"

"I can transport it, Landon," Dante said. "Through Purgatory, like I did for Rose."

"You want to carry Abaddon through Purgatory?"

"Only for a split-second, yes."

"Isn't that risky?"

"Yes, but we have to do something."

"Where is the Fist?" Rose asked.

"Central Park," I replied. "Turtle Pond."

"I can do it," Dante said. "Let's go."

I heard a thump behind me. I spun around. It was Alyx, back in human form.

"I killed everyone I saw," she said. "I - Landon!"

Her face twisted in warning. I didn't know why, and I barely had time to react. I began to turn around again, knowing the threat was behind me. Except I didn't understand because only Rose and Dante were behind me.

I felt the knife begin to dig into my neck, the force of it too strong to be typical.

Then a grunt and the knife was gone. I finished turning, finding Bradford on top of Rose, his knife to her throat.

"I don't think so, ghost bitch," he said.

Rebecca had taken Rose, and she had been about to stab me in the back. Again.

Rose's eyes fluttered as Bradford began to recite an exorcism. He paused when she fell limp.

"Which way?" I asked, knowing that Rebecca had fled.

"That way," Bradford replied, pointing down.

That had to be where Abaddon was.

"Alyx, stay with Rose. Don't let anything happen to her."

"I should be with you."

"I'll be fine. I need Bradford to spot Rebecca and Dante to move the prison. Please?"

She smiled because I asked. "Yes, my love."

The three of us took off at a run.

Execution

38

We made our way to the first stairwell we found. There were three piles of ash around it already, clinging wetly to the surface of the ship. We started to descend, feet clattering on the metal rungs.

"How are you able to stay here so long?" I asked Dante.

"I'm not. I have been coming and going the entire time. Rose is a treasure, signore. She may be mortal, but she is tireless. A rare find."

"Yeah, she's pretty great," I said. "Are you okay right now?"

"I am well, Landon. Get me to the prison, and I will bring it to Central Park for you. Then you can meet me there."

"If we make it. Abaddon isn't bound to the prison anymore."

"What do you mean?"

"He can break it open any time. He's been waiting for me."

"Waiting?"

I didn't understand it either, but it was what it was.

We reached the first deck. Bradford had seen Rebecca go below the surface, but he had no idea how far she had travelled. If we needed to search every deck, we would be here forever.

"Do you know which deck?" I asked Dante.

"No, signore. We saw them load the prison onto the ship. It is a rune covered wooden box just big enough to fit a man, with more runed chains wrapping around it. There is a blade mounted inside which sits in Abaddon's gut and draws out his power, while at the same time keeping him healed. Whoever holds the hilt gains the power."

"A sword that steals Divine power?" I said.

"Yes. It is an ancient relic, predating the Canaan Blades. I had thought it was long lost to this world."

"Apparently not. Do you think maybe next time you could tell me about missing relics with that much power beforehand?"

"As I said, it never occurred to me what the artifact was because we all thought it long destroyed."

"Great. Just great. Well, there's only one other way I can think of to find him."

And I hated it.

And I wanted nothing to do with it.

And I did it anyway.

"Abaddon," I said, internally, closing my eyes and pushing my voice through our bond.

There was no response.

"Abaddon," I said again, pushing some of my power through.

I felt a wave of confused nausea hit me. The demon still didn't answer.

"Abaddon," I said a third time. I pushed harder, sending my energy through the link and into the demon. He wanted me to come so I could set him free? Maybe I couldn't end him just yet, but this was going to be his best chance.

I felt dizzy once more, and I fell against the side of the corridor. I felt Dante's hands on my a moment later, but they turned numb against me. I was only halfway within myself, and halfway somewhere else.

Not somewhere else. Someone else. Abaddon. I was there, inside whatever passed as his soul. I could feel him around me. The power radiated like the sun. The only other time I had felt this much was inside the Box.

"Judith," Abaddon said, his voice soft.

I opened my mouth the reply before realizing he wasn't speaking to

Execution

me. I could hear him speak? That didn't seem right.

"Judith," I heard again.

His power was all around me, but none of it was coming at me. He was distracted by something, wide-open for me to eavesdrop.

"I told you I would come, Abelard," I heard a second voice say. It was ethereal. Corporeal.

Rebecca.

"I'm sorry," Abaddon said. "I didn't believe you."

"It is well. I understand."

"I'm sorry."

"You've told me that a thousand times. I told you, I forgive you. I'm here. I've been here, all of this time, waiting for you. A spirit, waiting to be joined to my lost love."

"I killed you."

"And by killing me you brought us together for an eternity."

"I want to end. I want to be done with this existence."

"No. Please don't leave me, Abelard. Please. Not now, when I've finally found you."

"But Judith."

"Please. If you're truly sorry, you won't go."

I could feel his hesitation. Rebecca was baiting him, too, and he was falling right into her trap. How did she know about his lost wife, the one he had killed in a fit of rage?

"Abaddon," I said again, pushing a little bit harder. "You can't do this. We had a deal."

He heard me this time. I felt his power turn on me, overwhelming me and throwing me violently from his soul. I snapped back into mine, the pain of it a thousand lances across my entire being.

"Landon," he said. He was different than he had been before. He sounded more put together, more intelligent. Like the way he had in the Box. "My apologies, diuscrucis. I have reconsidered our bargain. Ten thousand years aren't long enough for me to make good on the wrongs I have done to my Judith."

"You'll destroy the world," I said.

"If she wishes it, yes. That is of little consequence now. I have long believed my love lost to me. I have long been remorseful and regretted my actions. I have suffered, and in that suffering wished to end. I suffer no more. I care not if humankind suffers in my stead."

"She isn't your lost love," I said. "Her name is Rebecca. She's a-"

"Do you question me?" Abaddon said, sending some of his power through the link. My entire body turned cold, and my vision began to fade from the sudden shock and pain.

I did question him. She wasn't Judith. I knew that for a fact. How could I prove it to him?

"Tell me where you are. Let me come to you, and I'll prove it," I said.

Abaddon was silent, though his power swirled within me, a maelstrom ready to unleash.

"Abaddon?"

The demon's voice was cold and calm.

"I have decided, diuscrucis. I absolve you of your promise. Consider our bargain satisfied."

I didn't have time to say anything else to him. One moment the bond was there, strong enough to choke me. The next, it was completely gone. The link shattered, leaving me feeling momentarily cold and alone.

It had been bad before.

It was much, much, much worse now.

39

"Landon?"

Dante's voice echoed in my ears. My vision was blurry, but it started to clear as I shook my head.

"Landon, what happened?" he asked.

I opened my mouth to speak.

The boat began to shake.

"Abaddon," I said. "He's free."

"What?" Dante said.

"Damn Rebecca. She convinced him that she is the ghost of his dead wife. Can you believe that?"

The boat shook harder. I heard screams from further below.

"Down. He has to be down," Bradford said.

"Dante, you don't need to be here anymore," I said.

"I can help you."

I glanced over at him. He couldn't help me against Abaddon, and he knew it.

"Okay, fine. I'll return to Rose. We need to get her out of here."

"Good enough," I said. I pulled myself to my feet, feeling oddly empty without the demon's bond weighing on my soul.

The boat shook again, a little harder this time. I wasn't sure why. Abaddon's power didn't work like that. It was something to worry about later. We had to do something to stop Abaddon before he escaped.

The question was, what?

Bradford would be immune to his power. As for me? I was hoping he wouldn't kill me outright. That he would give me a chance to talk. It was a naive hope, but it was all I had.

"Come on," I said, leading the Nicht Creidem back to the stairwell. We ran down the steps, taking two at a time, following the source of the shouting.

Bradford didn't feel it as we drew closer. He was lucky. One step and I was fine. The next, and I felt a cold tingle growing within me, getting worse with every subsequent movement forward. The fear. It was part of Abaddon's power. From a distance, you felt frightened. Closer, you were terrified. Closer still, and midnight tendrils of paralyzing darkness would circle around you, envelop you, and finally wrap you up and take you in, feeding on your fear and your soul until there was nothing left but an empty husk.

It was a lousy way to go.

I fought against it the only way I could think of. I relaxed into it, letting my power sit neutrally on top of me like a blanket, accepting the demon's energy and asking it to change. I could almost feel it washing over me, cold one side, room temperature on the other as it was converted. I wasn't able to stop it all, but it did allow me to continue the descent.

"You okay, bro?" Bradford asked as we grew ever nearer.

I could feel the darkness of him, and I knew we were almost there.

"You don't feel it at all?" I asked.

"Feel what?"

Right now, I would have traded all of my power for that. "We're close. His power is slamming me pretty hard."

"Oh."

"Any sign of Rebecca?"

"Not so far. When she's in spirit form, she can float through walls and all that shit."

Execution

"Why did God think ghosts were a good idea? It seems pretty unbalancing to me."

"I don't think most ghosts turn so evil."

Rebecca was almost too evil. It was beyond what I had ever expected she would do.

We exited out of the stairwell and into the engine compartment. Massive turbines occupied both sides of the area, vibrating and thrumming while they worked to turn the ship's propellers. There was a light at the far end, spilling out of an open compartment.

Abaddon was standing in front of it.

I almost collapsed at the sight of him, my efforts to quell his power lost for a moment in the immediate. He wasn't the well-dressed warrior I had met in the Box. He was the dark and nearly formless demon, the black soul that stretched out in a shifting tide of pure death, reaching for whatever it could kill and eat and destroy.

"How do I kill it?" Bradford asked, holding up his knife.

I laughed at him. "You may be immune to his power. He's got a thousand years on you. He'll take that knife and jam it right into your eye."

Bradford didn't seem bothered by the comment. "Okay, bro. So what do we do?"

"Do you see Rebecca?"

"Nope."

Abaddon was stationary, his tendrils whipping around him as though he were in a storm. He looked like he was waiting for something. What?

There was movement at the other end of the engine room, and a second bulkhead door swung open. Abaddon's form shifted slightly to see what it was, as did Bradford and me.

Randolph Hearst entered the space, followed by half a dozen of his henchmen. It was easy to see that the vampire had drank heavily of Abaddon's power. His skin was dark as night, while his eyes burned a luminescent white. Wisps of the dark energy swirled around him with every step.

He leaped from the top catwalk down to the floor, landing a dozen feet in front of Abaddon.

"Sheeeeee's baaaaaaccckkkkk," Bradford said, pointing at Hearst.

Abaddon's tendrils reached for the vampire. Hearst reached into his pocket, withdrawing an unevenly shaped stone.

"What is that?" Bradford asked.

"A Riftstone," I replied. An escape route. A way to go from here to any other demonic rift on the planet.

Rebecca had to have known Hearst had the stone, surely to use for his own timely escape. Now she was going to use it to evacuate Abaddon.

I took one long breath, pulling in my power and holding it. "Can you handle the drop?" I asked Bradford.

He nodded. "I got the power, bro."

I hated timewalking, and I had a feeling this one was going to get me killed. I had to do it, though. The only thing I could imagine was a lifeless world where Rebecca and Abaddon lived in sick bliss. Either that or God on his knees and letting her into Heaven to stop her from destroying everything. Rebecca. In Heaven?

Both of those images sucked.

I pulled time ahead of me and pushed it behind. As I stepped forward, I appeared directly in front of Hearst, reaching out for the Riftstone while still trying to fight against Abaddon's power. It wasn't my intention to stay anywhere near the demon. I just wanted the damn rock.

I got my hand on it, too, before the combination of Hearst and Abaddon's power slowed me down. Rebecca yanked her hand away, and a solid punch to my midriff sent me bouncing off a piston. I fell onto my stomach, coughing up blood.

"Landon," Rebecca said. "That was a nice move."

She dropped the Riftstone onto the floor, mouthing the incantation that opened it. Then she started walking toward me.

I tried to pull myself up, slow to recover from the hit. I wanted to heal, but the timewalk had weakened me, and I was struggling to resist Abaddon's power. I was barely on my knees when Rebecca approached.

"I'm sorry it had to be this way," she said, holding her hand up, claws extended and dripping with Abaddon's poison.

For the second time in an hour, Bradford fell from the sky. His feet

Execution

slammed into Rebecca, knocking her back and away from me as he landing on his rear.

"You," she said with a hiss, planting her feet and pouncing at him.

"What did you think of that move, bitch?" Bradford asked, catching Rebecca and turning, throwing her hard against the side of an engine. She landed on her feet; teeth bared, her eyes wide in confusion.

Bradford's shirt had a claw-shaped tear straight down the center. There was no blood. No decay. His immunity was obvious.

Could Rebecca take him in a straight-up fight?

Maybe.

Maybe not.

"Abelard, we're leaving," she said, deciding not to try. "Landon, a little parting gift for you. Have fun with Randolph two-point-oh." She smiled and then vacated the premises. I couldn't see her in ghost form, but Bradford could, and his head turned to watch her go.

She and Abaddon entered the Rift and vanished.

40

I struggled to get to my feet, my body and mind exhausted from the time walk. I kept my eyes on Hearst, who was regaining his consciousness after Rebecca's possession.

"Landon?" he said, his white eyes locking on me. He looked truly scary in the dim lighting of the engine room.

"Randolph," I replied, putting up my hands. "I don't want to fight you."

Hearst looked past me, toward the compartment where Abaddon had been stored.

"What the hell happened?" he asked.

"Rebecca possessed you."

"Where's Abaddon?"

"Gone. She took him."

"Son of a... I knew I couldn't trust that bitch; that's why I brought Abaddon out here. How the hell did she know where to find me?"

I looked back at Bradford, who shrugged in response.

"She followed me," I said. "I was looking for Rose."

"Rose? Who's Rose?"

"The girl from the deli," I said, getting angry.

Execution

He thought for a second. "This high, big tits?" he asked.

I rolled my eyes. "Yes."

"Dammit. I told Rebecca to get her, too, but she refused."

"You killed Elyse," I said. "She was a friend of mine."

"If you cared that much, you would have kept your part of our agreement."

I heard a few light taps on the floor behind us. I glanced back to see that Hearst's goons had joined the party.

"You knew I wasn't going to just let you run around with Abaddon. I told you I would keep out of whatever you were doing, not that I wouldn't try to find a way to stop it."

"Now you sound like a demon."

I kept one eye forward, and the other on the approaching vampires. Bradford was watching them too, staying close to me.

"Rebecca just ran off with Abaddon," I said. "What are you going to do about it, Hearst?"

He flashed a dark, toothy smile. "First, I'm going to kill you. Then I'm going to find Rebecca, and I'm going to kill her. Simple."

I was afraid he was going to say that. I barely rolled away from him as he leaped toward me, landing amidst his henchmen and spinning on his heels. I was tired and weak, and he was super-powered.

It wasn't going to be pretty.

I couldn't do this on my own. Not where I was right now. Bradford was immune, but he wouldn't survive being choked out or having his neck snapped.

"Come on, Landon. You can do better than this."

He waited for me to get up. He even kept his subordinates back. Bradford was standing in the middle of it, trying to decide what to do.

"I recommend getting out of the way," I said to him.

He shook his head and pounced on one of the vampires. I took that as my cue to go on the offense, throwing my power out at Hearst. It hit him hard and knocked him back a few steps, but he recovered too fast, hissing and coming at me again. I caught his arm in mine, turning him and pushing him away. He was fast, he was strong, and he didn't really know how to fight. It was my one hope of winning.

I heard the fracas to the left as Bradford did his own damage, killing one of the vampires before he was tackled by two others. I needed him alive to help me see Rebecca, so I backed away from Hearst, grabbing them by the neck and throwing them away from the Nicht Creidem.

"Damn it, Bradford. Get the hell out of here."

"Dude, you can't fight them all alone."

"We can't fight them together, either," I said.

They were forming up again, and I could tell Hearst had no intent of coming in solo a third time. I pulled my power in, feeding it into my lungs.

"Alllyyyxxx," I shouted, extra loudly. It echoed off the surrounding steel, loud enough that the vampires grabbed at their ears.

I took advantage of the opportunity, taking the stone from my pocket at throwing it at the closest vamp. It changed into the spatha as it flew, embedded itself deep into the demon's neck.

Bradford followed close behind it, grabbing the hilt a moment later and wrenching it free. He put his arm out to deflect a claw, swept his leg to knock the vampire over, and brought the sword down in its belly.

Hearst roared and leaped at me again. I brought my power up ahead of me like a shield, but he was stronger than I was right now and it served only to slow him. I fell away, barely escaping a poisonous claw before he embedded Abaddon's decay inside me.

I scrambled to my feet, barely avoiding his next attack. Had Alyx heard me from all the way down here? I could only hope so.

"I had everything planned out," Hearst said, stalking me. "I was using Rebecca to drum up support down below. You know, they don't take me seriously in Hell. I'm just a blood counter to them. I've always been the second fiddle. The nerd."

He came at me again. I batted his hands away. He caught me with an elbow, and I fell back a dozen feet, landing hard.

"Do you know what it's like to be so close to the power, but never drink it?" he asked. "To watch everyone around you become something more while you're still just you?"

"No," I replied.

Execution

The answer incensed him even more. He came at me a fifth time, launching an attack with a speed and fury I couldn't match. Maybe Alyx hadn't heard me, and now I was going to die.

I did everything I could to deflect his attacks until I just couldn't keep up anymore. In a last ditch effort to save myself, I used my power on my shirt, changing its structure and letting his claws bounce off the hardened material. It was a delaying tactic, nothing more.

I continued to backpedal, searching for Bradford behind Hearst. The Nicht Creidem had to get away. He had to get to Dante and Alyx and Rose and tell them what had happened. I knew they wouldn't give up even if I didn't make it. They would find Rebecca and Abaddon.

I finally spotted him. He was on the ground; his knife buried in his chest.

He wasn't moving.

Shit.

My anger flared. Or maybe it was a renewed sense of desperation. I caught Hearst's next blow, holding his wrist tight. He tried to dislodge me with his other hand, and I caught that one, too, my arms folded over one another, gripping him in a tight cross. He struggled against me, his strength immense. I refused to let go. The two remaining vampires were done with Bradford, and they started coming our way, seeing their boss in trouble. I had to do something, quick.

I let Hearst go. He was pulling against me so hard he stumbled backward, bouncing into his cronies and falling to the ground. I clenched my teeth, reaching out with my power, wrapping it around one of the massive engines beside me. Could I move that much weight?

It was do or die, and I didn't want to die.

A horrible groan preceded the block of steel as it shifted its position, lifting into the air and rotating. Hearst bounced to his feet, ready to charge me again. I released the engine and threw my power out, knocking him over and at the same time pushing Bradford well beyond the landing zone.

"Hold this for me, will you?" I said, action-hero style, as gravity regained the humongous turbine, bringing it down on top of the three vampires.

They vanished beneath it, a spreading pool of blood that sizzled and turned to ash the only sign of their passing.

41

I wanted to check on Bradford. Instead, I fell to the ground, completely exhausted. A moment later, Dante appeared directly in front of me, his hand on Alyx and Rose's shoulders.

"Landon," Alyx said, running over and kneeling beside me.

"Landon, are you okay?" Rose asked.

"You're late," I said, glaring at Dante. "Really, really late."

"My apologies, Signore. We ran into some trouble on the deck."

I looked at Alyx. "You ran into trouble?"

"More of Hearst's vampires. I had to be careful they didn't touch me."

I nodded. I was happy she was safe.

"What happened down here?" Dante asked.

"Rebecca took Abaddon. She had a Riftstone. I don't know where they went. Hearst was under there."

"You're saying Abaddon is gone?"

"Yeah. He broke the bond. He doesn't want me to destroy him anymore. He thinks Rebecca is his dead wife."

"Why would he think that?" Rose asked.

"Because she told him, she was, and he believed it. Alyx, can you help me up?"

"Of course."

She put her arm under my shoulder and lifted me easily to my feet. She helped me walk slowly around the engine to where Bradford was resting. I fell to my knees, leaning over him.

"He's dead," Alyx said.

Damn. I was afraid of that.

"He thought he was invincible because he was immune to Divine power," I said, checking him. It wasn't the knife that had killed him. They had broken his neck, just like I had worried they would.

"Did you say immune?" Dante asked.

"Yeah, why?"

"That isn't possible, Signore."

"I tested it out myself. Nothing Divine could hurt him. He didn't even feel it."

Dante stared down at the dead man. "Do you know if he had children?"

"He said the Nicht Creidem used him as a stud for a while until he fizzled out. He said some of the kids survived, but most of them didn't make it. Is there a point?"

Dante looked thoughtful and distant. "Probably not," he said at last. "It is of little concern right now."

"He was the only one who could see Rebecca," I said. "I don't know how we'll ever find her now."

"That should be easy," Rose said. "Find Abaddon."

"Yes, but I mean when she tries to run. She's too dangerous to be having her way with the mortal world."

I looked at the third-eye on Bradford's forehead. "Dante, do you know where to find a ring or a necklace or anything that has the third-eye on it?"

"Not offhand. I can consult with Alichino."

"Yeah. Go and do that. Make sure you write it down. He's been worried about you, you know."

"The demon? He simply tolerates me."

"Maybe that's how he acts. It isn't how he feels."

"I will contact you when I find something. Be safe, all of you."

Execution

Dante disappeared.

"We don't have time to go on a treasure hunt," Rose said. "Abaddon is loose, which means it's only a matter of hours before the entire world starts falling apart." She glanced back at the engine. "I wish I had gotten to be the one to crush Hearst, after what he did to Elyse."

"I know," I said. "On both counts." I kept staring at the scar on the Nicht Creidem's head. I needed a third-eye to see Rebecca. Dante might find one, but how long would that take?

A macabre thought wormed its way into my head. In other circumstances, I might have ignored it. Desperate times.

"I have an idea," I said. "It's going to be a bit gross."

"What is it?" Alyx asked.

I reached out and pulled the knife from Bradford's chest. I put it against his forehead and began to cut.

"We need an eye," I said. "This is the only one available."

Rose wrinkled her face but didn't say anything. Alyx seemed intrigued.

"I can do a better cut," she said, one of her fingers extending into a claw.

I removed the knife, and she reached down and slowly traced along the skin, cutting around it. When she was done, she lifted the patch of flesh away and held it up to me. The sight made me a little nauseous, and her ease of handling the skin was a lot less than sexy. The next part would be even worse.

"Put it here," I said, tapping my forehead. Alyx did as I asked, positioning the eye against my head.

I used my power to push the flesh tighter against my skull while at the same time pushing my skin over it, fusing Bradford's skin to mine. It took a little doing, but as I worked the graft on, I began to feel a change in sensation coming from the stolen mark. It tingled against me, and when I looked around, I could see wisps of energy floating in the air that hadn't been there before.

"I think it's working," I said.

"Great," Rose replied. "What about Dante?"

"What about him?"

"We could use his help."

"To do what?"

"Stop Abaddon, maybe? What is it with you and him, anyway? He keeps trying to do the right thing, and you treat him like he's nothing but an errand boy."

I felt the anger, but I wasn't going to let it get the best of me. Not with Rose. "It's a long story. The bottom line is that the Beast was his fault."

"From what you've said, it seems like the Beast was either nobody's fault or everybody's fault."

"How do you figure that?"

"He fooled everyone. So either everyone is culpable because they didn't figure it out, or nobody is because he was just that good at it. Blaming one person who was doing the best they could-"

"Dante did more than that. He was a Servant of the Beast for a while."

Rose paused, but only for a moment. "Which he clearly regrets, no?"

"Yes."

"Then why do you have to keep punishing him? He comes every time you call. He does everything he can to make it up to you. He told me how sorry he is, but that he can't seem to get that through to you."

I stared at her. I knew her well enough to know she wasn't going to back down. She was right, anyway. It was about more than just the Beast. It was Dante who had sent me back here to live this life, and the raw, selfish truth of it was that I hated him for that. Maybe I had saved the world. Maybe I was the only one who could do it. It had been more hurtful than happy. I had suffered more than I had succeeded. Finding things to care about helped, but it only went so far.

Especially when those things wound up suffering, too.

Maybe that was why I had fallen for Alyx so quickly and so easily. Maybe she was the one creature who might suffer less with me than she had before me. Maybe she was the one thing that could share this life and be better for it. She seemed happy in her loyalty to me, happy to live for it, and to die for it.

"It's complicated," I said at last.

She rolled her eyes. "Bullshit, Landon. Let's call off the pity party and optimize our efficiency."

I nodded a little less than enthusiastically. "Fine, but we need to save him until we need him. The fresher he is from Purgatory, the stronger his power."

Rose smiled. "Okay. You're the boss."

I couldn't help but laugh at that.

"Should we get out of here?" Alyx said.

"Not yet," I replied. "I want to check out Abaddon's prison. At the very least, I want the sword."

I got to my feet, still a bit shaky. Alyx took my arm and helped support me while we crossed back over to the open compartment.

The inside looked as though a bomb had exploded. There were bits of metal and wood everywhere, scattered around the space along with the ash of dead demons. I scanned the debris, looking for the blade Dante had told me about. If it could sap Abaddon's power, I was sure it would come in handy.

"I don't see it," Rose said. "Maybe Abaddon took it with him?"

"He wasn't holding it when he left," I replied.

"It must have been slagged, then."

I pushed some of the splintered wood aside, revealing a hilt with no blade attached.

"I found a piece of it," I said, dismayed.

"Here's another," Alyx said, lifting a shard of metal with angelic scripture on it.

"This might be one," Rose said, finding a third piece.

"Let's collect as much of it as we can find. We might be able to put it back together."

We spent the next ten minutes gathering the shards and collecting them in my jacket. Then we headed back up to the deck. I had no idea where Gervais had gone, or if he were coming back. I expected we would have to find another way off the ship.

I was only half surprised to find the NYPD chopper waiting for us when we arrived topside. I had known Gervais was going to do something I didn't like, and he hadn't disappointed. He was standing in front of the helicopter, and he waved us over when we popped out of the stairwell.

"Landon, you're still alive. Good."

"You didn't have to kill them," I said.

"I know, but it was boring being out here while you were having all the fun. Do you need a ride?" He shifted form, becoming the pilot. "I won't be missed for a few hours at least."

"Just take us back over to the island," I said. "We'll figure things out from there."

"Affirmative," he said, giving me a weak military salute.

He always had to be an asshole.

42

"So, what next?" Rose asked.

We were back at my apartment. It had been four hours since Gervais had airlifted us back to Manhattan, and I had needed a little bit of downtime to recharge.

I had escaped to my bedroom and fallen out of everything almost instantly. Alyx was curled up against me when I woke, alert and waiting for me to come around. She greeted me with a kiss that brought me back to life in an instant, and now we were trying to decide on our next play.

"We can't stop Abaddon until we know where Rebecca took him," I said.

"Obviously," Gervais said.

"He also can't stay hidden for long," Rose said. "His power will start destroying things whether he likes it or not."

"Again, obviously."

"Even if we do find him, he's more powerful than any of us," Zifah said. He was sitting on the sofa behind Rose, his eyes shifting down to look at her bosom every few seconds.

"Is this going to be a meeting for statements of the obvious, or will we have some true mental exercise?" Gervais asked.

"What's your problem?" Rose said.

"Perhaps I don't want to lose this world to an upstart vampire ghost, eh? You should feel the same way."

"Gervais is right," I said. "Even if his motives are self-serving. Let's look at what we know. First, we know we need to get Abaddon out of action before he either destroys humanity or Rebecca uses him to get into Heaven."

"I still can't see how that plan will work," Rose said.

"It won't, which is part of the problem. Second, we know the only way to do that is to get him into the Fist of God. So let's start there. How do we get him into the Fist? Is it as simple as opening the latch and pushing him in?"

"Cain believed it was," Zifah said. "With the runes he created, and the ring." He pointed at the ring I had taken, still on my finger. "Get the demon inside, and it will do the rest."

"Are you sure it will work?" Alyx asked.

"I'm not going back to Hell to ask Cain, so who knows."

"If we don't have anything else to go on, let's assume it does," I said. "So third, we know we need to get Abaddon and the Fist of God to the same area."

"Central Park?"

"It doesn't have to be Central Park, but it would make it easier not to have to carry the armor around."

"Dante can teleport it," Rose said.

"Four," Gervais said, "We need to do something about Rebecca. How do you kill a ghost?"

"I can kill her," I said. "If I can get close enough to her."

"Oh?" Gervais said. "This is new. Do you think you will be able to do it when the time comes? Or will you feel sorry for your old flame once more?"

There was no doubt in my mind or my voice. "I'll do what I have to do. She had her chance to change, and she chose not to."

"The eye should help you get close," Rose said.

"It looks disgusting, by the way," Gervais said. "Though I commend you for the effort. I'm pleased to see I am rubbing off on you."

I put my hand up to the third-eye, feeling the marks in Bradford's flesh. It was my flesh now.

"Speaking of close, we also can't get too close to Abaddon," Rose said. "His power will destroy us before we can do anything to him."

"Yeah," Zifah said. "It has to be an ambush or a trap or something. If he sees it coming, we'll never get it done."

We were all silent for a few minutes while we considered our options. The number one problem was that of us all, only I could get near the demon, and even then not for very long and not without devoting a lot of my energy to protecting myself from him. Whatever we did, we would have one shot at getting it right. No rehearsals, no margin for error.

"I have an idea," Gervais said, breaking the silence.

I raised my eyebrow at him. Any idea of his was bound to be designed to work out in his favor.

"I don't hear anyone else volunteering," he said, smiling politely.

I didn't have a solid plan either. "Okay. Let's hear it."

"You said Abaddon thinks Rebecca is his wife?"

"Judith. Yes."

"We don't need to do anything to Abaddon. We capture Rebecca and bring her wherever, it doesn't matter. When he comes to rescue her, we throw him in the Fist."

I stared at him.

"What?" he asked.

"That's it?"

"It is a good plan."

"If all of your plans are like this, I'm not surprised you never actually succeeded in taking over the world."

He sneered at me. "There is nothing wrong with my plan, diuscrucis. Find Abaddon, catch Rebecca, use her as bait, profit."

"Finding Abaddon won't be a problem," Rose said. "What about catching Rebecca? How do you catch a ghost?"

"Yeah, Gervais," I said. "How do you catch a ghost?"

"I don't know. There must be some way. What if you knock out the person she possesses before she can get out?"

"I would think that would force her out," I said. "I could be wrong."

"It's a bad plan," Zifah said.

"Oh?" Gervais said. "Do you have another suggestion?"

"Not yet. It doesn't matter. You can't catch a ghost, case closed."

I didn't want the two demons to start arguing again. "Rose, do you have Dante in your contact list?"

"I have the number he called me from before he showed up here."

"Good enough. Can you dial it?"

"Sure." She pulled out her phone and hit the screen a few times.

"What's this about?" Zifah asked.

"I asked Alichino to do some digging on ghosts. Maybe he can help us settle this."

Rose put the phone on speaker.

"Hello?" Alichino said, his voice scratchy on the other end of the line.

"Allie, it's Rose," she said.

"Hey sweet cakes," Alichino said. "Call for a date?"

"Alichino, it's Landon," I said.

"Oh. Hey, Landon. Thanks for sending Dante back to check in with me. You didn't have to tell him I missed him, though. You made me look like a sap, and I have a reputation."

"No you don't," I said. "I'm calling about ghosts."

"What about them?"

"Did you do the research I asked you about?"

"You asked me to do something?" I heard the sound of shuffling papers. "Oh yeah, here it is. I was trying to figure out why I was Googling for spirits. What do you want to know?"

"How to catch one," I said.

He hiss-laughed at the other end of the line. "Catch one? You planning on renting an old firehouse and buying a hearse?"

"Funny. I'm serious. I need to catch a ghost."

"Shit. Okay. Let me see." He paused, shuffling notes. "Do you have a third-eye?"

"As a matter of fact, I do."

"Really? I wasn't expecting that. Okay." He shuffled some more. "Do you have a metal box?"

"What kind of metal box?"

"Any kind. As long as it's metal and has a lid."

"I can get one."

"Okay. Get some dirt from a church, and line the bottom of the box with it. Get the ghost in the box, close the lid, and sprinkle salt on it."

"Are you screwing with me?" I asked.

"Nope. I got this online. It has to be right."

"Dirt and salt?"

"Okay, maybe it isn't one hundred percent accurate, but every part of mortal legend has a real origin, usually stemming from the Divine. The point is, I bet it can be done. Get the box and bring it to an angel. I'm sure they would know what to do with it. Ghosts are more Heavenly than demonic."

"Not this one," I said. "At least not anymore. Thanks, Allie."

"Yeah, no problem. Rosie, this has to be worth a date, no?"

Rose laughed. "Maybe."

Alichino's voice rose in pitch. "Maybe? Sure. I'll take what I can get. Laters."

"Bye Allie," Rose said.

"Well, there you have it," Gervais said. "Find an angel and ask them how to catch Rebecca."

"Before I do, does anyone else have any better idea?" I asked.

It was crickets all around.

"Alyx, would you like to go for a run?"

"With you? Absolutely."

"Rose, keep an eye online for anything that shouts Abaddon. Gervais, Zifah, watch the news for the same."

Gervais was already watching the news. He flashed me a thumbs up.

"Be careful, Landon," Rose said as Alyx and I headed for the door.

"I always am. Except when I'm not."

43

Twenty minutes found us back at the airport. It was an exhilarating ride, a quick dash through the city, some of it traversed on rooftops with Alyx making massive leaps across busy streets and scaling up and down vertical faces. I enjoyed it as much as she did, laughing at the freedom, strength, and power that she put on display.

It ended too quickly, and we found ourselves back inside the terminal, bypassing security and moving toward the food court once again. I knew I could probably find an angel somewhere else, but I would have to go looking. I already knew Jane would be here.

I found her laying on a bench near Gate 21. She was projecting herself as a weary traveler, splayed out on the bench with her luggage behind her head. There was no sign of any other angels, and that worried me.

"Jane," I said, coming up behind her. I was masking Alyx's aura, keeping her wrapped and neutralized in my power. There was no point in causing another scene.

She sat up and spun to face me, her hand out to summon a sword. The action told me a lot about her in very little time. For one, she wasn't even close to new at the angel thing if she were experienced enough to keep her blade remote.

Execution

"Who are you?" she asked, eyeing both of us.

She didn't remember our meeting.

"My name is Landon Hamilton," I said.

"The diuscrucis."

"Yes. We met about a week ago. You wouldn't remember."

She stared at us without summoning her sword. "I remember something happening. I was mad at Saul for starting a fight."

"With Alyx here," I said. "She's a Great Were."

I could see the uncontrollable fear flash through Jane's eyes.

"It's okay, she's with me," I said.

"We're mates," Alyx said. "I won't hurt you unless Landon asks me to."

She didn't seem to get much comfort from that.

"What do you want from me?" she asked.

"Abaddon," I said.

"I should have guessed. All of the others have been returned to the Sanctuary to prepare should he begin his assault on the world."

"Good idea. He's escaped from his prison."

"I knew he would. Nothing but the Box could ever have held him for long."

Would the Fist of God hold him permanently? There was only one way to find out.

"It's worse than that. He's working with a ghost. Her name is Rebecca. He thinks she's his dead wife."

"A ghost?" She shook her head. "That can't be. Ghosts work to redeem themselves and earn their place in Heaven."

"Yeah, she tried that. From what I've heard, it didn't go too well."

She didn't look happy about that news. "Dark spirits are a rarity, and very difficult to control. You should understand how and why that potential exists."

"Balance. I know. I came to ask you if you know how to catch her?"

She looked up at my forehead. "You have a third-eye. You can see her. That's usually the hardest part."

"So, she can be caught?" I asked.

"Trapped? Yes, of course, though I've never done it myself."

"In how many years?"

"For me? Three hundred seventy two." She smiled. "I don't feel a day over three hundred. I don't think any of us has ever had need to trap a spirit. They are uncommon enough as it is, and most fulfill their obligation and are brought to Heaven. What does she want with Abaddon? Let me guess, to destroy the world?"

"Actually, no. She wants to blackmail God. A place in Heaven in exchange for humankind."

"That's preposterous."

"I know. It's still the truth. Will you help me?"

"I'm not supposed to leave the area. We're on high alert."

"Just tell me how to catch her, and I'll do the rest."

"It doesn't work like that, Landon. Only an angel can catch a ghost."

"Is there any dirt or salt involved?"

"Dirt, yes. Salt, no. I really shouldn't leave."

"Can't you call someone else to take your watch for you? Jane, I have a plan to take Abaddon out of play, but that doesn't happen without getting Rebecca first. If you help me with this, the seraphim won't need to be on high alert anymore."

She looked uncertain. "My Lord may not approve of me helping you."

"I think He'll be a lot happier with what I'm going to do than what Rebecca wants to do."

She considered for a few moments more. "Very well. Meet me at Saint Patrick's Cathedral in twenty minutes."

I felt an immediate lump in my throat. "Saint Patrick's?"

"Is that a problem?"

It was where I had stashed the Grail. It was where Sarah had slaughtered a dozen innocents to retrieve it. I didn't have good memories of the place.

It seemed fate was forcing me to relive a past I wanted to forget.

"No. It's no problem," I said at last. "Alyx, can we make it in time?"

"Of course, my love."

"We'll see you there," I said. "Remember."

She nodded resolutely and then vanished in a stream of light. She was

Execution

going back to Heaven first. To get a replacement? Or was I going to be walking into a trap of a different kind? I never knew for sure with the Divine.

"Thank you," I said to Alyx. "For everything you're doing for me."

She smiled brightly. "I'm happy to do it." She paused. "And a lot more."

I kissed her once, unable to resist. "Soon," I said, remembering what Bradford had said. It wasn't like that. It would never be like that. "Let's finish this."

44

Jane was already at Saint Patrick's when Alyx and I arrived. She was standing out in front of the church, a large, metal box covered in scripture cradled in her arms.

"I had to return to Heaven for this," she said, holding up the box. "There is only the one. Follow me."

She headed up the steps to go into the church. I paused behind her, my mind flashing back to the past. This wasn't the same thing. I looked at Alyx. Nothing was the same.

I started up the steps.

"Landon," Alyx said, remaining behind. "I can't go in there."

"Yes, you can," I said.

"I'm a demon. I can't."

I paused. I had actually forgotten. The cathedral was protected from demons by powerful scripture. It was the reason I had hidden the Grail there, and the reason the Beast had used Sarah to retrieve it.

"I'm sorry," I said, going back to her. "The scripture doesn't know the difference between a truly evil demon, and a lovely one like you. Remember, you decide who you are and what you do. It isn't predefined for you."

"I'll wait for you here," she said. "At least I know you'll be safe enough in there."

Even if the angels wanted to jump me, I would have to attack them first. They had to know I wouldn't fall for that one.

"If they want to start something, they'll start with you," I said. "Don't let them, no matter what they say."

"I won't."

I kissed her forehead and ran up the steps to catch up to Jane.

"Really, diuscrucis? A demon?"

"Save your judgement for someone who wants it," I said. "She has a good heart."

"Is it her heart you're truly interested in?"

I felt my anger flaring, and I forced it back down. Was that how they were going to try to bait me?

"That's none of your business. I don't answer to you, or to God."

"Everything answers to God. Even Lucifer."

"The Beast didn't."

She rounded on me, her face turning red. "Do not speak of that in here."

I smiled. Who was baiting who?

We walked the length of the cathedral and then exited through a side door, out into a small garden. It was a calm and peaceful place, a rarity in the middle of Manhattan.

"What are we doing here?" I asked.

"I told you, we do need dirt." She placed the box on the ground and fell to her knees next to it. She used her hands to dislodge some of the grass and place it to the side. Then she began scooping soil from the ground and dropping it into the box. "Consecrated soil. It will hold the spirit that gets too close to it, and give us time to close the lid."

"Did you tell the others what I told you?" I asked.

"About Rebecca? Yes."

"And?"

"It isn't an open and shut case, if that's what you're asking."

"You mean He might submit to her demands?"

"Not God, no. He isn't the only one who decides who enters Heaven."

"Michael?"

"Yes. He may decide to allow it if it means saving humankind."

"How can he even consider that?"

"With the hope that Heaven can change her when being a spirit couldn't. It's called faith, diuscrucis."

"I know what faith is," I said. Josette had faith. Sometimes it seemed like she had too much of it. "I still think that's a bad idea."

"It's a good thing it isn't your decision."

"And yet you're still helping me."

"We would prefer not to have her, of course."

"Of course."

Jane finished dumping dirt into the box, covering the bottom of it an inch deep. She put the lid back on and returned to her feet. "We have everything we need except the spirit."

"That's it?"

"When we catch her I will say a prayer that will bind her to the soil more strongly."

"Sounds good," I said.

"Once the trap is sprung and Abaddon is contained, I will take her to the Sanctuary for reconciliation."

"What? Reconciliation, as in penance? As in, you get another chance?"

"Yes."

I opened my mouth, ready to tell her about my plan to destroy Rebecca. I realized it was probably better if she didn't know about that up front.

"Okay," I said, choking slightly on the word.

We retreated back through the church to where Alyx was waiting. I wasn't surprised to find Saul out there with her, leaning against the side of the cathedral and staring at her.

"Really?" I said, turning to Jane.

"A test. Nothing more. Saul, go."

The second angel turned his head at Jane's voice, but didn't leave right away.

Execution

"Saul," she said again, more sternly.

He started walking toward Alyx.

"Saul," Jane shouted.

Alyx glanced over at me, and then back at the angel. She didn't change. She just stood there. Saul approached her, getting within a foot of her. It was close enough that she could run him through with her claws before he could blink.

Jane started forward. I put my arm out to stop her. "It's okay," I said.

Saul said something to Alyx. I could see the anger skip over her. She turned her entire body, facing away from him. He said something else, moving with her to stay in her face. She folded her hands over her chest and turned again. I knew she wanted to rip his throat out, but she was controlling it.

When he followed a second time, I was done.

"That's enough," I said, casting out my power and using it to pull him roughly away from her. He fell onto the sidewalk, attracting the attention of some of the pedestrians.

"That counts as an attack," Jane said next to me.

"Is that how you want to play it?" I asked. "The two of you against the two of us?"

"No. I want to help you stop Abaddon."

She descended the stairs, grabbing Saul by the arm and saying something to him. He nodded miserably and went into the cathedral.

"Are you okay?" I asked, reaching Alyx.

"Yes. I'm fine. I'm proud of myself for not giving in to him."

"I'm proud of you, too. I told you that you're lovely."

"I'm impressed," Jane said, catching up to us. "I didn't think it was possible."

"I told you she has a good heart."

Jane looked Alyx in the eye. "Perhaps you truly do."

45

We made our way back to my place. Alyx ran while Jane took to the skies, gliding along and easily keeping pace with her. We rejoined the angel on the rooftop, and I brought her down the fire escape and in through the window.

"Rose," I said, entering the apartment. "Anything?"

Zifah and Gervais turned their heads away from the television to check out Jane. I could see the fiend shudder at the sight of an angel.

"You should be careful of the company you keep, diuscrucis," he said.

"Are you talking about yourself?" Zifah asked. He hopped onto the back of the sofa and stared at Jane. "I've never seen a real angel before."

Jane turned to face me. "Landon, your house is full of demons."

"You know what I am," I said.

"I'm not a demon," Rose said, standing up and approaching us. She held her hand out to the angel. "Rose. Nice to meet you."

She took her hand. "Jane." She turned back to me again. "I'll wait outside."

"Hang on a second. Do you have anything?" I asked again.

"The All Blacks are winning 23 to 14," Gervais said.

"Actually, I do," Rose said, glaring at the demon. She led me over to her laptop.

"Landon," Jane said, motioning toward the window.

"Can't you deal with them for two minutes?" I asked. "You won't fall for sharing the same space."

"Yeah, toots," Zifah said. "We don't bite. Unless you want me to, that is."

She sighed but stepped closer to Rose.

"What do you have?" I asked.

She turned the screen so I could see it. "I've been mapping some random police reports that have been coming in. They've been finding corpses in the street that match Abaddon's MO."

"The street? Like he's just wandering around? If he were out there, he'd be leaving hundreds dead, not single bodies."

"Maybe he's able to contain it? Or maybe sucking some of his power away made him a little less deadly? I don't know. He isn't wandering around. The trail leads right to this building."

She tapped a few keys and zoomed out. I groaned.

"You know it?" she asked.

"Yeah. It's the Solen family's penthouse uptown. Rebecca took Abaddon home."

"She's taking this wife thing a little far, don't you think," Gervais said.

"Does Abaddon even have a penis?" Zifah asked.

"She knows I'll track her down," I said. "She doesn't care. It's a message that she isn't afraid of me." Of course, she didn't know that I had found a means to trap her. I bet that would have changed her plans some. It was a point in our favor. "She should be. We can catch her."

"Ah, now I understand why you brought Ms. Goody-two-shoes," Gervais said.

"It was your plan," I said.

"Landon, what about the sword?" Alyx asked. "Maybe Jane knows how to repair it."

"Sword?" Jane said.

"Abaddon's prison," I said. "They were drawing out his power with a sword. It shattered when he escaped, but I kept the pieces."

I retrieved the bits of metal from where we had left them in the kitchen. "Do you think you can do anything with them?" I asked the angel.

She picked up one of the pieces, her eyes growing wide. "Do you know what this is?"

"I already told you, we-"

"Landon, this is Archangel Uriel's sword. It was thought destroyed during the War in Heaven when Lucifer was cast down."

"It steals Divine power."

"Yes. Uriel used it against the fallen angels, taking their power and adding it to his own. It made him nearly invincible. I can't believe it has been here this entire time."

"It's in pieces now."

"It can be fixed, but not here. Only Uriel himself may be able to repair it."

I plucked the shard from her hand. "We won't be letting him do that," I said. "I don't need Uriel coming down here to start powering up again. The question is, can we use it against Abaddon?"

"In this state? No. It is worthless. If it were whole, it might be able to steal enough of his energy to make him manageable."

"It was jabbed into his gut for over a week," I said. "He still seems pretty strong."

"Demons wouldn't be able to draw the power out, only absorb what was absorbed into the blade. It's the difference between touching the surface of the water and submerging yourself in it."

"Do you think I would be able to draw it out?" I asked.

"You should."

"Wouldn't you have to get close enough to stick him with it first?" Rose asked.

"Yes."

"We can worry about that after we get him contained," I said. I handed the pieces of metal back to Alyx, who returned them to the kitchen. "Rebecca knows I know where she is. She's going to assume I'll come for her."

"So how do we catch her if she already knows you're coming?" Jane

Execution

asked.

"She's expecting me. Maybe even Alyx. She won't be expecting you." I pointed at Zifah. "Or you."

"Me?" Zifah said. "I told you, Landon, I don't want to get involved."

"That's too damn bad," I said. "There's no point in you being here if here is going to go the way of Hell, and that's what's going to happen if you don't help me."

"Look, you're a nice guy, and your girlfriend is hot, and your other friend is even hotter. I don't care if this Rebecca gets into Heaven. It doesn't concern me."

I wanted to strangle Zifah. "It concerns you because if you don't do it, I'm going to kill you."

"Really, Landon?" Zifah said. "You're resorting to-"

He started choking as I wrapped my power around his scrawny neck. "I don't like threats, which should tell you how important this is to me. Let's say God lets Rebecca into Heaven. Guess what? Abaddon is still here on Earth."

I let him go. He rubbed at his neck dramatically.

"All I need you to do is distract Rebecca and give Jane a chance to swoop in and get her into the trap. You said you were a master sneak."

"Well, of course, I am."

"Then will you do it?"

He growled softly for a few seconds. "Fine. I'll do it. On one condition."

"What's that?"

"I want a steady supply of popcorn."

Demons. "Okay."

"What about me, diuscrucis," Gervais said. "I don't seem to fit into your plans."

"You'll be waiting back in Central Park. We'll bring Rebecca there, and when Abaddon comes, you'll help me get him in the Fist."

"How am I supposed to do that?"

"I don't know, this was your plan, remember? I trust you'll think of something."

"We can call on Dante, too," Rose said.

"I plan on it. It's going to take all of us to get this done. Are you with me?"

I didn't get much of a response from the assembly of angel, demons, mortal, and other.

"I said, are you with me?"

"Yes," they said, catching on.

"Pathetic. Are you with me?" I shouted.

"Yes," they shouted back.

"Good. Then let's save the world."

Yeah, it was hokey. But what was wrong with that?

46

Alyx and I were standing across the street from Rebecca's penthouse three hours later. It had taken a bit of time to fine tune the details of our plan and to get it organized. Rose had called on Dante and filled him in, and everything was supposedly in place. The fact that I was relying on not one, but two demons made me nervous. Very nervous. Especially since one of those demons was Gervais.

Luckily, Rebecca was keeping Abaddon to herself. For the moment at least. I could feel the demon's power, even from the distance, so I knew he was up there. I wondered what they were doing? Playing house, as Zifah had suggested? Who was Rebecca possessing to do it, and how could they survive anything like that?

They were lewd thoughts for another time. Like never.

"How is he not killing everyone in that building?" Alyx asked.

I kept staring at the penthouse. I could see there was a light on up there. "I don't know. Maybe he's learned to control it better? Or maybe Rebecca told him not to kill anyone." I turned my wrist to check the time. "Are you ready?"

She nodded. "As ready as I'll ever be."

She looked amazing in a red dress that hugged her athletic form. It flowed to the floor, with slits along the sides to give her legs some clearance to move. I was wearing a tuxedo, looking good in it, if I did say so myself. The charade wasn't for anyone, but the vampires I knew would be guarding the lobby. We had to make it past them and into the elevator without making a scene and giving ourselves away. I could hide Alyx's aura as long as she was close enough to me, giving us the appearance of plain, ordinary, wealthy mortals. The kind that might live in the building below the penthouse. I could hide any aura that was close enough.

"I have to say, this is the best ride I've ever gotten," Zifah said.

He was the reason for the long dress. He had his arms wrapped around Alyx's leg, clinging to the inside of her thigh where he wouldn't be seen. It had to be a dream come true for the little demon to get that close to Alyx's groin.

"Keep your appendages to yourself," Alyx whispered. "Or I will eat you."

"Okay, okay," Zifah said.

My phone vibrated. I didn't need to check it. "That's the signal."

We made our way across the street. I kept my arm around Alyx's shoulder, holding her close and playing it that we were a little bit drunk and amorous. We paused a few times to share an overly passionate kiss, and it was all I could do to stay focused on the task instead of falling apart at the taste of her.

"Good evening Jeeves," I said, reaching the front of the building. The doorman was a were though none of the mortals around would know it.

He sniffed me quickly, not picking up Alyx's composition through a strategic scent of booze and perfume.

"Good evening, sir," he replied, opening the door for us.

We had cleared the first hurdle.

We strolled into the lobby, continuing our facade of drunken laughter, embraces, and nearly pornographic kissing. There was a part of me that wanted to save and savor it for the bedroom. It was an important part of the mission, and I wasn't one to shy away from doing what needed to be done.

We made our way past two vampire bellhops and another vamp guard who had the black teeth of one who had drank from Abaddon's fountain, reaching the elevator banks by drawing a lot of the right kind of attention. People looked at us out of the corner of their eyes, embarrassed and curious at the display. They probably thought we were a pair of celebrities the way we were carrying on, left to wonder if the paparazzi had taken a day off, or fallen asleep.

I pushed Alyx against the wall, kissing her while my hand found the button to go up. She growled softly against me, her teeth catching my lip and biting tenderly, her tongue tracing the flesh.

"I'm ready to forget about Abaddon," she whispered in my ear.

I swallowed hard. Maybe this hadn't been the best approach? "Stay focused."

"I'm focused on you."

"I know. Stay focused on the mission."

She giggled softly beneath my kiss. "I love you."

The elevator dinged, and the doors slid open. There were five other people waiting to go up, but when I turned Alyx into the car and shoved her back against the wall, and she wrapped one of her legs around me, they decided to wait for the next one.

We shifted as soon as the doors were closed, keeping up appearances for the surveillance cameras. I moved her close to the control panel, hitting the button to bring us up to the floor three below Rebecca. It was the best we could do without having access to a private elevator.

We made out all the way up, which seemed like it only took a few seconds. I was sweating beneath the collar of the tux, and another part of me was making itself a little too apparent, much to Alyx's enjoyment.

Finally, the doors parted, and we slipped together out into the hall. As soon as we made it into the corridor, we pretended to trip and fall, winding up splayed out on the rug and fake laughing like a pair of idiots.

That was Zifah's cue to abandon his hiding spot. He departed from beneath the dress, blending in with his surroundings so completely that I could barely make him out in front of the wallpaper.

We were fairly close to Abaddon, and his power was enough to ruin my earlier predicament. It was also enough to disguise Zifah. I stayed on the floor, still laughing while I pushed open the elevator doors just enough for him to climb into the shaft. He would head up to the penthouse while we circled from the outside. It was up to us to provide the distraction that would allow him to sneak in.

"Ready for round two?" I asked.

She kissed me one more time and slowly dragged herself to her feet. "Yes."

Execution

47

We made our way down the hallway. There was an apartment at the end that was directly below one of the windows in the southeast corner of Rebecca's penthouse. From what I knew of the layout, it was a full-length window that went directly into the bedroom. It would be thick, bullet-proof, demon-proof, and angel-proof.

It wouldn't be me-proof.

"Do you think anyone is home?" Alyx asked.

We were holding hands, still walking a little crookedly for effect. I had spotted the cameras in the corners, and I knew the viewers had to be Solen goons; vampires or the Turned. We ambled to the end of the corridor and bounced up against the door. I made a motion like I was fumbling for my card, making sure to hover over the security panel and obscure what we were really doing.

I didn't need to do anything with the panel. Instead, I reached out with my power, finding the locking mechanism inside the door and turning it. The door clicked, and I pushed it open.

It turned out; someone was home. I had barely gotten inside, pulled the door closed, and separated myself from Alyx when I heard the unmistakable sound of a shotgun being primed.

"What the hell are you doing in my apartment?"

We both looked at him at the same time. He was middle-aged, handsome, wearing a pair of silk pajamas. He looked pissed. His television was on, and a can of beer was sitting on an end table.

Did he always keep a shotgun right next to his sofa? What were the odds of walking in on that?

"What?" I said, still playing the drunk.

"You're in my apartment," he said again.

"This is my apartment," I said.

He shook his head. "You lousy drunk. How did you open the door anyway? Did I forget to lock it again? Go on, get out of here."

"I like him," Alyx said to me, running her hand along my chest and playing it sexy.

"Him?" I asked.

"Me?" the man said.

She slid away from me and moved slowly toward the man. He kept his shotgun up but didn't make a move to blast her. It was a good thing for him.

She reached his side, putting a hand on his face. "Do you want to play with us?" she asked.

I wondered if the guy watched porn, and if he did, what he was thinking right about now. If the stakes weren't so high, I would have thought the entire thing was amusing.

"Wha- What do you mean, play with you?" the man asked.

"Come on, Kevin, don't be shy," Alyx said, looking at me. I guess I was Kevin. "Say hello to our new friend."

She smiled mischievously. She may have had a good heart, but she was still a demon, and sometimes it seemed she just couldn't help herself.

I walked over to them. The man was slowly lowering the shotgun, clearly confused. I put my hand on his arm suggestively.

"What do you say?" I asked him in the most seductive voice I could manage. To an onlooker, it was probably hilarious. "If my wife wants you, I want you."

The statement seemed to disgust him. His face wrinkled, and he tried

Execution

to take a step back. "You perverts. Get away from-"

Alyx hit him in the temple, just hard enough to put him out. We lowered him gently to the floor.

"You're enjoying this a little too much," I said.

"You looked like you were enjoying it, too."

"No, I wasn't."

"Yes, you were."

"You started it."

"Yes. It worked, didn't it."

I couldn't argue with the results. The occupant was disabled, and we had our path up to the penthouse. "Come on."

We made our way over to the window. I gazed into it, down to the city below. Then I cast my attention to the top of the opposite building. I could just barely make out Jane perched on the edge of it, watching.

Then I took a step back. Alyx replaced me, her finger growing into a long, sharp claw. She pressed it against and then into the glass, quickly cutting away a piece large enough for us to climb through.

"Hold on tight," I said, stepping up to the opening.

The wind rushed in from outside, adding atmosphere to the effort. Alyx wrapped her arms around my neck and chest and clung to me while I focused my power, using it to press us against the side of the building and keep us from falling as I climbed out.

I didn't see it, but the activity should have sent Jane from her current position to the next one, a secondary skyscraper on the western side.

I had just started scaling the glass exterior of the building when the screams began to rise from below.

48

I looked down. I had a moment of instinctual panic when I realized how far I was from the ground, before remembering that I couldn't fall to my death. To a lot of pain, yes, but my head would have to be totally crushed to not recover.

I scanned the street. It took me a few seconds to find the source of the screams, though I should have guessed before I looked.

Vampires.

Lots of them.

They were coming out of the building's parking garage, at least a hundred strong. They pounced on the mortals with reckless abandon, grabbing them, biting them, dropping them and continuing on.

Rebecca was making her move.

We were out of time.

"She's starting the attack," I said. "We need to get up there before she comes down with Abaddon. Forget the original plan, we have to distract her."

She wouldn't put the demon on the streets right away. She couldn't without killing her own. They would clear the area, and then he would descend as backup. The angels would confront him, and they would die

Execution

unless they submitted to her demands. And some of them would die. Michael wouldn't agree to let her in without trying to stop her first, but I knew Heaven had nothing that could handle the demon. Not without Avriel and his Box.

"Your turn," I said to Alyx.

She kissed me on the cheek, her face growing and elongating as she did. She released herself from my back, planting her claws on the building and climbing it easily. I scaled the wall below her, a little slower in my ascent. She reached the penthouse window in seconds, drawing back her arm and slamming a massive fist into the heavy glass. It didn't shatter the first time, or the second, or the third. She was reaching back for a fourth punch when a dark tendril began to ooze through the cracks she was making.

"Alyx, watch out," I shouted, feeling the urgency. I planted my feet against the building, pushing off with my toes, using my power to send me springing up to her. I got a grip on her arm with one hand, reaching out to the tendrils with my other.

The fear and pain nearly overwhelmed me before I was able to calm myself enough to reverse it. The tendril evaporated against my skin, dissipated by my passive will.

"Swing me," I said.

Alyx grunted, pulling me back and swinging me forward, toward the window. I could see the dark tendrils of Abaddon's energy filling the bedroom. He wasn't there, watching us, but he knew we were coming. So did Rebecca.

Good.

The window came in fast, cracks spreading across the entire pane. I threw my power out ahead of me, pushing against it with more force than even Alyx could manage. It exploded in a spray of shrapnel that peppered the king sized bed with the rumpled sheets and dead, naked, female vampire laying in the center. It blasted the large armoire, and the priceless art that hung on the walls.

I landed inside, right in the middle of the darkness.

"Alyx, stay back," I said.

She wouldn't be able to survive in the mess. I wasn't even sure I could.

The tendrils shifted, coming toward me like a nest of vipers. I felt the overwhelming fear of the demon, his power a gale force against my own. I had to stay calm. I had to stay within myself and let it come.

The darkness snapped at me, leading edges biting at my flesh, falling away as it struck it. Cain had no idea what he had done by stringing me up and forcing me to get myself down.

I owed Zifah more than a steady stream of popcorn for helping show me the way.

I waded deeper into the room, even as the darkness eased up around me, pulling back through the doorway I was about to pass out of. Seeing the room clear, I heard Alyx enter behind me, back in human form in order to fit the space more easily. I paused, waiting for her to catch up.

"How?" she asked.

I answered with a smirk and took her hand. We followed behind the retreating blackness, and I knew what we would find when we got to the end of the poison-brick road. I could only hope our entrance had been enough of a distraction to get Zifah inside unnoticed.

We came out into the main living space. The memories came rushing back to me all at once. Merov's party. Rebecca's entrance. The blood fountain and the demon Reyzl. I blinked them away, noticing that the windows had been replaced, as had the furniture with something a little more Rebecca's style. How long had she been living right under my nose and I hadn't known it? Had she been here almost as long as I had?

Had she been watching me the entire time?

"Diuscrucis," Abaddon said. His voice was deep and smooth and wise, more like I had experienced it in the Box. He was standing in the center of the room, his darkness wrapped around him like a cloak, his head shrouded by it. My heart was pounding, the fear of him threatening to make me turn and run with every moment that passed.

Rebecca was next to him. She didn't have a host. Not anymore. The host was back in the bedroom, dead. Before or after? I had no idea. I wouldn't have imagined it was even possible.

"I can see you," I said, her soul forming an ephemeral outline of the

Execution

demon she used to be. It was a bit rough around the edges, as if it wanted to fall apart at any moment.

"I knew you would come," she said. Her voice was a high-pitched whine in my ears. "I wanted you to come. I wanted you to see it."

Abaddon's head had turned to look at her. He could see her? Without a third-eye or did he have one somewhere in the blackness of his being?

"You need to stop this. Rebecca, you're killing innocent people."

"Innocent? No one is innocent, Landon. Everyone has done something that they are ashamed of, or that they regret. Why should they be welcomed to His Kingdom, while I suffer as this?"

"They have remorse for what they've done."

"I had remorse once. Where did it get me? Trapped in this world, doing His bidding. Trying so hard to be what He wanted me to be, and being turned away over and over again. Because of who I am? Or because of what I am?"

"You think God is shutting you out because you're a demon?" I asked. "That's ridiculous. He gave you a chance before you ever deserved one. You're the one making a mockery of it. You're the one who doesn't get it."

"But I will get it. With my dear Abelard's help, I will end this nightmare. He promised he would deliver me to Heaven, even if he has to destroy the entire world to do it. I'm holding him back to send a message to the angels. If they refuse? The world will shrivel up and die."

I didn't answer right away. Alyx was tapping her foot on mine. It was one of the signals we had decided on for her to let me know when Zifah had opened the window. She could smell the outside air coming in.

"No," I said. "You're going to watch your Abelard die."

49

Of course, there was no way I was going to be able to kill Abaddon that easily. It was a stupid, empty threat, and on its own it would have been laughable.

When I summoned the obsidian spatha and dove at the demon, any thoughts Rebecca had of laughing were put on hold.

I nearly managed to dig the blade into Abaddon's flesh before he could get his own, midnight dark sword up to parry mine. He did it smoothly, hardly concerned about the attack, the rest of his form remaining still, his dark energy staying under control.

That wasn't good enough. He had to fight.

I threw my power out at him, forcing him to unleash his own or fall back. Fear spread away from him like a cape, the darkness swinging out and back toward me like the tide. I held steady against it, letting it wash over me, showing him I could defend myself even at this close range.

"Good," he said, clearly impressed.

I punched him in the face.

He wasn't expecting it. Even I hadn't been expecting to connect. The force of the blow knocked him over, and I didn't waste any time charging again.

Execution

"No," I heard Rebecca scream. The shrillness of it distracted me, and I turned my head to see what was happening.

Jane had landed next to Alyx and had the box laid on the floor, the cover open. She was speaking in Seraph, an earlier form of Latin, her hands glowing as they touched the metal container. I saw Rebecca's spirit, being pulled toward it as though she were trapped in a vacuum cleaner.

"Abelard. Help me."

She sounded desperate. Our plan was working.

Abaddon grunted beneath me, hitting me hard with his power. He had been holding back, at least, a little. He wasn't now. The dark energy blasted through my defenses, sending needles of pain through my entire body and forcing me to shiver in sudden fear. His sword came up at me, and I barely managed to block it in time. He kicked out with a foot, hitting me hard and throwing me backward.

Jane wasn't done yet. I pushed out with my power, flipping myself over and landing on my legs. Abaddon was up, and his tendrils stretched out toward the angel.

Alyx changed, letting out a short roar and tackling the demon.

"Damn it, Alyx, no," I said, a new fear entering my heart. She managed to distract the demon, preventing his darkness from reaching Jane, but she wasn't going to survive his touch for long.

I reached out with my power, throwing her off him with enough force that she blasted through the wall and into the kitchen, a massive clatter of pots and pans following. I charged Abaddon again, replacing her in the melee, leading with my blade.

"I'll kill you," Abaddon said, his voice angry and raw. Before, he had been almost civilized. That time was over. The pure evil was pouring out. "I'll destroy this entire world."

"Not if I can help it," I said. "Jane, can you hurry up?"

I risked a glance to see what she was doing. Rebecca was gone. The lid was on the box. The scripture was glowing. She was rising to her feet, wings spreading to take flight, the trap in her arms.

"No," Abaddon shouted again.

The power of his voice sent a wave of panic through me, and my entire body went numb. Jane reacted the same way, her wings dropping to her sides, her hands slipping on the trap.

I forced myself to stay calm, letting my power dissolve the demon's. Tendrils of darkness spread out toward Jane once more. Too fast. I couldn't stop them.

Alyx burst from the kitchen in one massive, impossibly quick leap. Her arm was out to her side, and she barreled past me, catching Jane in her massive hand before the evil could reach her. Jane barely reacted to it, the fear still controlling her, and she would have lost the trap if Alyx's hand hadn't closed around it as well.

Then she was beyond us, tucking her head and letting all of her weight and power slam into the window, the same window I had used to escape from Reyzl years before. It crumbled beneath the force, and then she was out of the building, fifty-plus stories above the demonic slaughter below.

She disappeared a moment later, tumbling toward the earth. She was a Great Were. She would survive the fall, even if it hurt when she landed.

"What have you done?" Abbadon cried, getting his hand on my shoulder and throwing me back again.

I hit the wall hard, bouncing back and charging. He was going to the window, and I needed to buy Jane and Alyx some time.

I was almost on him again when something caught my eye from the corner. A dart, thin and long and dark. It buzzed past my ear, vanishing in the darkness of the demon.

Everything stopped.

Abaddon's tendrils dissipated. The dark cloak around him nearly vanished as well, leaving his human form momentarily visible. He was nude and black as night, even his eyes. He was lean and perfectly formed, as though he had been made from a Greek sculpture. He also clearly hadn't been a slouch in fulfilling his husbandly duty with the spirit of his dead wife.

One of Zifah's needles was poking from his neck. He pulled it out, examined it for a moment, and tossed it aside.

"What have you done?" he asked me again. Already, his power was returning, and his cloak began to reform. Zifah's poison had slowed him,

Execution

nothing more.

It was enough. Jane flew past the window, holding the trap. Abaddon saw it, too.

"I will stop at nothing to get her back, diuscrucis. Nothing. I will destroy everything on this Earth, everything that you love, until you return her to me."

"She isn't your wife," I said, trying one more time. "She's using you to get what she wants."

"She is my Judith. It does not matter to me if she is the original. I care not for details. Long have I desired a reason to continue, as even you have been unable to end this existence for me. Now it is here, and you seek to take it away? No. I have purpose again, Landon. Do you not understand that? So many years and there is a point to the chaos and death and killing. There is fuel to my fire. You will die. This world will die. She will be free, and He will take her into His Kingdom. He will take me as well. That is the price."

I wanted to say something. Anything. That last statement put my ability to articulate anything on hold. Abaddon in Heaven? Even Archangel Michael would have to know how impossible that situation would be.

"If you want her back, I'll give her to you," I said. "Central Park. One hour. A duel. If you win, she's yours. If I win, you let me imprison you once more."

"I can end you now. This world cannot stand up against me."

"I know you. I know there's still a shred of honor in you, despite what Lucifer made you into. Central Park. One hour. I'll be waiting."

I felt Zifah's weight on my foot, though the demon was still blending with the surroundings. I reached into my pocket and double-tapped my phone, sending a prepared text.

Abaddon was seething. The tendrils of darkness had returned, and they writhed and twirled around him, snapping forward at me like cobras before retreating and undulating once more. I didn't know if he would attack, and I wasn't about to take the chance.

Dante appeared right behind me. His hand landed on my shoulder, and

I felt the tug of his power as he pulled me away.
    Abaddon would come.
    He had to.

Execution

50

We reappeared back in my apartment. Zifah immediately hopped off my foot, while I ran over to the window to look for Alyx.

She had to be okay. She was a Great Were. She could easily survive a fall like that, assuming she hadn't grabbed the side of the building and climbed down.

I timed it in my head, the distance and her speed. She should have been back.

A soft flow of air, and Jane landed on the fire escape in front of me, still clutching the trap with Rebecca inside.

"I can't believe that worked," she said, smiling at me. It was the first time I had seen her smile.

"Did you see Alyx?" I asked.

"She is fine, Landon. She was delayed killing some of the vampires that were attacking the people."

I felt my heart lurch. "Those vampires had Abaddon's power in them."

"She was careful."

Careful enough? I had to trust that she was. I didn't own her, and she was trying to do the right thing.

"Are you serious, Landon?" I heard Zifah say behind me. He hopped up on the window sill a moment later. "Challenging Abaddon to a duel? That wasn't part of the plan. He'll beat the living poop out of you."

"Thanks for the vote of confidence," I said. "I don't plan on dueling him. At least not to a finish."

"Oh. Cheat to win? I get it. I'll take one ticket to that main event."

"Zifah, you did well back there. Thank you."

The demon lowered his head. "I figured, what the heck, you know? But did you see that? Even Cain fell to my poison. Not Abaddon. He shook it off like a minor inconvenience."

I had seen it. It didn't make me happy.

"Jane, can you head up and scan the streets for Alyx?" I asked.

"She'll be okay," Jane said.

I was going to push when I saw her turn the corner. She was still in demon form, running hard. I made a quick scan of her for injuries. There were none.

She bunched her hinds and leaped up the fire escape, changing into human form midair and catching the railing as she hit. She smiled as she vaulted over it, leaning into the window to hug me.

"You're okay," she said. "I was worried about you."

"I was worried about you," I replied. "Are you hurt?"

"No. But Landon, something is wrong."

"What do you mean?"

"The mortals. They saw me."

"Some mortals will always Awaken when the Divine are right in front of them."

"No, Landon. Not some of them. All of them. There were police. They stopped their cars and shot at me."

I didn't know what to say. That should never have happened. It had to have something to do with Abaddon's power being siphoned into the vampires who were attacking the people in the streets.

"Did you kill all of the vampires?"

"I think so."

"Then it should be over. The mortals' Awakening, I mean."

"I hope so, for their sake. They were terrified of me."

"I would be too if you weren't on my side."

"Signore," Dante said, joining us at the window. "We don't have a lot of time."

"Jane, you need to hurry back to Heaven and warn Archangel Michael. Abaddon doesn't just plan to help Rebecca get a pass. He wants to join her there."

Somehow her pale face turned more pale. "What?"

"Exactly. We both know that can't happen. He won't be able to take her without him. He needs to know that."

She nodded, holding out the trap to me. "Very well. Take this."

I collected it in my hands, feeling the soothing warmth of the seraphim power against it. I could see Rebecca's soul inside it with the third-eye, bound to the consecrated soil.

Jane lifted her head toward the sky, vanishing in a beam of light a moment later.

"Dante, Alyx said the mortals were able to see her. All of them. Do you know why that would be?"

He furrowed his brow as if he were concerned, but shook his head. "No. It must be a side effect of Abaddon's power."

"That's what I thought. It seems strange though, doesn't it?"

"Perhaps not. Mortals who are exposed to the demon's power have always died in the past. It may be that one cannot be near it and survive without Awakening."

I got the feeling he wasn't saying everything, but I didn't dwell on it. We had little enough time to prepare for Abaddon to arrive in Central Park.

I pulled my phone from my pocket and called Rose.

"We've got the package. Are you in position?" I asked.

"Ready and waiting," she replied. "Not that I'm enjoying being stuck with Gervais for this. He's already made at least a dozen lewd comments about me and my sister." She made a sound of disgust. "I can't wait to be done with him."

"Just keep an eye on him. You know he can't be trusted."

"I know. I am."

"Great. We'll be there soon."

I hung up the phone at the same time Jane landed back on the fire escape. She didn't look pleased.

"It is up to us, diuscrucis," she said. "Michael will not allow Abaddon into Heaven under any circumstances. If we cannot contain him, he and the other archangels will attend to the matter personally."

That meant they would come down from Heaven and join the war between good and evil. One of the first things I had learned was that the archangels getting involved on Earth was bad. As in, Armageddon bad.

"Hey Landon, check this poop out," Zifah said.

I spun around. He had turned on the television. The news was showing a live scene of the carnage on the streets outside Rebecca's apartment. There was blood and bodies everywhere, though things seemed to have quieted down. The headline under the image said, "Are Monsters Real?"

"Shit," I said. "This is turning into a real mess."

"Yeah," Zifah agreed. "Look at that." He pointed to the lower left corner of the screen. "It's about to get worse."

I followed his finger. The camera was just barely covering the entrance to the apartment building. A flow of dark tendrils was just beginning to stretch out from it.

"Time to go," I said, feeling a chill at the sight. "He's on his way."

Execution

51

We took separate routes to Turtle Pond. Jane carried the trap via air, while Alyx roamed the streets, in part to test if any other mortals were affected by Abaddon's presence, and in part to ensure there were no other pockets of vampires attacking the city. Zifah and I went with Dante, making the instant trip from my living room to the balcony of Belvedere Castle, where Rose was waiting for us, a pair of binoculars in hand.

"He's coming," I said to her.

She wasn't startled by our sudden arrival. "I figured he would be."

"Where's Gervais?"

She passed me the binoculars. "Near the pond, over at that tree. He's been doing something to it for the last hour. Scratching some kind of runes into it."

I took the gear and peered through them. I could see the demonic scratches covered the entire trunk of the tree. Whatever it was for, it was intricate, the kind of stuff only a former archfiend like Gervais could manage.

"How do we know those runes aren't meant to catch you?" she asked.

"We don't, but if he grabs me and not Abaddon, he's as good as dead."

"Don't get too close to it anyway."

"I'll try not to."

I handed the binoculars back to Rose. Jane came down next to us a moment later.

"Where do you want it?" she asked, holding out the trap.

"I'll take it," I said. "Stay back here, out of sight. If I look like I'm in trouble, do something to help me."

"That is all?"

"Unless you have a better idea."

She shook her head and took a couple of steps back.

"Signore," Dante said. "If you are in trouble, I can grab you and get you out, as I did before at the apartment."

"No. I need to stay close to the trap. I can't help Gervais with whatever he's doing if I'm too far away."

"Understood. Please accept my moral support if that is all I may offer."

"Thank you, Dante. I know we've had our moments, but I'm glad you're here."

The poet smiled, even though I wasn't sure how much of that I meant and I didn't know if he could tell I was lying somewhat. "Me too, Landon."

Alyx came bounding through the park less than a minute later, leaping up onto the balcony and returning to human form.

"Did you have any trouble?" I asked.

"No, Ma... My love." She smiled at her almost slip. "It seems normal where Abaddon's power has not been. I don't believe Rebecca had time to order the full assault."

"Score one for the home team," I said. "I'm going to check on Gervais and get in position." I opened my arms, taking Alyx in them. "I love you."

"I love you, as well," she said, nuzzling my neck. I closed my eyes, taking in the feel of the contact. "If you die, I will avenge you. Even Abaddon will not be able to stop me."

"I know." I backed away from her. Was that a tear in her eye? I hope she had more confidence in me than that.

"Good luck, Landon," Zifah said.

"Yes, Signore. Good fortune," Dante said.

Execution

"Godspeed, Landon," Jane said, handing me the trap.

"Thank you all," I replied, taking it from her. "Be ready for anything."

Then I pushed, leaping from the balcony and coming down a dozen feet from Gervais and his tree.

"Ah, Landon. You have finally arrived," the fiend said. "It took you long enough."

"What is that?" I asked, pointing at the tree.

"My special surprise for Abaddon. Believe it or not, I had prepared it way back when I freed him from Avriel's Box, just in case he was not as amenable to release as I had been hoping. It will distract him."

"Distract him how?"

"Does it matter? When you fight him, get him close to the tree. I will activate the runes, and you will use the few seconds you have to retrieve the Fist and put him in it. Yes?"

I reached out with my power, sending it into the pond and finding the Fist of God there. I didn't trust Gervais. I knew whatever was going to happen; it wasn't going to be everything I was expecting.

What choice did I have? I couldn't worry about Abaddon and the fiend. "Okay."

"Good. Good. And Landon, should you die, I will mourn you." He smiled. "I always wanted to be the one to do it, and I don't want to lose this world."

"At least, we can agree on that last part," I said.

"That is Rebecca in there?" Gervais asked, pointing at the trap.

"Yeah, she's in there."

He came close and rapped his knuckles against the lid. The scripture burned him, but he didn't seem to care.

"Serves you right for your failure, Rebecca," he said. "I hope you never get out of there."

I didn't know if she could hear him or not. I pulled the trap away. "Just get in position. He's on his way."

"Of course," Gervais said. He jumped, grabbing the limb of the tree and climbing into the higher branches where he couldn't be seen.

I walked fifty feet away from the tree, staying close to the edge of the pond. I put the trap down on the ground, leaning it against a rock so it would be visible from a distance.

Everything was in position.

There was nothing to do but wait.

52

We didn't wait long.

I knew he was coming long before he appeared. His anger was in full bloom, and the world around him felt his wrath. The sky darkened, the wind picked up, and the grass began to die beneath my feet, everything around me becoming dead at his proximity. I could only guess at the number of innocents who had fallen to his power as he had traveled from Rebecca's apartment. Thousands who had done nothing more than be in his path.

They were unfortunate casualties. I hated to be callous, but their deaths would hopefully save millions of others.

I glanced over at Gervais' tree. It too had succumbed to Abaddon's power, the trunk turning gray, the leaves wilting and hanging from dark branches. Gervais was hiding up in it, and he managed to remain that way despite the change. The runes remained visible and ready, carved into the bark.

I stood beside the trap, stone in hand, heart pounding an intense rhythm against my chest. The fear was reaching me as well, and I relaxed my power against it, letting it wash away. I could manage it for now. Would I be able to once he was on top of me?

I looked up to Belvedere Castle. The others had vanished, gaining some distance to escape the power. Was Rose still watching Gervais for me? I hoped so.

He crested a small incline, appearing before me, draped in his cloak, its tendrils spreading out two hundred feet ahead of him, writhing and twirling, snapping like snakes or scorpion tails. His face was hidden behind it, his form ethereal and inhuman. I stayed calm. I had to stay calm.

It was time.

"You came," I said, as the tendrils shrank back toward him and he neared my position.

"You knew I would come."

"I don't want to fight you."

"Because you know you will lose. This was your challenge, diuscrucis. Your decision to make. I did not ask for this."

"You asked me to destroy you. You made me promise."

"And I released you from that promise."

"I haven't released myself."

He chuckled, soft and low and terrifying. "And you have found a way, now that I wish to survive, to join my Judith in Heaven?"

"I have," I lied. Why not? "God will never let you ascend into His Kingdom. Archangel Michael will also not allow it. He would consider Rebecca, but never you. You destroy all that you touch. All that you become close to."

"That is not my fault. Lucifer made me this way."

"Did he make you destroy Judith when she was still alive?"

His silence was all the answer I needed.

"She's here," I said, tapping the trap with my foot. "If you want her, you need to get past me."

"Very well. Let us do battle with honor."

A sword sprouted from his hand, a black thing made of pure evil and death.

The obsidian spatha appeared in mine. I crouched into one of Josette's favorite stances, glancing over at the tree again. I only had to get him close.

Execution

He bowed to me, so I returned the gesture.

Then he attacked.

He kept this power contained, at first, coming at me only with the sword. He was good, ridiculously good, and we had done this dance once before. I had lost that time, and within seconds, I knew that if I tried to fight him straight up, I would lose this time as well.

I fell back, barely able to get the spatha in position to deflect a flurry of thrusts and jabs and cuts. I managed to turn my back to the tree, keeping my feet going and doing everything I could to avoid being hit.

"You were better last time," he said, his sword arcing over and nearly cutting through my neck. I barely bent myself to avoid it, kicking my leg out toward his knee, only to find it immovable. I pushed off, throwing myself backward to avoid a second attack, landing on the grass a few feet closer to the tree.

"I don't use the sword much anymore," I said. I was tempted to use my power, to throw him back with it, or pull his legs out from under him. What would be the point? Perhaps he would submit if I stabbed him, or perhaps he would simply release his contained power and batter me to nothing with it.

"It shows."

He caught my blade with his, throwing out his hand and catching me in the chest. The blow knocked the wind out of me and sent me another ten feet back toward the tree. I smiled inwardly. He was helping me, and he didn't know it.

Perfect.

I scrambled back to my feet, charging him before he might notice the runes. He brushed my first three attacks aside without effort, but I managed to catch him in the arm with a fancy move Josette had only used when she was sure it would win the day. He cried out in surprise but didn't slow, and I had left myself wide open. The sword came in at my heart.

I pushed against it with my power, throwing his arm wide and ramming him with my shoulder. He stumbled back a few feet and paused.

"It that how you want to fight, diuscrucis?" he asked. He sounded disappointed in me.

"I would have lost right there."
He chuckled darkly again, his power beginning to swirl around him. We were ready for round two.

Execution

53

I had been losing sword against sword. I was completely outmatched when it came to his power versus mine. He hit me with a whirlwind of dark energy, fear and death and terror unlike anything I had experienced before. I fought to deny it, to transform it, to let it wash past and remain unaffected.

It was impossible.

My heart pounded faster than any living mortals could survive. My skin broke out in a cold sweat, and my eyes became blurry with panic. I threw my power out at him, and he swatted it aside with his like it was nothing more than a nuisance.

Round two?

That was a joke.

I had turned the fight into a massacre.

I stumbled backward, heading for the tree, desperate to get away from the onslaught. It wasn't a question of whether or not he would defeat me. The only question was if I could double-cross him before that happened.

Honor?

There was no honor in desperation.

"I like you, diuscrucis, and so I will give you a chance," Abaddon said, hitting me with another wave of power and knocking me to my knees.

I glanced back at the tree, still twenty feet away. Was I close enough? I couldn't be. If I were, Gervais would have done something. Wouldn't he?

"A chance?" I asked, buying time to recover from the blow.

"Surrender. Tell me that I have won, and I will spare your life. I will take Judith, and we will complete our plan without your intervention."

I didn't answer right away. He was giving me a chance to catch my breath. Why not? We both knew I couldn't win. At least not fairly.

"I can't," I said. "Don't you understand? The entire world will burn. Everyone will die. You and Rebecca still won't be in Heaven. I'd rather die trying to stop it, then to watch everything I care for wither to nothing."

"Good," he said. "If you had agreed, I would have labeled you a coward and drained you more slowly."

He stepped toward me again. I bounced back to my feet, crouching low, sword out and up. His tendrils whipped around and shot at me, and I sprang up and forward, a heavy, hard charge right at him.

I avoided the tendrils, knocking his sword aside and getting into his guard. I stabbed down with the spatha, and his hand came up and caught the blade.

I had made it further than I expected. I yanked the sword back, unwilling to lose it, hitting his shoulders with my feet. I pushed off him, making him lose a few steps while I carried myself back. I had seen Josette pull of a similar move when she had fought Ulnyx, though she had managed to stab him, and I had failed in that.

I landed at the base of the tree.

Abaddon recovered from the move, bowed to me with respect to the effort, and started toward me again. His power shrank back into him.

He was ready to finish it.

So was I.

I reached out with my power, finding the Fist once more and pulling it up from the bottom of the pond. Abaddon didn't notice. He was so focused on me, and all the action was happening at his back. I dropped the armor on the grass behind him, undoing the clasps that held the prison closed.

I heard Gervais' incantation above me. The fiend remained hidden in

Execution

the slack branches of the tree, but the runes began to glow with hot fire. I did my best to fake surprise until I caught movement over Abaddon's shoulder.

Rose was running my direction at full speed, pointing up into the tree.

My blood turned cold in an instant. If she was coming, it meant Gervais was doing something I wasn't going to like.

And then it happened.

Abaddon came up short, his power exploding out from him, sending dark tendrils writhing past me. "Avriel," he shouted, his voice harsh with rage.

"Diuscrucis," I heard a voice say, and my cold blood froze to ice.

I turned slowly, not quite believing it, but powerless not to.

"Hey there, pardner," the Beast said. His face was twisted into a scowl, and he was reaching for me with one large, electric hand. The other was holding a head.

Charis' head.

I froze.

"Landon," I heard Rose shout.

Then he was on me.

Not the Beast. Gervais.

He landed behind me, grabbing my arm.

"My apologies, Landon," he said, his lips right against my ear. "But I am what I am."

With one quick, precise motion he cut off my right hand.

I wanted to scream in pain, but I didn't. I was still as he bent down and grabbed the hand, pulling the control ring from my finger at the same time he morphed into the vampire he had killed.

He didn't look back. He sprang over Abaddon, who didn't even seem to notice him in his quest to fight the angel he thought he saw.

Rose had her dagger out, and she tried to intercept him. It was a brave and stupid thing to do, and he didn't even slow, slashing her across the chest before reaching the Fist. He hefted it easily in one hand, the vampire's strength becoming his own, carrying it away from us.

Rose fell to the ground, the demon's poison leaving her still.

I wanted to scream out in frustration. I wanted to rip the whiny little French asshole's head from his skinny, demonic body.

I didn't understand. What the hell was he doing, anyway? He had the Fist. He had Abaddon. All he had to do was grab the distracted demon and throw him in the armor.

Except he didn't.

He kept going until he reached the trap.

Rebecca? Did he want Rebecca? Why? It didn't make sense.

No. It did make sense. He didn't need Abaddon in the Fist to control him. Not if he had Judith. He would use her to make a deal with the demon, and all would be well in his twisted world.

"Abaddon," I said, fighting to block the Beast's voice from my head. "It's a trap. We were both tricked."

He wasn't responding. Damn it.

I grabbed the spatha from the ground with my remaining hand, ignoring the blood and pain from the empty stump. I could regrow it later. I had other business right now.

"Abaddon," I shouted again, skipping in and grabbing him by the neck. He noticed that, and his attention shifted to me. "We've been had. Turn around."

I let him go, and he spun to see Gervais drop the Fist of God next to the trap. He picked up the trap, his hands sizzling from the scripture as he did, and brought it close to the armor.

Time. There was no time. Abandon's power lashed out toward Gervais, but he had gone too far, and as soon as Rebecca was trapped he would stop Abaddon's attack. He would turn the demon on me, and he would win. Maybe not right away, but he would find a way.

I clenched my jaw in frustration. There were no more choices. No more options. I had given Gervais a little bit of leash because I needed his help. Should I be surprised he had bitten me? I had to salvage what I could of the mess.

"I'm sorry," I said to Abaddon, as I plunged the spatha into his back, continuing to push it through as my hand sank into his flesh. I could sense the core of his soul with the third-eye, and I dissolved the sword, moving

Execution

my hand up to it and wrapping my fingers around it.

He tried to spin again, but I held on fast. I felt the white-hot fury of his evil in my grip, and I made myself calm around it. "Rest," I said, willing the power to transform, to change, to balance. "Rest."

Abaddon screamed. The sound of it echoed across the park, so powerfully sad that even Gervais paused in what he was doing at the sound of it.

I had never considered that I could do this before Gervais had forced my hand. But why not? Rebecca was a spirit, a free soul, and I could destroy her in the same way. I could destroy any soul like this if that were my will.

The power began to fade away from him, dissipating and sinking back to Hell. Within seconds the cloak and tendrils were gone. A few more and his black face became human again. I remembered it from our meeting in the Box.

"Diuscrucis," he said, his eyes old and sad. "Judith."

"She isn't Judith," I said. "She never was."

"I... I feel..." He paused, tears springing to those eyes, turning more human by the second. "Free."

He smiled. There was no malice in the smile. No evil intent.

"Thank you, diuscrucis," he said. "Thank you."

The last of his soul transformed to my touch, and his body fell away in a burst of light. It rose and dispersed, headed not to Heaven, but to join the rest of the universe.

He would know peace at last.

I wasn't so lucky.

54

I scanned the area for Gervais.
Of course, the bastard was gone. So was the Fist.
The trap lay open and discarded in the grass, the soil spilled across it. Empty.
I turned my attention to Rose. I ran over to where she was laying. I knelt beside her, fighting my own tears.
"Rose," I said. "Rose."
She was dead.
I let the tears come then. I crouched over her, lamenting everything the universe had made me. Foremost of all, a failure. I had hoped to help mankind learn to save themselves. I had only managed to get my first and only student killed.
I felt a hand on my shoulder.
"Signore," Dante said, his voice low.
"I failed her," I said.
"No, Signore. You saved her. You gave her purpose and pride."
"The demon that killed her sister killed her, and he got away with the Fist."
"Yes. It is unfortunate. But you stopped Abaddon, and I know you will

Execution

stop him."

"I'm not going to settle for stopping him," I said, getting back to my feet and facing the poet. "I'm going to end him like I did Abaddon. I have the power, and I know how to do it."

"That is the Landon I know," he said, smiling. "Do not worry too much about Rose. She will be with me, and you know I will take care of her."

"Her soul is in Purgatory?"

"Si, Signore. Unfortunately, she can't return from there to see you, but I will tell her how sorry you are."

I shook my head. I could picture what she would say, and how she would say it. "I'm sure she knows."

Jane and Alyx joined Dante a moment later. Alyx jumped into my arms, holding me tight and kissing my cheek. She was soaking wet.

"He took Rebecca and the Fist," I said to the angel.

"You stopped Abaddon from reaching Heaven. That is a good day's work."

"Did you see where Gervais went?"

"He jumped into the pond," Alyx said. "That's why I'm wet. I followed him. He had hidden a rift under there. He took the Fist through it."

"He put a rift underwater? I didn't think he had the power to make his own rifts."

"He doesn't," Alyx said.

I closed my eyes, sighing. "Zifah?" I asked.

"Yes."

They had been quarreling the whole time they were together. It was all one big lie.

I really, really, really hated demons.

Alyx kissed my cheek again.

Okay, I hated most demons.

"We have to find out where they went."

"I will contact Alichino," Dante said. "We will work on it. Again."

"Jane, what do you intend?" I asked.

"I will inform the archangels of the outcome, and of the demon Gervais' betrayal. Beyond that, I do not know. I suspect we haven't seen the last of each other, and I would prefer not to forget about this."

"You won't," I said, making it so. "I may need your help again."

"As long as you are fighting on the side of good, you can call on me anytime."

"Thank you."

Jane bowed to me, her wings spreading behind her as she did. Then she took to the sky and vanished once more.

"I want to get out of here for a while," I said. "Away from New York. There's too much destruction here. Too much chaos. You saw the television. Something is going to change, and we need to be better prepared for when it does."

"I have a place in Mexico," Alyx said. "It looks like junk from the outside, but it can be rather cozy. It also has access to an incredible network of information."

"A good place to track down Gervais from," I said. "And to monitor the situation with the mortals. Are we going to see an escalation in the number of Awake, or will this be an isolated incident? Dante, will you bring us there, and then pick up Alichino and return?"

"Of course, Signore. Tell me the location, and I will make it so."

"I just need to do one more thing first."

I pushed the earth aside, right next to Turtle Pond. Then I lifted Rose's body and placed it in the hole, covering it over. I bowed my head, as did Dante and Alyx. I didn't say anything. There was no need. She had moved on from the vessel. This was tradition and respect, nothing more.

Then I nodded to Dante, and he put his hand on my and Alyx's shoulder. In an instant, we were standing in a junkyard in Mexico, formerly owned by the fiend Espanto.

"I will return," Dante said, vanishing again.

"Are you sure you want to stay here?" I asked, taking Alyx's hand.

"Yes. I want to make good memories here, to wash away the bad ones."

"Then let's go home."

Execution

55

It took a few days to get the place back under control. Most of the servants had fled when Cabal arrived to announce the new Mistress, and the remainder had fallen into what I could only describe as a state of confused hopelessness. They were so used to being a slave to the demon that without him, they didn't know what to do with themselves.

We worked to renew that purpose with them, first by getting them fed and clothed, and then by returning them to their old tasks. Their familiarity with Alyx was a help, as was the fact that she had formerly been under Espanto's control as well. They looked up to her like children, and she took to them as a mother would to her young, always treating them with kindness.

It was such a drastic change from anything I had ever seen in a demon. It was a major change from how she had been when I had freed her. Whether it was killing Espanto that had changed her, or if it was seeing what mortals went through at the hands of the Divine, I didn't know. I was proud of the ways she was growing and maturing. I was proud of the free creature she was becoming.

Alichino took over the information network that Espanto had run. He delighted in the capabilities of the fiend's systems, and he swore that he would be able to find Gervais wherever he went with it. I told him that was his only goal. Gervais had double-crossed me for the last time. He had also killed Rose, and while Dante had delivered her message that it was okay, I wasn't going to let that go.

Beyond that, I had a bad feeling that if his power was growing, he was going to make another move on Sarah. I had no question that he still lusted after her power, and now that he could feed on the Divine and capture their abilities, I was worried that he would attempt to do the same to her.

It was a lot to be concerned about.

I forgot about all of it when Alyx and I finally got some time alone together, in a room we had converted into a bedroom far from where Espanto had taken her for his twisted play.

"You promised me," she said, putting her hand on my chest and looking up at me. "As soon as Abaddon was contained. Or destroyed. I've waited four days for you." She smiled. "I don't want to wait anymore."

I looked down into her big eyes. I could feel her desire.

"I don't want to wait anymore either," I said.

And I didn't. I had spent my entire human life as a virgin, and even after becoming Divine and falling in love, there had never been a chance to be with Charis. Even though we had a child in the Box, we had never actually made love.

I was always waiting for the right time. The right person. I thought that was Charis. There had never been a chance. A month ago, I never would have guessed that person would be a demon. Bradford could think what he wanted, but he had a messed up view of intimacy that I was glad I didn't share. I loved Alyx. As furiously loyal as she was to me, I knew I was to her as well. I had seen her true spirit and the goodness of it. It was still tinged with evil, but then, so was I.

It made things a little more interesting. A little more exciting.

I leaned down, picking her up below her rear and lifting her to my height. She wrapped her arms around me, her lips finding mine. I held her while we kissed, releasing every ounce of passion I had for her soul into every motion of my mouth and hands.

She rocked against me, tugging me off balance so that we fell together

Execution

onto the bed. She laughed, and I laughed too. Her hands worked to get my shirt off, and I did the same. My body was shivering with excitement and desire. I don't know if I had ever wanted anything more.

"I love you," she said, her hands soft on my bare chest.

"I love you, too," I replied, feeling the shape of her with my palms.

Our lips met again, and I sank so far into the smell and touch and taste of her that I only heard my cell ringing with the barest of consciousness.

"Leave it," she said in a soft growl, nipping my ear.

I tried to ignore the sound of it.

I couldn't.

I knew the tone.

It was Sarah.

"I have to answer this," I said. "I'm so sorry."

She rolled off me, nodding. "I know. It's okay."

I sat up, grabbing my phone from my discarded pants. I hadn't even noticed that Alyx had taken them off. I hit the answer button.

"Sarah?" I said. "What's up?"

"Landon," Obi's voice was a fearful whisper on the other end of the line.

"Obi? What's going on?"

"Landon, we've got a problem, man," he said. "You need to get over here."

"Why? Obi, tell me what's happening."

I could hear his breath on the phone. He was scared. I was sure of it. "Sarah's gone. It doesn't make any sense. She killed Brian and took off with Adam. What happened to him, Landon? What made him fall?"

"Adam?" was all I managed to say. Every part of me had gone numb.

"Just get here, okay?" Obi said.

I looked at Alyx. She could tell I was scared, and she was waiting for me to tell her what we were going to do next.

"Hang in there," I said. "We're on our way."

M.R. Forbes

Join the Mailing List!

"No," you cry. "I will not submit myself to even more inbox spam. I have quite enough garbage coming in from people and places that I care a lot more about than you."

"But," I reply, "if you sign up for my mailing list, you'll know when my next book is out. Don't you want to know when my next book is out?"

"Eh... I'll find it on Amazon."

"True enough, but you see, a mailing list is very valuable to an author, especially a meager self-published soul such as myself. I don't have a marketing team, and I don't have exposure in brick and mortar stores around the world to help improve my readership. All I have is you, my potential fans. How about a bribe?"

"Hmm... Keep talking."

"Picture this... giveaways, a chance at FREE books. There is a 10% chance* you could save at least three dollars per year!"

Silence.

"Where'd you go?" I ask. "Well, I'll just leave this here, in case you change your mind."

Execution

http://mrforbes.com/mailinglist

* For illustration only. Not an actual mathematical probability.

Thank You!

It is readers like you, who take a chance on self-published works that is what makes the very existence of such works possible. Thank you so very much for spending your hard-earned money, time, and energy on this work. It is my sincerest hope that you have enjoyed reading!

Independent authors could not continue to thrive without your support. If you have enjoyed this, or any other independently published work, please consider taking a moment to leave a review at the source of your purchase. Reviews have an immense impact on the overall commercial success of a given work, and your voice can help shape the future of the people whose efforts you have enjoyed.

Thank you again!

About the Author

M.R. Forbes is the creator of a growing catalog of speculative fiction titles, including the epic fantasy Tears of Blood series, the contemporary fantasy Divine series, and the world of Ghosts & Magic. He lives in the pacific northwest with his wife, a cat who thinks she's a dog, and a dog who thinks she's a cat. He eats too many donuts, and he's always happy to hear from readers.

Mailing List: http://bit.ly/XRbZ5n

Website: http://www.mrforbes.com/site/writing

Goodreads: http://www.goodreads.com/author/show/6912725.M_R_Forbes

Facebook: http://www.facebook.com/mrforbes.author

Twitter: http://www.twitter.com/mrforbes

M.R. Forbes

<<<◇>>>

Printed in Great Britain
by Amazon